Truth is Key

ALSO BY PHYLLIS DEWEY

BOOK SERIES:

THE MYSTERIES OF BELLA ROSE ESTATE

1. LEAVING CAME EASY
2. SECRETS IN THE ATTIC
3. THE HIDDEN TRUTH
4. STANDING ALONE
5. TWO UNLIKELY SOULS
6. TRUTH IS KEY

NON-FICTION:

HER TURN – ONE WOMAN'S POSITIVE JOURNEY THROUGH HER FIRST YEAR OF GRIEF

Truth is Key

The Mysteries of

Bella Rose Estate

Book #6

Phyllis Dewey

This book is fiction. Names, characters, places, and incidents are the author's imagination or used fictitiously. Any resemblance to actual persons, living or dead, events, or locales is entirely coincidental.

Dedication

Truth is Key, this final book of The Mysteries of Bella Rose Estate, is dedicated to my fictional characters, Sara, Heather, and Andy. They have brought this story to life as they developed in my mind and throughout this series.

Their dedication to family and determination to overcome challenges inspired me to keep their story going.

It is time to let them live without me but to live on in your minds.

To you, my readers –

As you have read this series and this final book, I hope you have taken this family into your hearts. When you reach the end and close this book, I hope you will remember Sara, Heather, and Andy and the life around them. The characters, the situations, the mysteries, and mostly the love and acceptance shown to all who touched their   lives.

Prologue

Guests that no one seemed to notice quietly checked out of the manor. Sara had been so busy working on the family history that she did not realize she had not seen them after they checked in. She assumed Heather, or at least Andy, had seen them during the breakfasts they provided their guests.

It was not until later that the mystery couple came to light and intrigued them.

The family was always busy with guests and raising their ever-growing families. Friends were becoming family. And the family continued to grow.

Sara's work on the family history continued to lead to more discoveries. She never totally forgot about the keys. She knew there could be more to be revealed. She just did not know how or when. Or, for that matter, by who.

Chapter One
Clues

Heather was intrigued about finding the key in the guest room after the mysterious couple checked out of the manor and left. She returned to the room to do a deeper cleaning and search for more clues they may have left behind. Their next guest would arrive the next day, limiting her time to search.

Heather asked Rachelle to join her to help speed up the cleaning process and to have an unbiased witness if they found anything. She explained the situation to Rachelle, who was happy to help.

Two hours later, Rachelle picked up a journal from inside the trunk at the foot of the bed.

"Don't the guests usually leave the journal on top of the trunk or on the dresser when they leave?"

"Yes, if they have written in it, they sometimes leave it on the pillow. Why?"

"This beauty was inside the trunk. Seems these guests wanted to hide it."

"Maybe they didn't want it to get lost while here." Heather kept working without looking in Rachelle's direction. Until she heard Rachelle's next words.

"I like the new cover pattern on the journals."

"What new pattern? We've not changed them since we began the tradition." Heather walked to where Rachelle stood holding the journal and reached out for it. Rachelle handed it to her without hesitation.

"This is not ours."

They both sat on the edge of the bed. Heather looked at the front and back covers of the little journal. Then she hesitantly opened it to the first page.

She read the first words handwritten in flowing cursive with blue gel ink. The words formed a simple title. Rachelle looked over and saw the words Heather was reading –

The Truth Will Set You Free.

"What does that mean?" Rachelle asked.

"Maybe it's a story they were writing. It's not our company-supplied journal." She closed it. "We'll give it to Sara to read if she wants to. She may want to contact the guest and return it without reading it. Let's see if they left us anything else." Heather set the little book on the chair near the door.

Two hours later, the two ladies left the room with the cleaning supplies, the journal, and two old photos they found in the nightstand's top drawer tucked inside the front cover of the Bible the family supplied to each room.

Deep in thought, Sara did not hear the faint knock on her office door. A louder knock pulled her into reality. She called out for whomever to come in.

Heather walked in, followed by Rachelle.

"You could have just come in. You don't need to knock first."

"We didn't want to surprise or pull you from your thoughts if you were writing," Rachelle said.

"Although what we have to show you will at least disrupt your thoughts." Heather handed the journal to her older sister as she blurted out the words.

"What's this?" Sara looked at the cover. "Whose is this?"

"That was found inside the trunk in the room where the mysterious guest stayed," Rachelle said.

"And these two photos were tucked inside the Bible, still in the nightstand's top drawer. Do you recognize them?" Heather handed the photos to Sara.

"This is the gentleman who registered. I am assuming this one is of his wife." Sara studied the photos.

"Didn't you say the gentleman was an older man?"

"Yes, a little older. Why?" Before either lady had time to say anything, Sara knew the answer. Neither of the other ladies said a word.

"This is the gentleman. That I am positive about." Sara turned the photo over.

The white border scalloped edge framed the picture. The photo was faded but had always been a black-and-white print. The print shop's lettering was gold, and its date was 1921. The photo of the lady was the same style and had the same year written on the back.

The people in the photos themselves were the same as the mysterious couple. There was a slight age difference, but they had the same hairstyle and clothes. Maybe the year written was wrong. Sara felt an overwhelming feeling, almost faint. She had no words.

Chapter Two
Solitude

Turning left instead of right sometimes makes all the difference in Andy's travels and life.

As Andy continued along the road, he reached the end of town, turned left again, and kept going. He knew he did not want to stay on the main roads. This was his week to get away. No contact with anyone. He had packed for a week away, and his vehicle was set up, so he could sleep in it if he wanted to. And since he did not want anyone to know where he was going or where he was at any given time, he was not putting anything on a credit card. He was being careful not to even spend cash where there may be any cameras showing his face.

He laughed as he thought about traveling that way. It made him sound like a criminal trying to hide from the law. All he was doing was hiding from his family and his reality. His history from childhood had stuck with him. He was afraid it would stay for life. He hoped his family would understand any time he had to run. He knew that this trip would not be his last.

Andy continued to drive for the next three hours. He had stayed off the interstate roads by taking random side roads. Some would consider him lost. He considered himself on an adventure. It was not the first time he had run this method. It always led him to the most interesting places. As he thought that, he saw a road sign that caused him to turn right and head toward the town that stated it was a town of free spirits and adventurers. He had to see what they were all about.

He drove slowly through town to get a feel for what was there. It did not take him long to drive along the town's main street. He decided he would turn around and go wander around for a while. At the end of town, he found a park, and instead of driving back, he parked his car and got out to explore.

He heard music playing a short distance away when he stepped out of his car. He looked around and saw a small group gathered around a man playing a guitar and singing. He walked over to the group and stood there for a few minutes. Then he left the group and headed downtown. He was getting hungry and wanted to find a small mom-and-pop restaurant. Locally owned places made the best food. Much better than the corporate chains where most people ate. It did not take him long to find a tiny place to eat. He opened the door and was greeted by a small in stature young woman. She walked him past the buffet and drink stations to a table near the back. He felt isolated there but soon found it was the perfect spot to sit and watch the other patrons and the workers. The acoustics were bad in the room, so he could hear a lot of conversations simultaneously. That had been a curse all of his life. He could hear what most people either could not hear or understand when there was any distraction in the room. He had a very active and precise hearing capability.

He looked over the menu and ordered a Reuben sandwich and fries. Karen would have given him a hard time about his food choices, but not many things on the menu captured his interest. From the sign, the place closed before five that night. That was okay; he was only in town long enough to grab a bite to eat and stretch his legs.

While eating, he noticed a sign outside about a hiking trail. When the waitress returned, he asked about it. She told him it was a popular trail and fairly easy to hike, adding that she and her husband had hiked it several times. He finished eating, asked for water to fill his water bottle, and headed for the trail. He parked his car and grabbed his backpack, which held his water bottle, phone, binoculars, snack bars, compass, knife, and other safety items. He never used it at home. He rarely went hiking anymore. For some reason, he had brought it along on this trip. At the trailhead, a sign said the hike was five miles round trip. He shook his head. He might not need his backpack for that short hike, but he secured it on his back and began to hike.

About halfway up the first incline, he realized how out of shape he was. He rested against a tree for several minutes as he gazed over the view. A lake sat at the bottom of the hillside. Homes were built around the lake. A few boats were out on the water, while most were tied to docks. It was the beginning of autumn, and he assumed some people had taken their boats out of the water for the season.

Further up the trail, he stopped again. The view showed a small town below. He figured he would drive through it when he left this area and continued his solitary journey. A few families were headed back down the trail. He kept moving forward, anxious to see the view at the end.

When he reached the end, he sat on the bench and surveyed the land around him and the valley below. It could take a person's breath away. Another hiker joined him and began a conversation by asking him if he had ever seen such beauty. Andy was about to say no when he realized he had it at home. The view from the gazebo at Bella Rose was just as spectacular. He began to tell this stranger his story. About where he lived, his days of running away, and his current reason for being there. The stranger let him talk. When Andy finished, the stranger looked at him.

"Man, you have it made. A beautiful home. A wife and children who love you. Siblings and family who love and care about you. Go home, Man!"

Andy didn't say a word. The man was right. He had everything and more that any person could want. So, why was he running?

"I can't go home yet. I may have everything, but they don't have all of me. I need to find my missing piece."

"Your missing piece?" The stranger pointed to Andy's heart. "That is your missing piece. Stop holding it in. That is your missing piece. Let go, Man. Let them see the real you."

Andy listened and remained silent. Let go. Was it that simple? How did a person just let go of things? How could some people do that when he couldn't? He never had been able to let things flow off his back. He was always analyzing things. He never had been able to let go. It was his nature to hold things in. Until the urge to run became so strong he had to run. It was never a case or a thought of letting go, which would be enough to clear his mind. Other people could, but not him.

Andy turned around and hiked back to his car. The words from the stranger lingered. "Go home, Man." He put his backpack in the car and drove away. Still headed away from home.

Over the next several days, Andy took roads that led to more hiking trails. A few small towns that he explored touched him. They were full of friendly people. In his quest for quiet solitude, he discovered his need for people. The days of hiking alone gave him time to think. His thoughts always concerned home, family, Karen, and his children. He thought about his past and wild, carefree days, as some people would call them.

He returned to the first hiking trail and the little restaurant on his last day before going home. He walked inside, and the same waitress greeted him. She smiled as she seated him.

"Did you find yourself yet?"

Andy smiled and nodded his head. "I think I have. It took the words of a stranger and a few extra days out on the roads and trails, but, yea, I think I've found myself. How did you know that was what I needed?"

"That stranger was probably my grandfather."

"He wasn't old enough to be your grandfather."

The waitress smiled and asked if she could sit down and tell him a story. He motioned for her to sit across from him. She motioned to another waitress as she sat down. The other lady brought over two glasses of water and a Reuben sandwich, even though Andy had not even looked at the menu this time. He smiled and nodded his thanks as the waitress began to speak.

"Yes, that man's my grandfather. He has been offering advice to hikers for years now. I hear so many stories about how the stranger helped someone. Mostly they are people who are looking for answers to life. Some don't want to keep living. Others are just bewildered about their future. Some are just mentally lost."

Andy listened but shook his head when she stopped talking. "He helped me, that I know. It didn't take a lot of words. However, he was not your grandfather."

The waitress smiled. "Yes, it was Harry. You see, Harry lived here all of his life. He raised his family to be the best they could be. In the early nineties, Harry was killed on that trail. Another hiker shot him for no reason. He is buried at the foot of the trail. Since he died, hikers have stopped here and told us how a young man took the time to talk with them and offer bits of life's wisdom."

Andy's eyes opened wide, and he felt a cool air brush past him. His hands started to shake. The waitress reached out and held his hands from shaking. Her smile and the beauty in her eyes calmed his spirit.

"You were one of the chosen that Harry knew needed to be touched by his wisdom. You are blessed."

"Blessed? More like spooked." Andy felt the need for a strong drink.

The waitress looked up above Andy and softly whispered, "Okay."

"Okay, what?" Andy asked, bewildered.

"Harry says you do not need a drink. You need to go home to your family."

The blood from Andy's face drained. He stared at the waitress. He lowered his eyes and noticed her name. Susan reached over and placed her hands on his forearm. "Everything will work out, Andy."

The next day Andy drove home. He would never forget his encounter in that small town. He now wondered if the town was even real. He knew Harry was a figment of his imagination. Maybe the whole town was.

~~~~~~

Karen rushed to the door when she heard her husband pull up to the house. She stood on the front porch and watched him. Andy ran up to her and wrapped his arms around her. "I am never running again. Not without you by my side. And until the kids are grown, they will be with us wherever we travel."

"Welcome home, my love. I guess you found yourself while you were away?"

"I found Harry. Rather, Harry found me and sent me home."

Karen pulled away from him and looked into his eyes. No words, just a look.

"Don't ask. You will never understand. Know that I am a changed man. I am finally who I need to be, and you and all the family need me to be."

Karen wrapped her arms around him. "Welcome home, my love. Welcome home."

Together they walked into the house where their children were waiting.

Chapter Three
Carpenter's Star

The next day new guests arrived that were assigned to the room of the mysterious guests. Sara found it odd that someone had requested a particular room, but she registered it in their name since it was available. The couple was planning to stay a week.

The name on the reservation was Mr. and Mrs. Leon Watson. They were a younger couple, Sara estimated to be in their twenties. With no children. At least none that were with them.

She asked what their plans were to see if she could suggest places they may not already have on their agenda. Mrs. Watson told her they planned to explore cemeteries, old homes, and old nature trails.

"Interesting locations. Any particular reason?" Sara asked out of curiosity. The idea of them visiting cemeteries caught her interest.

"Old family tradition. We love to search for families, hear their stories and imagine their lives. Our ancestors loved to leave clues behind, almost like a treasure hunt. We find it fascinating when we find something that connects unsuspecting family members together through their past."

"Enjoy. If you have any questions, feel free to ask any of us here. My family has been here for the last four generations. I am working on our family history through the journals I found on our estate."

"Very interesting. We may want to sit down with you while we are here to listen to your story."

"My siblings and I would be glad to join you one evening."

"We shall plan on it." Mr. Watson took his wife gently by her elbow and escorted her out of the office toward their room. Sara found it odd that they knew where it was, then remembered the website had the layout of the manor included in the information.

When the couple left, Sara reached into the top drawer of her desk. She pulled out the fancy journal and pulled the photos from it. Mr. Watson resembled the older gentleman in the photo. She wondered if it was her imagination or if they were somehow related. She then shrugged her shoulders and returned them to the drawer without looking further. She had work to do on her family history.

Sara sat at her computer and began to write the next chapter. "Truth is stranger than fiction." She spoke the words as she typed. "Could the truth be the key to happiness and answers? And could learning her family's truth set them free from the stresses they each seemed to be having this year?" She stopped talking while she typed from the words on the latest family writings she had discovered.

Heather came into the office without knocking as Sara was lost in thought.

"Have you seen the new guests? Oh, of course, you have."

Sara stopped typing and turned to face her sister. "Of course. Why?"

"Did you see the resemblance between the two men?"

"Yes, I took note of that. I am not assuming anything, though."

"Why not? Did you assign that room to them, or did they ask for it?"

"They requested it, and I let them have it since it was available. Had it not been open, they would have taken another room."

"I think they are connected to the previous guests, that's all." Heather sat down as though she was going to stay a while. Sara stared at her, giving her an eye full.

"I'm sorry. I guess I should go and get my work done." Heather stood and left the office. She walked the long way around to her house, which involved walking down the hallway in front of the new guests' room. Their room, number three, was named the Carpenter's Star Room. As she walked in front of the door, the lady opened it and stepped out, almost running into Heather.

"Oh, excuse me. I didn't mean to rush out of the room and run into you. I didn't expect anyone to be here for some reason." Mrs. Watson said. "Hi, I am Mrs. Watson." She held out her hand for Heather to shake.

"Hi, I am Heather. My siblings and I are the owners, so you never know when we will be walking around the property." She had no idea why she added that last bit of information. It sounded like a warning.

"That is fine. We expect to run into people while we are here. It is good to meet you. My husband and I are on our way downtown if you will excuse us from not chatting longer."

"Of course. I won't keep you." Heather replied. She continued to walk down the hallway to the door at the end that led to her home. Heather turned her head as she made her exit. She still felt there was something odd about that couple.

Mrs. Watson told her husband about her running into a lady named Heather. "We must check into her and see what she is all about. She said she was one of the owners."

"Oh, yes, three siblings own the estate now. From what my grandfather said, there is a story between them and our

15

family. Somehow they are connected. He wants us to find out how."

"How interesting. First, we need to check out the local cemetery. I also heard this little town has haunted homes and businesses."

"Yes, from what I read, there are several."

They arrived downtown, parked their car behind the old courthouse building, and began walking. Today's mission was to observe the buildings, read the signs, and watch the people. They knew a person could learn a lot without saying a word.

Chapter Four
Extension

Terri noticed a young couple walking on the sidewalk in front of the café. They were dressed differently than most visitors in town, but with the storytelling event approaching, she did not think much of it. She suspected that at some point, they would visit her café, and she would find out more about them. Few visitors were quiet when they came in. They were either full of stories or of questions.

A few minutes later, Steven came in and mentioned the couple Terri had seen.

"Did you see that young couple walking down the street?"

"I did. It is almost time for storytelling. Maybe they are here early."

"Oh, Yes. I forgot it was that time of year already. That would explain it."

"Explain what?"

"The way they were looking at all the architecture. It was intense."

"That is interesting. Maybe they want to use it in their stories."

"Maybe. If I see them again, I will invite them to the lounge one evening while they are here. Maybe they can tell us a short story or sing a song."

"Good idea. Most people stop in when visiting the area. You may want to call Sara and see what she knows. Several of the storytellers stay there."

"I might ask Ben and Heather what they know. Barbara has invited them over for dinner tonight."

"Let me know what you find out."

"I will."

The café got busy with regular customers, and neither one thought about the young couple again until the next day.

~~~~~~

Mr. and Mrs. Watson walked arm in arm throughout the town the first day they visited. It was the same as Mr. Watson's grandfather had told them, although some things were new in keeping up with modern-day growth.

The owner of the coffee shop stopped Mr. Watson and offered the couple a free specialty coffee. Mrs. Watson responded by nodding her head. Mr. Watson gave in and accepted a cup for each of them. One sip and they both could tell this was a very special blend to make the flavors they tasted. When Mrs. Watson asked what the secret was, the answer was simple. "Love."

The couple smiled, walking and enjoying the coffee and the friendship shown by those who lived and worked there. Mr. and Mrs. Watson did their best to blend in with the other people in town but quickly realized they were dressed differently. Luckily they saw the advertisement for the storytelling and pretended to be early for the event.

That night in the guest room, Mr. Watson pulled out the photo album he had brought along that had once belonged to his grandfather. Inside were photos of his grandfather as well as great-grandparents.

The couple leafed through the pages adding note papers to the photos of things they had experienced. Mrs. Watson wrote a list of the places they still needed to find. The older man from a previous generation wanted his grandson to discover his background. He had a story to tell, but it was up to Mr. Watson to live it without the benefit of written words. A picture was worth a thousand words, his grandfather had always told him. He was told to go discover. "Find my father's true story."

And discovering was what the two of them planned to do. Accidentally landing there during storytelling was going to be a bonus.

Sara was still sitting and writing in her office when the young couple walked in. She asked what she could do to help them. Mr. Watson asked if there was any way he and his bride could extend their stay through storytelling weekend. Sara smiled. She shook her head but added that since they were already in a room, she would make arrangements for her other guests, and they could remain.

"Are you certain it will not put you out?"

"I am sure. The other guest I was going to put in that room will be fine staying at my second choice. They are repeat guests and love an adventure."

"If you are sure. That is greatly appreciated."

"You are welcome. Did you enjoy your time in town today?"

"We did. Tomorrow we are returning to town and visiting other places we have heard we need to see while we are here."

"If you have any questions, feel free to ask. I have lived here most of my life, and my family started this estate many years ago. So we have a history here."

"Thank you so much. We have already found everyone to be helpful and friendly. Most places are not this friendly and helpful without wanting something in return."

"We are a small community and close-knit. For the most part, anyway."

Sara made a note as the couple left the office. She needed to call Joe and Nicole to see if they would be comfortable staying with her and Randall for storytelling. She assumed they would love it.

Chapter Five
Suspicions

Joe and Nicole were thrilled to spend their week with Sara, Randall, and Gayle. They knew it was close enough to the manor that they would still benefit from Andy's cooking. The breakfasts were always a treat to the guests. Joe always enjoyed meeting the other guests each morning. It was in his nature to attempt to figure people out. It was his life's work, but he found it more fascinating when they were unaware of what he was doing. That was part of why Joe was successful in his counseling work.

When Sara was talking with Joe about her need, she explained why. It was not due to just another guest. This was for a guest with suspicious behavior. She said it was not bad or wrong behavior, but she did not feel at ease with them. Joe understood the unspoken request in her voice. She wanted him to secretly check them out. To find out what they were all about, what they were up to, if anything, since they were in the area so soon after the mysterious guests, and why they requested the same room. Joe loved a challenge, whether he got paid or not, for deciphering them. He rarely talked of his specialty unless it was with family or close friends. Over the years, he had counseled the Fairchild family about so many things that he considered them close friends.

When Joe and Nicole arrived, they were invited to the family dinner. Mr. and Mrs. Watson were also invited. Sara had only invited those involved with figuring out the mystery of the journal, the photo, the particular room request, and those she thought could help.

21

"So, what brought the two of you to Bella Rose Estate?" Joe asked while they were waiting for the dinner that Andy had made for this special occasion.

"We found out about it through my grandparents. My grandfather recommended we stay here. He said his father, my great-grandfather, had been in this area and knew about Bella Rose Estate."

"Interesting. Most people happen upon this place and only stay for a few days. I am sure Sara and her family appreciate you wanting to stay longer than originally planned."

"We are thrilled that she could accommodate us at such short notice. Thank you for being willing to stay elsewhere."

"It is our pleasure. We have known Sara and her family for as long as they have owned this place after their parents died within six months of each other." Joe offered more information than he needed to.

Joe knew if he could share so much, this couple would be more willing to share what they were all about and why they were there. Joe sensed they had a mission beyond a simple vacation. It was brought on by more than what Sara told him. He could feel something about them when they walked into the dining area. When it was mentioned that the grandparents wanted them to stay there, it made Joe wonder what the connection was.

"Sara tells me they did not get to spend much time with your grandparents when they were here."

"No, sadly. My grandfather had several things to take care of in town and did not get time to socialize as much as they would have liked. That is one reason they suggested we stay here. They said it was a wonderful place and hoped we would take the time to explore more than they had."

"Does your grandfather have a connection to this area?"

"He said he did, but his father had more of the connection. He did not elaborate on any details. He said he would discuss it with us when we returned home. He has a hard time keeping things to himself once he is asked for specifics."

"That may be why he did not spend time with us. Maybe he is hiding something." Heather spoke up.

Everyone looked at her. What had made her say that?

"What? Has no one thought of that yet? I mean, why were the journal and the photo left behind?"

"What photo?" Mr. Watson asked. His attention was drawn to Heather and intensified when he looked at the other faces around the table.

"And what journal?" Mrs. Watson added. She also noticed the body language of everyone.

"Rachelle and I found a journal and two old photos in the room while cleaning after your relatives left. I gave them to Sara for safekeeping."

"May we see them?" Mr. Watson asked.

"They are in the safe. I don't know who they belong to. They may not be from your family. We don't always clean as thoroughly as we did this time." Heather replied to help Sara. She knew her sister was not ready to release the treasures to anyone before she had time to read more of the journal.

"Yes, I have put them safely away until we contact previous guests to locate the true owners." Sara covered herself. She knew all too well who they belonged to. Looking at Mr. Watson was all she needed to know that he was related to the man in the one photo.

"That makes sense." Mrs. Watson said. She did not want her husband to make a scene. They had a mission. One that required discernment.

Andy interrupted all the conversation and thoughts when he served dinner. Karen poured fresh coffee for everyone and joined the rest of the family to eat. The children were all sitting at their table and not paying attention to the adults.

Gayle was thrilled to be included at the adult table this time. She felt so grown up this year. Hearing the conversations piqued her curiosity. As she ate, she repeatedly looked at the new guests. What was it about them?

Chapter Six
Young Detective

Gayle decided to do some investigating of her own the next day. She had seen what her aunt Heather had found and wondered if the new guests had left clues in their short visit. Gayle had been intrigued with researching since she was a small child, learning about the discoveries about the family she was adopted into. Maybe she was destined to become a detective.

Gayle waited until the coast was clear, and the young couple left for the day before she asked Heather if she could help clean the rooms that day. Heather was thrilled any time Gayle asked and agreed to let her help. Without thinking or asking, she told Gayle to start in the young couple's room and just do a quick cleaning. She added that it did not need the deep clean like she and Rachelle had done a few days prior. All it needed was the bed made, fresh towels, vacuuming, and a quick dusting.

Gayle took the cleaning supplies with her and entered the room. At first glance, she didn't see anything out of the ordinary. Quite the contrary. The couple had even made their bed before leaving. The towels were folded and placed on the counter by the bathroom sink. Their clothes were placed in the dresser drawers and hanging in the closet. Their shoes were neatly placed under the edge of the bed. Their toiletries were neatly arranged on the bathroom sink vanity.

Gayle took care of all the normal cleaning and then noticed the wallet sitting on the dresser, partially hidden by the tray of coffee supplies. She carefully examined how it was placed, then gently removed it. She glanced around the room as if someone might be watching her, then opened it.

Inside were the driver's licenses for both of them. Roman Leon Watson was the man's full name. Jennifer Marshall-Watson was the woman's name. Gayle glanced at the other information, then folded it back and replaced it as she had found it. She wondered why they never mentioned their first names around anyone. All she knew them as was Mr. and Mrs. Watson. And why were they out without their licenses? No one ever went anywhere without their ID. Gayle found both details odd for a young couple.

"Gayle?" Heather called from the hallway. "Are you still in the Watson's room?"

"I am just leaving," Gayle said as she opened the door and walked out. She closed the door and made sure it was locked before stepping away to join Heather.

"So, did you find out anything new about them?"

"What do you mean?"

"I know you well enough. You wanted nothing to do with cleaning today. By the way, thank you for doing it, though. You wanted to see if you could find any information on them."

"I think it is a family curse. I have watched you and mama and wanted to be a part of it all my life. And yes, I discovered their first names and that they are traveling without driver's licenses today."

Heather shook her head and smiled as she raised her hand to give her niece a high five. "Good work, kiddo. You will make a great detective one day. What are their first names?"

"I will not tell."

"Oh, you are good! Now, tell me."

"His name is Roman Leon Watson, and her name is Jennifer Marshall-Watson," Gayle whispered close to Heather's ear.

"Interesting."

"But what does that mean?"

"I have no idea. More investigation is needed. In the meantime, little one, we have rooms to clean." Heather handed her a new dust cloth.

Gayle smiled and took the cloth from her aunt. This was going to be fun. She was going to be a part of the silent investigation. Eyes and ears open, twenty-four/seven. She followed Heather to the stairway to work on the rooms upstairs. As she turned the corner, she saw the front door open and watched Roman Watson walk in alone.

Heather touched Gayle's arm. "Discreet," she whispered. "Always stay discreet."

"Right." Gayle turned her gaze and followed her aunt into the next room. Her curiosity continued, but she knew she would solve the puzzle if she took her time.

Roman did not stay in the room long and put something into his right pant pocket as he walked out the front door.

After Heather and Gayle finished cleaning the remaining rooms, Gayle helped put all the supplies away. Heather said she was heading home to give Ben a break with the kids. Gayle snuck into Roman and Jennifer's room as Heather walked out the door. She immediately looked on the dresser to see if the wallet with the licenses inside was there. That was still there. She could not figure out what Roman may have taken on his way out. What could be more important?

Gayle took one more look around the room and left. She would need to take her time if she was going to find out the mysterious connection between them, the previous guests, and their family estate.

Sara watched as her daughter left the manor. She shook her head, wondering why Gayle was interested in helping Heather clean. She rarely cleaned her bedroom. Kids are always changing, thought Sara. She loved her daughter, no matter what stage she was going through. And she had gone through several since being adopted several years ago.

The phone rang, interrupting Sara's thoughts.

"Hello, Bella Rose Manor, Sara speaking."

27

"Hello, Ms. Sara. How are you?"

"I am doing well, Mr. Williams." Sara laughed. It was not often that her husband called and pretended to be a stranger. Sara always knew his voice, even when he tried to disguise it.

"That is good to know. I was wondering if you were doing anything special this evening or if you would be interested in joining me at the Lounge for dinner and some dancing."

"Dancing? Mr. Williams? It has been years since we went dancing. What is the occasion?"

"I heard through the grapevine in town that Adam has a new group playing. A band instead of the usual karaoke. I thought we'd support them and check out the newest hot spot."

"Sounds good to me, my love."

"Who is this love you speak of? Do I know him?" Randall laughed at his jealous attempt.

"I will never tell," Sara replied with a sneaky expression. "You will have to trust me and find out tonight."

"It will give me great pleasure to find out. See you later, Ms. Sara."

Sara hung up the phone and smiled. She loved how Randall found ways to keep their romance alive after all the years they had been together.

Chapter Seven
Antiques

Roman caught up with his wife downtown. She had been shopping in one of the antique shops and found items Roman had mentioned his grandparents owning. She had them in her hands when he walked into the store.

"What do you have there?" He looked at them briefly. "We don't need any of these."

"No, but I have heard you talk about some of these things. I wanted to show you how much they cost." Jennifer set them on a cleared side table.

Roman picked up the first item and turned it over to see if a name was imprinted on the base. There it was. His great-grandmother's name. He smiled as he turned it toward Jennifer. "She'd be proud that this is priced so high. I remember it being in my grandparent's home when I was younger, and no one thought anything of it except it was a kitchen tool, although Grandma told me it was an heirloom.

"Funny how things change over the years. Look at this recipe book." She handed it to her husband.

He stared at it for a moment. Then took it from her. "This one we are keeping."

"Why?"

"This is the exact same one my great-grandparents gave my grandparents on their wedding day."

"How do you know it is the exact same one?"

"Look inside at page thirty-two."

Jennifer opened it to that page. A message was written in black ink near the center of the page. Jennifer read it while her husband attempted to hide a tear.

"If you have reached this page, know that you are more than a friend. You are a friend to be cherished."

"My grandmother wrote that before she gave this book to her neighbor before she was married."

Jennifer closed the book and tucked it under her arm. That treasure was going home with them.

Roman did not protest. He knew what else was hidden in that book. He would have insisted on purchasing it if his wife had returned it to the table.

"It is time we get going. I want to see a few other places this afternoon before it gets too dark out here."

"Okay. I'm right with you. I will put this in the car and catch up with you."

"No, bring that book with you. I am not letting it out of my sight until it is in our room."

"Why, because of that short message?"

"No, there is more to it. I will explain it to you when we get back."

"Okay. You know I will remind you until you do."

"Yes, my love. I know how you are. This time I won't complain."

The pair left the shop and walked toward the end of town. They had one more stop to make.

When they returned to the manor, they were met by Sara and Heather. Jennifer entered their room and placed the recipe book on their bed before joining her husband, Sara, and Heather in the great room.

"Did you all enjoy your time in town today?" Sara asked.

"We did. It was a time of discovery. So many old things I remember my grandparents had, some that belonged to their parents."

"I know. We hear that remark a lot. Andy has a few older kitchen tools that he uses. He says some of them work better than the modern inventions."

"I agree. I learned how to cook using the old tools."

"And he is a good cook," Jennifer added. She placed her hands on her husband's forearm.

Roman looked around the kitchen where they had migrated once the topic of the kitchen tools came up. He spotted the antique key in the corner, hanging on the wall by the back door.

"Where did you find that key?" he asked.

Sara reached up and took it off the hook. "This old thing? Andy found it when we were on vacation. She lied. It was not the same key, but it was similar.

"My grandfather had one very similar. I thought maybe this was a match. He used to talk about the special keys his father used. He kept the ones he could find after his father died."

"What did he use the keys for?"

"He used to make furniture. Most of what he designed used a key like this, but each one was unique. None of the keys worked in two separate pieces. So there were a lot of keys around his place. Us kids always wanted to play with them, but Granddad would not let us touch them, let alone play with them."

"I can imagine the mess it would be if you mixed the keys around."

"Oh, yes. As kids, we did not understand, but as an adult, I certainly do. I wish we knew what piece of furniture that key goes to. Have you found any furniture on the property that did not have a key to open it?"

"We did have a few pieces in the attic that required a key, but we found them all with some extra searching. I wonder if there are more pieces we have not found?"

"Either that or the pieces have been destroyed over the years. And like every red-blooded American, the keys were saved."

"That is so true. Men back then did not like to throw away anything they 'might need someday' away."

Sara laughed. She remembered her father saving and collecting the smallest and oddest things. Old screws, nails,

31

tile, roofing, measuring tapes, saws, hammers, and screwdrivers. Glen had multiples of many tools.

The group returned to the great room before Roman and Jennifer said they would get changed and get some dinner. Sara asked them if they had eaten at the Downtown Café yet. They said they would go soon.

Roman and Jennifer discussed their plans for the Storytelling celebration while they ate dinner at a local restaurant just outside of town. They had not planned on being there for the event, but once they heard about it, they knew they had to stay and hear the stories, get to know some of the storytellers, and assure that their stories were at least partially true.

Jennifer had observed her husband talk with a few local men and a few of the early storytellers already in town. She knew he was not sharing their story, just assuring others were not touching on it and making it a fable. Somehow he would find a way to tell his story while there. He always did.

Later that night, while they lay in bed talking quietly, Jennifer asked him about the key they saw in the kitchen.

"Were you telling the truth about what your great-grandfather used the keys for? Was each one different? Seems it would have been easier to have all the keys alike."

"Yes, I am very sure. He did most of the work on his own during that time. Each piece was unique, and he had several customers. So he believed each key had to be different."

"That is so impressive. I'd like to hear the story behind the keys."

"In time, dear. In due time. We need to let it ride its course as long as possible if we can. No talk of the key for a while, Okay?"

'Okay. I don't understand, but I will deal with what I must do."

"You are an amazing person, Jennifer-Marshall Watson."

"You are too, my love. We need to get some sleep. I have a feeling tomorrow will be busy. The people start arriving for the storytelling."

Jennifer rolled over, away from Roman. She was tired and in total understanding of his need for quiet.

Chapter Eight
Whispers

The town was buzzing with activity when Terri arrived at the café. She appreciated her private parking spot behind her business. Before entering through the back door, she walked around the side to gaze down the main street. She knew it would only be a matter of hours before it was so busy and full of traffic, and then just people, it would be difficult to see the asphalt. She had grown to love this event. So many people from around the world entered the little town she now called home. She knew she would learn a lot from the people without attending a single show. Many ate a meal at the café. Others she walked among after work. All anyone had to do was pay attention with eyes and ears.

They had added the Lounge this year and wondered if it would draw more people in. She and Steven discussed closing it during the event but decided to stay open all night if the people continued to come.

Adam agreed to stay to sing karaoke and run the sound for the one night they had a band playing.

As Terri was about to open for business, she noticed Roman and Jennifer walking up the steps. She opened the door and welcomed them in.

"Good morning. How are you doing today?" Terri asked them as she did all her customers.

"We are doing wonderful. Sara told us to stop here at least once while we were in town. We decided to beat the crowd later in the week."

"You made a wise decision. Come on in." She let them in and looked outside to see if anyone else was on their way before closing the door.

"The menu is written on the wall. Read over it and let me know what you would like to eat. What may I bring you each to drink?" Terri pointed to the wall as she spoke.

"I want to try your raspberry sweet tea. I have heard a little about it."

"Ah, it is one of the popular drinks. Made fresh each day. I will be right back with it." Terri went into the back to pour their drinks. Her other help had not arrived yet, and she was getting concerned. There was no way she could run the café on her own.

A few minutes later, her help arrived. "So sorry we are late. The traffic got us. There was an accident at the end of town."

"Oh no. Did anyone get hurt?"

"Not that we could tell, but the road was blocked, and we were stuck at a spot we could not turn onto another road. It would seem easy to do with all the ways to get around this town."

"Not always. I am glad you were not involved and made it in." She then told them who their first customer was and walked past them to deliver drinks to the young couple.

As she approached their table, she noticed Jennifer was rubbing Roman's arm, and he looked pale.

"Are you okay?" Terri asked as she set their drinks down.

"Yes, he is fine," Jennifer said. "He gets flashbacks sometimes."

Terri assumed it was service related and thanked him for her service.

"No," Roman shook his head. "Not service related. Just an old memory. Your menu reminded me of something."

"Oh," Terri turned to look at the menu. "A favorite dish from childhood?"

"Something like that," Roman said. "I'll be okay."

Jennifer had no idea which item on the menu on the wall brought the memory. She imagined the clue or even the answer was in the recipe book. It had to be. They placed their order and then ate in silence after it was delivered. Jennifer did not pressure Roman for answers regarding the flashback.

The day continued at the Café with a steady stream of customers. Steven arrived mid-afternoon to open the Lounge. Adam arrived even later to start the karaoke. Terri noticed something different about the two of them. She could not put her finger on it.

Barbara walked in after getting off work and told Terri she was there to help for the night.

"You are a godsend."

"Not really. I figure being here is the only way I'm going to see Steven all week."

"That may be true. I am glad Adam often works with me. Makes it more fun."

"Agreed. Anytime Steven and I can spend time together is wonderful." Barbara looked at Terri and noticed something in her expression. "What's going on, Terri? You look perplexed."

"I don't know for sure. Steven and Adam both look or act a little different today."

"Maybe because of the crowds they expect or the long hours ahead?"

"Maybe." Terri walked away to wait on more customers. She shook her head to push out any suspicious thoughts running through it. Now was not the time for such things.

Barbara watched as Terri went to work, then walked into the kitchen to see how she could help. She looked at Steven and Adam from the side swinging door into the Lounge. She had noticed something about the two of them over the last couple of weeks. There was more to her being there that night than wanting to spend time with Steven.

The music was loud, and the crowd was more than they had ever had. Terri was thrilled. She sat with Barbara watching the men in their lives work together.

"Those two have such a special bond. Most men don't have that. They may have met under not so great of circumstances, but they have achieved great things since."

"Yes, they have. I am proud of them."

"I am amazed at what Steven has done for me. I would not be here if it were not for him. He literally saved my life."

"And I am glad he did." Terri reached over and put her hand on Barbara's forearm. She had become a great friend in a short time.

Terri looked at the clock. The party was going strong, and it was well past two in the morning. She was so tired. She knew she could trust the guys and decided to leave the rest of the night in the capable hands of Adam and Steven. She told Barbara she could stay if she wanted to, but she was going home.

"I will stay for a little bit longer. You have had a long day, and several more coming. Go. Get some rest."

"You are right. I need my beauty sleep." Terri laughed. She headed for the men with the key, then remembered they had their own. All she had to do was tell them she was leaving.

As Terri approached Adam, she noticed a customer standing next to Steven, saying something right into his ear. He smiled and nodded his head. He looked over at Adam, who also smiled.

Terri didn't say a word. Whatever it was, it was none of her business. They were adults. They could handle anything. She went to Adam and told him she was going home to get some sleep.

"I don't blame you, my love. You have been here forever. Get some sleep. I will try not to disturb you when I get home." He looked around at all the people and laughed a quick laugh. "I may be getting home when you wake up." He leaned over and kissed Terri's forehead. She was too tired to raise her head for a better kiss.

Barbara decided she needed to go home too. She spotted Steven looking at her and smiling. She walked over to him and told him she was going home.

"Get some good sleep. I am going to try to get these people to leave. I've never known such night owls. I thought I was bad when I was still into my party days."

"You are older now."

"Have you looked at this crowd? They are not so young."

Barbara looked around. He was right. A lot of them were older than they were. They were, however, a different breed.

"True. Well, good luck. I am leaving them all in your capable hands."

Steven kissed Barbara and held her for a few minutes longer. "Sleep well."

Barbara left through the back door and drove home. She had seen the same thing Terri had before she left. She couldn't get the image out of her head of the lady whispering into her husband's ear.

Chapter Nine
A Story to Tell

Sara was still awake and in the office when she heard Roman and Jennifer walk in. The young couple had been in town all day and late into the night for the festival.

Sara was always amazed at the people who flocked to town to listen to stories that may or may not be true. No set type of person attended. They came from all around the world. She usually wandered through downtown during Storytelling, attended a few events, and talked with people. She had missed the first day but planned to go on the second day this year.

In the meantime, she kept an eye on her guests who were there for the festival. She had not seen most of them since early that morning. When Roman and Jennifer returned, she met them in the great room as they walked through to their room.

"Good evening," Sara said. Jennifer was surprised but laughed.

"I didn't mean to scare you. I thought you saw me."

"I did see you. But I've been listening to stories told today, and you startled me."

"Some of those stories can be frightful. Especially the ones late at night. I've been down there most years. Didn't make it today."

"You will need to go on the last night of the festival if you don't go any other time."

"Oh, and why is that?"

"That is when Roman is telling his story."

"You have a story to tell? Is it true or a fable?"

"You will need to attend and decide for yourself," Roman added to what his wife had told Sara.

"Then I will do my best to be there. I enjoy the stories my guests tell. I usually hear them while they stay here, but being part of the storytelling could prove interesting."

"I look forward to seeing you there," Roman said. He touched his wife's elbow to get her to move.

"I guess we are done for the night," Jennifer commented as she took steps toward the hallway. "We will see you in the morning."

Sara nodded her head without saying a word. She noticed the physical communication between the young couple. It was not something she would normally pay attention to, but there was something about this couple that intrigued her from the moment they arrived. She made a mental note to keep her eyes open. There may be something to worry about. Chances were that it was nothing.

Sara closed and locked her office door and left the manor through the side door. She walked home, illuminated only by her phone's flashlight. She was used to the path and could have done it in the pitch dark. She knew Randall would worry, so she always had a light to use.

The next morning Sara joined the guests in the kitchen for the meal Andy had made. She smiled when she saw that he had made one of his one-pan breakfasts but added so many extra things that it looked like he had prepared a feast.

After breakfast, the guests said they were headed to town for the festivities. Roman and Jennifer had been noticeably absent. Sara knew they had not gotten in until well past midnight and asked Andy to set aside meals if they were hungry when they woke up. Andy gave her a funny look but agreed. He would have thrown the food away if it were not for that.

"Why are you so concerned with them eating?" Andy asked.

"I'm not really. I am concerned about them overall. There is something about them that have my cat hairs raised a little."

"That is a phrase I have not heard in a while," he grinned and shook his head. He had not heard that since his mother said it when he was little. He cleared the table and put the leftovers in containers for Roman and Jennifer.

The street was empty at this early hour when Roman and Jennifer began walking down the center lane. No matter where they went, their goal was to find time in the day to walk down the middle of the road and not be in anyone's way. This little town was easy to do, even during a festival.

They left the road and walked into the large tent at the end of town. Another storyteller was waiting for them at the front.

"Good morning. I assume you are Roman and Jennifer?"

"Yes, we are. We are so glad you were able to meet with us today."

"I understand you have a story to share that is not on the schedule. One that needs to be told?"

"Yes, on both counts. Our story involves many of the residents who live here. It has a history not heard before by most. And those that have heard it still do not believe it."

"As you stated last night during our conversation. Are you able to authenticate your story and the people involved?"

"I can account for the people. I cannot prove the story one way or another. That is where your trust comes into the picture. The people who need to hear this will be surprised when it is presented."

"I am intrigued. As I told you during our phone conversation, I will put you in the lineup for the last night of the festival."

"I appreciate that." Roman took Jennifer's hand and led her out of the tent.

"Are you ready to share your story with the world?"

"I don't know. I know it needs to be told. I know the family involved needs to hear it. I understand your question, though. Are they ready to hear the truth?"

"Only time and telling will answer that. In the meantime, I think we need to play it carefully and not draw suspicion to us and what we are doing."

"Agreed. We need to act normal."

The day continued, and more and more people arrived. The town was alive with shoulder-to-shoulder people by the time evening was upon them. Stories had been told. Food had been consumed from food trucks and local restaurants. Music played from the side street and on the garden hill. Everyone was enjoying the annual celebration.

Except for one mysterious person. A man who blended into the background. No one noticed him as he quietly wandered the streets and backside of town.

When the night engulfed the joyous sounds, the lights of celebration, and the musical notes of songs and instruments, he quietly walked away and disappeared behind the entryway. His name was engraved on the top iron archway.

He didn't notice being followed.

Chapter Ten
Beach Life

The ocean's waters lapped at their feet. The beach had been welcoming every morning since Jay and Carrie moved there. The sun had come up behind them as the day dawned from the east. They were blessed by the evening sunsets over the water most nights.

Walking along the beach had become a normal routine for Jay and Carrie. Tamara lay sleeping while Jay carried her in her carrier, lifting her when the water threatened to splash too high. Carrie walked ahead of her family, looking for special rocks to add to her collection. She turned and smiled at the man who had brought her happiness over the past few years.

Jay saw her smile and smiled back. He had searched long and hard to find the lady who would complete his life. He thought he had found the love of his life once before, but after that relationship ended, this beauty walked into his life, and everything changed. He stood in his tracks, watching her. She was the answer to his prayers.

A wave crashed into his leg and made him jump. He never let go of his daughter's carrier. She was his precious cargo. The littlest love of his life. Carrie laughed as she watched him. He had a way of making life easy and carefree.

Carrie walked back to be with Jay and Tamara. She picked her daughter up from the carrier and walked with Jay for another fifteen minutes.

"I need to get to work," Jay said as he turned to walk to the car.

"I know. You have beauty to capture and stories to write."

"Always."

"We can take another walk along the beach this evening."

"I look forward to it. It never gets old, you know that." Jay leaned over and kissed his wife. Never gets old, he thought as he took one last look at the beach. He closed his eyes for a brief moment. Maybe it was getting old. He shook his head as he got inside his car and started the engine. He then put the car in reverse and went off to capture his next group of photos for a future story he might publish.

That thought never left him as he worked that day. Maybe it was getting old. Was it time for a change? Would Carrie accept his idea? Was she ready for a change? After work, he parked his car in the garage and sat for a few minutes. Nothing like the present, when it was heavy on his mind, to discuss it. He learned a long time ago to voice his opinion. Keeping secrets or things bottled up inside was not good for him, nor anyone around him.

"Welcome home," Carrie greeted him with a frosted mug of beer. It was not always how she greeted him, but it had been an extra hot day, and she knew he had been out in the elements.

"You have read my mind." Jay took the mug and walked into the living room to sit down for a few minutes. Carrie joined him with a glass of wine. Jay looked at her and wondered why she had a glass of wine already in her hand. That was not her style.

"Okay, what is up with you?" He asked. Jay sat up and leaned toward her.

"Nothing," she tried to cover up her thoughts.

"I know that is not true. Spill it. What is going on?"

"I have been thinking recently and debated saying anything, but today as I watched you on the beach, I think it is time."

"Time? For what?" Jay sat straight up. What was she about to tell him?

"We need a change," Carrie began. She hesitated long enough to get a quick reaction. When there was none, she knew she had to speak her mind.

"I think we need to move." She held up her hand to stop Jay from saying anything. "I think we need to move close to Jeff. He is your family, and you need him."

Jay looked at Carrie without saying a word. His mind was flashing through the thoughts he had been having. How had she deciphered that from his recent actions? Had he accidentally said something?

"What makes you say that?"

"It is so obvious. You have a longing look in your eyes. I don't know if it is the need for a new area or if you need to reconnect with family and old friends."

There it was. *Old friends*. That is who or what had been on his mind. However, he was not about to mention any names. He continued to look into her eyes in silence.

"Am I right? Do you want to move?"

Jay took a deep breath and stood up. How could he tell Carrie what was on his mind? Would she understand? Of course, she would. She knew all about his life. She had accepted what he had to offer as the best he could give her. She had agreed.

Carrie knew someone else would always hold a piece of his heart. She also trusted him to never act on it. That love was a special love that two people of opposite sexes rarely share. She was wise enough to know he needed her. The *other* her.

Jay took a sip of his beer. His eyes diverted from her, and he gazed out the window. He could see the beach in the distance. He reached for Carrie's hand to draw her into him.

"Let's go for a walk. Can you call the neighbor to watch Tamara?"

"I already have." Carrie smiled.

Silence filled the space between them as they began the walk. The water lapped onto the sand. Sandpipers darted along the edge of the incoming balance of a wave. Jay's heart ached.

"I cannot believe you would agree to move to Tennessee. You love the ocean and beach life."

"Yes, I do. I love you more. While you were away for those six months, I told myself that wherever you were or wanted to be, I would support your decision. I will be by your side. As long as you wanted me to be."

"Why say it that way? I will always want you by my side."

"I know you will. But I want you to know I will be fine if you are happy."

"I will only be happy with you by my side." Jay put his arm around her shoulder. "Now, let's talk." He guided her to a bench, and they sat side by side, watching the sun slowly lower into the horizon.

Chapter Eleven
Moving

Terri had just returned home when her cell phone rang. It was Angela.

"Hello, Sis. What's going on?" Terri acted normal. A call at this hour from her sister was anything but normal.

"Hi. I know it's late, but Jeff just got off the phone with Jay."

Terri was immediately at full attention. "What's wrong?"

"Nothing, Sis. Boy, you are still hooked, aren't you?"

"No! I just know Jay would not call his brother unless something was wrong. Are his family alright?"

"Yes, Sis. Everyone is fine. I think." Angela added.

"Okay. So at this hour of the night, what is going on?" Terri calmed her voice. She did not mean to sound so concerned about her ex.

"Jeff told me that they are coming to Tennessee."

"I know that. They waited until Tamara was a little older to visit."

"No. Not for a visit. They have decided to move here."

Terri stood up. Move here? Her Ex? They had agreed. Why were they moving? "WHY?" Terri asked without hesitation.

"Jeff told me that Carrie knew Jay needed to be where he felt at home. Or something like that. He said Jay was unhappy, and Carrie would give up living on the coast to make him happy."

"Wow! I wonder what is really going on?"

"That's what I am wondering. But Jeff said there was nothing else to it. Jay wants to be near his family. And since Jeff is the only family they have left, here is where he wants to be."

"Well, I guess he can work from anywhere in the world, so that isn't a problem. What is your take on it?"

"I don't know. I thought you should hear it from me before you suddenly see them in the area."

"You make it sound like they are on their way here already."

"Almost. No, kidding. Jeff said they are coming for a visit first and then moving."

"So why was this such an urgent phone call?"

"I don't know now that I think about it. Silly of me to think you would care where they live."

"I am fine no matter where they live. So is Adam, if you are wondering."

"Okay. Good night, Sis."

"Goodnight." Terri hung up her phone. Her sister would never understand her relationship with Jay.

The next day Jay called Terri. When she answered, she immediately said she heard he was moving to Tennessee. In response, Jay laughed.

"I didn't think it would take long for the news to get to you. Sorry I didn't tell you first."

"It's fine. I am glad you are moving here. I am surprised she is giving up so much."

"I am too. This move is her idea. We plan to come next week to visit and see about the reality of a move. It may not happen in the end."

"Check it out. If I can help you with anything, let me know. Give Carrie my love."

"Thanks, Terri. That means a lot to me."

"We will always have...."

"Yes, we will," Jay finished without either one of them saying the actual saying they shared.

Terri went about her day. The festival was still going on, and there was a lot of work to do for all the visitors.

Adam noticed Terri watching him that night at the Lounge. He stepped away from the stage and asked her if she was okay. She looked at him and nodded that everything was fine. Then told him they would talk later. He was too busy to ask any other questions. He knew if there was an issue, his wife would talk to him about it.

As he walked back to the stage, he noticed the lady from the night before standing in the crowd. He glanced at Steven, but he was not paying attention. The lady approached him and spoke quietly. He nodded his head and pointed her towards Steven.

Steven smiled when he finally noticed the lady and motioned for her to come over to the end of the bar. She found an empty stool and sat down. Steven handed her a drink he had mixed for her, then walked away.

Adam watched from a distance as she took a sip but never let her eyes off Steven. Music was playing, and people were dancing on the small dance floor. Adam quickly lost his focus on the lady.

Suzanne sat at the bar, sipping her drink. She noticed Adam's stare but ignored it. He would find out who she was soon and why she was there. For now, Steven was the only one who needed to know anything.

Chapter Twelve
The Eyes

Steven finally closed the lounge at three in the morning. He had not known that late hour at a bar since his days in Seattle. It was fun to watch everyone and talk to many, but he was not used to the long work shift.

He shook his head as he walked to his car. Maybe he was getting old. He laughed at himself. That was a feeling he was not ready for. He had a lot of life to live left in him. He inhaled a deep breath of the pre-dawn air and drove home.

Thoughts of the lady at the bar kept sneaking into his thoughts. What was it about her? Why had he been the only person she spoke with? And what was her agenda? The words she spoke were deliberate. It was more than a casual conversation. She had a confident air about her. Not that she was stuck up in any way, but she was a no-nonsense lady. She knew what she wanted, and it seemed she was not afraid to ask for it. It was now up to him to help her. But he didn't know how. And the request for him to keep it between the two of them bothered him. He never kept things from Barbara, and he shared a lot of things with Adam.

Barbara was fast asleep when Steven tiptoed into their bedroom and eased into their bed. He smiled when he felt his wife's arm automatically reach over and rest on his chest. He held it there as he fell asleep.

Dreamland quickly overtook his subconscious. He was back in Seattle. Working the bar again. It was a busy night with rarely time for a break. Music was playing, and people were talking as they drank. A few couples were up dancing.

He smiled as he hoped someday to have someone to love like he imagined those couples had.

In the corner sat a lady. Alone. Her blonde hair was pulled back in a single ponytail at the base of her neck. She held up her wine glass near her face. He sensed she was deep in thought as her smile faded slightly. She had spoken to no one. A younger lady walked into the bar. The older lady watched her but never spoke to her. The girl, obviously not of legal drinking age, ordered a virgin mixed drink. Steven took her the drink and stood there a little longer than usual. Her eyes, a shade of blue he had never seen, accentuated by her red hair and teal blouse, were mesmerizing.

His dream faded. The noise of the bar drifted into silence. Steven slept. Barbara stirred.

When Steven finally awoke just five hours later, his head felt foggy. He knew he had not had anything to drink the night before but sensed something had occupied his thoughts. Steven slowly sat up on the edge of the bed. He glanced over and was glad Barbara was already up. He would not be disrupted as he tried to remember the dream.

His eyes opened as his thoughts cleared. His dream. It wasn't a dream. It was a memory. He had seen the lady from last night years before --- in Seattle. His eyes drifted around, envisioning the scene. The lady, then and again last night. Yes, she was a little older, but she was definitely the same person. He searched back. That younger lady. The red-haired one with those eyes…

"Good morning, sleepy head," Barbara entered the room with a fresh cup of coffee and interrupted her husband's thoughts.

He shook his head, erasing the visions like one would erase the drawings on an etch-a-sketch. "Good morning." He reached for the mug of coffee, took a sip, and set it on the nightstand. Then reached for Barbara's hand.

Barbara sat down next to him on the bed. "What time did you finally get home? I tried to stay up, but sleep overtook me."

"I finally closed the lounge at three this morning! It has been several years since I kept a bar open that late. It was fun, but I'm getting too old for that." They both laughed.

"Yes, we are getting older. More mature. More sensible."

"I never thought I'd be the sensible type." He smiled and drank more coffee. He needed to wake up. "What do you have planned for the day?"

"I need to go into the office for a while today. Then I hope to spend time in town. I love to people-watch and talk to the visitors."

"I may join you in town before I need to open the lounge later this afternoon." He set his empty cup down and stood up. "Time to get ready for our day." Barbara stood, and they hugged. Steven held her a bit longer than normal, but Barbara didn't mind. She missed their long hugs.

That afternoon they met in town and walked around amongst all the people. They were approaching the main tent when Steven gasped.

Barbara looked at him. "What was that about? What did I miss?"

"That lady over to the right. See her?"

"I see a lot of ladies. Can you be a little more specific?" Barbara shook her head.

"The redhead. Long red hair."

"Ah, yes, She's pretty. What about her?"

"I've seen her before."

"Was she at the Lounge last night?"

"No. And maybe it's not her, but I think she was in Seattle at one time."

"Really? You have a good memory if that's true. How long ago was that?"

"A long time ago. But, when you see her eyes, you will understand."

At that point, the lady turned to walk toward them, and Barbara noticed her blue eyes even at a distance. "Now I understand why you remember her."

The lady walked past them without saying a word. Steven turned to watch her as she walked away. What was it about her?

Later that evening, Steven was busy serving drinks at the lounge. Barbara stopped in and gave Terri a hand in the Café before it closed for meals. Customers could still order from a limited menu in the lounge. Most just wanted something to snack on while they drank and listened to music and karaoke. Barbara took a break and sat to watch the brave souls sing. That was something she would never be brave enough to try.

As Barbara returned to wash dishes in the Café, she was met by a tall blonde.

"Excuse me. I was not watching where I was going," the lady spoke.

"No problem. You are fine." Barbara looked up and noticed her eyes. She did her best not to overreact. The hair was a different color, but the lady's eyes were the same.

Barbara tried to shake the encounter as she washed the dishes and then helped wipe off the rest of the tables.

"Are you alright?" Terri asked. "You look like you have seen a ghost."

"No, I'm fine. I just ran into a lady whose eyes reminded me of someone else I recently saw."

"I am surprised anyone stands out that much with the crowd in town."

"This one certainly does. I can't help but wonder if they are the same person or at least related."

"They look that much alike?"

"The hair is different, but their eyes, their eyes are intense."

"Are you talking about the blonde lady?"

"The one is, yes. Why? Do you know her?"

"No, but she has been here for the past two nights." Terri cut herself off from saying more. She realized that the lady had spoken only to Steven and that she had literally spoken into his ear, not in a normal conversation.

"I wonder if Steven has spoken to her? He seemed shocked to see the other lady in town. That lady had red hair, but her eyes matched."

"You need to ask him."

"I will. He's busy now, and it's loud with the music. I'll ask him at home. I am not staying as late tonight. These late hours are for the birds." She laughed. "Well, not really. Birds don't stay up this late."

"You are right, though. I used to be able to stay up late and get up early. Not anymore. Too old."

"That is what Steven said this morning. We're too old for this." They both laughed as they finished wiping off the last table.

Chapter Thirteen
The Search

Roman met Jennifer at the front door of the manor. He reached for her hand to help her take the last step. She smiled at him. He was always such a gentleman. She knew his love for her was genuine. She rarely spent time away from him, but today she had the urge for some alone time.

"How was your time in town? Did you see anyone you knew?"

"How would I know anyone in this town? Plus, there are so many people walking around I would not be able to find anyone I knew if I tried. Have you been there today?"

"Only when we were there together. And you are right, the town is full of people. All kinds of people. I am enjoying seeing so many. Are you?"

"I love it here. I just wish we had more time to relax and enjoy it instead of being on the search for something your grandfather says is a connection to your great-grandfather. Do you honestly believe there is a connection hidden here in town?"

"Not in town. Here, at the manor. Or someplace on this estate. I can feel it."

They had walked to their room before finishing their conversation. Roman did not want to raise suspicions with the owners or other guests. Their mission had to be kept secret for as long as possible.

"So, where else do we need to look?"

"I heard Sara talking about a cemetery on the property. I feel something or someone may be there. That may be the connection or lead to it somehow."

"We could go locate that tomorrow."

"Did you notice that man last night that stood in the back of everyone else and then just seemed to disappear? I watched him for a while, and suddenly he was gone. No one seemed to pay attention to him."

"Sorry to say, I did not. Who do you think it was?"

"Since I am seemingly the only person who saw him," Roman hesitated. "I think it was my great-grandfather."

"But he's been dead for years!"

"Exactly. No one saw him because he is a ghost."

"A what?!"

"A ghost. Don't tell me you don't believe in ghosts."

"I never gave them a thought. Although I heard several people talking about how so much of this town is haunted. You may be right."

"I think we need to check it out. I will keep my eyes open more. Since you didn't see him, I won't ask you to keep a lookout. But if you do see something, let me know."

"Oh, believe me, If I see a ghost, you Will know." She laughed.

While Jennifer changed for their dinner out, she gazed at the mirror. Roman had asked if she had seen anyone she knew while in town. She had lied to him for the first time in her life. The person she had seen may or may not be who she thought it was, and there was no need to bring up that part of her life. Roman had rescued her when she was eighteen and never asked any questions about what had caused her to run. She disguised her pain over the years and even hid it from herself until today. The memories had flooded back. But it all could have been an illusion. So many tall tales were being told that one would begin to believe and want the imaginable.

Roman called her name and brought her out of her trance.

"I'll be ready in a few minutes. Where are we going for dinner?"

"I thought we would go to that BBQ place we saw just outside town."

"That sounds good. I know the south loves their BBQ." Jennifer immerged from the bathroom in a long flowing dress."

"You look good in that dress. You look like you belong among this group of people. Almost from the hippie generation."

Jennifer smiled. That was the look she was trying to achieve. She had found the dress at one of the vendors in town and hoped her husband would like the new look on her. He was often critical of what she wore and how she presented herself.

Roman had changed also. He had dressed casually so he could blend in with the country life of BBQ food. He had a knack for changing how he looked and spoke depending on what group of people he was with or what part of the country he happened to be in. His father had taught him that in the brief time he knew his father.

Losing his parents at a young age had not been easy. He made it a point to remember as much about them as possible. His grandparents did their best to help him remember his parents and to teach him more about life than most kids are taught. Life was short was one that he understood. Which was why he needed answers soon. His grandfather needed to know the truth.

An hour later, they were seated at a booth after waiting in line to eat at the Fire Station Restaurant. Roman had heard it was a good place to eat. The line was proof enough for them to believe the rumor. After they had eaten, they knew they would give it a good review. The owner had walked around and talked to everyone, learning a little about each group. That impressed Roman.

When Roman and Jennifer left, they walked around the area before going to their car and driving back to the manor. When they arrived, they decided to walk down the path to the gazebo before going to their room.

Sara and Randall were sitting in the gazebo when Roman and Jennifer arrived. They welcomed their guests and invited them to join them. As they all sat together, Randall pointed out all the mountain ranges and talked about the area. Jennifer sat and listened. She absorbed the beauty as the sun was ending its work for the day and setting behind the one mountain range. Jennifer smiled as the sun gave one last attempt at sending its glow over the earth below it. Sara smiled when she noticed the young lady experiencing what she had almost taken for granted. She turned to watch the last ray of sun leave and knew she should never ignore the beauty she was blessed with every day.

Together the four of them left the gazebo. Sara and Randall walked to their house. Roman and Jennifer walked back to the manor. It had been a full day for them. Tomorrow was going to be an adventure. One during which he hoped they would find answers to appease his grandfather.

The next morning the guests were treated to another well-planned breakfast by Andy. He rarely disappointed his guests with his meals. Sara joined them, but Randall had to get to the office early to meet a client. Roman shared his plans for the day about visiting the cemetery he had heard was on the property and asked if it was okay to see it. Sara said of course, and offered to go with them.

"No, but thank you. We have been interested in cemeteries for as long as I can remember, and there is something about small family ones that hold the most interesting details."

"We have discovered that this one holds secrets. We have deciphered some but imagine there are still some out there that we have not stumbled upon yet."

Roman looked at his wife, and they smiled. "That seems to be the case in all cemeteries. They are full of untold secrets. We enjoy making up stories about them when we visit them." He winked at Jennifer.

Roman and his wife walked through the opened gate and noticed all the grave sites before them.

"This is going to be interesting?" Jennifer said. "Where do we start?"

"We'll just follow the path around the edge and work our way to the center." He took her hand, and they began the slow walk, paying attention to each gravestone.

Each stone held a wealth of information if a person took the time to read it and take in the details of the stone itself. They hoped at least one would speak to them and answer their unspoken questions.

They noticed the gravestones to the left of the gate opening laid flat on top of the ground, while the ones to the right stood up as most gravestones in the country were. As they read the names, dates, and any message written on them, they realized the deceased buried with the larger stones were older. When they looked closer at the flat ones, they knew all the deceased were mostly infants. A few were older, but Jennifer commented that most were newborns.

"Why do you think there were so many infant deaths around here?" Jennifer asked.

"I am trying to remember what my grandfather told me about the manor and its original use. He said something about young children but didn't say they were infants."

"Maybe we should have brought Sara with us. I am sure she knows the story behind them."

"I would hope so since she owns the land."

"We will stop in and ask her when we get back."

"I would like to wait. I want to call my grandfather and ask him first. He may know. If he doesn't, maybe he can do some research before we get home."

"Okay. Plus, you don't want to draw attention to yourself and the reason we are here before it is time."

"Agreed. Speaking of which, I need to work on the story I will share at the last night of storytelling."

"Do you know which one you are going to share?"

"Not yet. I have narrowed it down to two. I will write them out tonight and see which one seems the best and does not take up all their time. There are several people telling stories while we are here."

"And you are not up until the last night. Some people will have already left, and many will be exhausted by then."

"That's okay. As long as the right people are there to hear it, I am okay."

"Are you going to tell me what you are sharing?"

"No, I need to keep it a total secret. I am so sorry. I hope you understand."

"I do. I would like to be included in the things you do once in a while."

"I need you to be in my background and support me when I need it."

"You know I will be. No matter what happens." Jennifer kissed him on his cheek as they reached the end of the cemetery and walked through the gate opening.

They walked hand in hand back to the manor. Sara was in the office and saw them approaching the door. She walked into the great room to greet them.

"Hello, you two. Did you find what you were looking for in the cemetery?"

"What we found was more questions. If anything, I need to call my grandfather to see what he knows." Roman replied. He did not want to ask Sara for the details. He wanted to hear as much as he could from his family first.

"Okay. If you would like, I can give you the details we determined from our findings." Sara said, wondering why they didn't want to ask her for the details.

"We thank you, but Roman wants to stick with his one source on this trip." Jennifer held her husband's arm with her hand to keep him quiet as she spoke for him.

"I understand," Sara said. She had more to say but kept quiet. Something told her there was more to this couple than they were willing to share or that she had figured out. "I will be around if you have any questions," she added.

"Thank you." Roman and Jennifer walked past her to their room.

Roman reached for his phone to call his grandfather.

Chapter Fourteen
More Clues

Suzanne sat on the bench in the middle of town. She had walked from her hotel room to avoid needing to find a parking space. The festival was in full swing, and people were everywhere, even in the early morning. Food trucks were set up, and a few were serving breakfast. She walked over to them and checked out the menus for later. Her fresh cup of coffee was enough to satisfy her for hours.

She watched as people walked around and talked with one another. She noticed that most people were in groups. Very few walked alone. She was one of the few who was on her own. She wondered how many had a mission other than attending the event. Was she the only one not interested in storytelling? She had her own story to tell if anyone wanted to listen. She was not ready to tell it yet, but she did have a story.

Instead of looking out of place sitting there, she had brought a book with her. She opened it and mindlessly turned a page. She was thankful for a sunny day and her sunglasses that hid her gaze. No one could tell she was not reading a single word.

Music began to play in the park. The band was practicing before their performance scheduled for that night. She wondered if that affected the business at the Downtown Café and Lounge. She had grown fond of the bartender in the short few days she had been there. He was a sweet young man. Plus, he was willing to help her when she had whispered her request. What stranger would be eager to help an older lady with such a secret?

She smiled as she listened to the band. She decided she may have to return that evening to listen to them.

As she turned another page in her book, she caught someone walking in front of her. She looked up and almost gasped. Suzanne did not expect to find the young couple out so early. She understood them to be night owls. Maybe all the excitement gave them little sleep. She kept her head down but her eyes up as she watched them cross the street and enter one of the stores.

She did find one problem with the stores in the town. They were small. A person could not sneak in and shop and not be noticed. For that reason, she stayed positioned on the bench and waited for them to return. Depending on where they went, she would follow them. There were enough people in town now that she would not be suspected of stalking anyone. That was the last thing she needed. She also had her cell phone she could pretend to talk on. She hated to see people on their phones so much lately but now found it came in handy. She wondered how many other people used it as a disguise.

Roman and Jennifer ordered their favorite coffee and Danish from the store and talked with the owner before they left. They didn't notice Suzanne as she stood up from the bench and followed them.

"Are we going to return to the cemetery today?" Jennifer asked Roman as they walked past the lady on the bench.

"I am still waiting to hear back from Grandfather. I left him a detailed message, so he may be doing some research before he calls me back."

"I would love to know the story about the different gravestones and why so many babies are buried there."

"I would too. I'm sure he will call as soon as he knows something."

Suzanne was puzzled. What graveyard were they talking about? What gravestones? Did it have a personal connection to them? It sounded like he had the connection, not the female that Suzanne assumed was his young wife.

She did not care about him. She wanted information about his wife.

Roman and Jennifer finished their coffee and tossed the empty recyclable cups in the receptacle on the corner. Roman picked up his phone when it rang a few minutes later.

"Hello, Grandfather. How are you this fine morning?" He listened for a response as Jennifer watched him.

"So sorry you have rain today. We have a beautiful, cool early autumn day here. What have you learned?"

Again a wait while he listened. Jennifer nudged his arm and motioned for him to put it on speakerphone. Roman pushed the button and took the phone away from his ear as soon as it switched over so she could hear the full conversation.

"I learned that the smaller gravestones were for stillborn and some babies that survived birth but did not live long."

"Why are there so many of them?" Jennifer asked.

"That I am still doing the research on. The other gravesites are for adults who died from various causes. Just the normal cemetery as far as that goes."

"Would it help if I sent you some of the names and dates on the stones? I know I sent you a rough idea of the span of years they included, but maybe some names would help narrow it down."

"That would help."

"We are headed back there now. I will text you the information I find and send some more photos too. Thank you, Grandfather."

"Don't thank me yet. Somehow I have a feeling those graves are related to us. I don't know how yet, but my father never told me many details about his time there. Maybe there is a reason he didn't."

"Now you are being mysterious. I never gave that a thought." Jennifer said as a shiver ran down her spine.

What if her husband had a connection to all that death? It was ancient history but could prove very interesting.

Jennifer turned as a lady walked past them. Her blonde hair was strikingly beautiful. Her walk was determined. She carried a book under her arm and a cell phone in her hand. Jennifer noticed that the lady was about her height and build and admired how in shape she seemed for the older age she assumed the lady was. She was about to speak to the lady when Roman interrupted his wife's thoughts.

"Ok, let's finish our walk in town and head out to the manor and the cemetery. We will inspect it closer, send information to Grandfather, and then figure out what to do with the rest of the day.

~~~~~~

Sara was sitting in her office at the manor, working on her book. She had just finished writing a chapter when the manor's phone rang.

"Hello, Sara speaking." The voice on the other end asked for the owner.

"I am one of the owners; how may I help you?" She scrunched her forehead. No one asked to speak to the owner unless there was an issue or trouble. She listened as the male voice asked about the cemetery on the estate.

Heather walked in as Sara listened. She motioned for her sister to sit down and wait for her. Heather took a seat and watched her sister's face. Something was going on. She forgot why she had even entered the office as she listened to her sister reply.

"I do have knowledge of the cemetery. Who wants to know and why?" Sara was cautious in her answer to the man's questions. Something about how he spoke bothered her, making her not want to reveal all the family secrets to this stranger.

"Yes, there is a history there. My family is working on finding the answers. Until we know details to be true, we prefer not to divulge any information beyond our family."

Heather gave Sara a questioning look. They were not keeping it quiet anymore. Why had Sara said that? Sara was busy writing about their family history and the history of the estate. They had all the answers. Didn't they? Heather wondered if she was missing something.

Sara talked with the man for a few more minutes without giving any details to him. When she could hang up the phone, the sisters stared at each other for a moment.

"What was that all about?"

"I have no idea. Some strange man was asking detailed questions about the cemetery. No one asks detailed questions. It was like he already knew a lot about it but needed to verify his information, or he was digging for more information he did not have."

"I noticed you did not tell him anything. Do you think he knows more than we do about it?"

"You read my mind. The man knows something. I don't know what. That is why I got his name and number. All he would give me was his first name, though."

"Well, that is interesting. I would say that indicates he somehow has a connection to it, and by revealing his identity, we may figure it out."

"We make a good detective team," Sara said and laughed.

Heather laughed and pointed to Sara's laptop.

"What?" Sara shook her head.

"All you need to do is enter his phone number into the computer, and you can find out who he is."

"You are right. We paid for that software program in case we needed it to do reference checks and research on guests on the chance we needed to contact them for damages to the rooms."

"This may make that purchase worth the money it costs."

Sara opened her laptop and looked at the number she had written down. Before she could enter the full number, the internet went down. "Well, crap. That doesn't happen very often."

"What happened?"

"The internet just went down! I wonder how long it will take to come back up?"

"I don't know. In the meantime, don't lose that number. We can research it later."

"Oh, I won't. Now, why did you come to my office?"

"Heck if I remember." Heather laughed as she stood up to leave. "When it comes to me, I'll be back. Good luck with figuring out the mystery caller." She walked out of the office and down the hall to return home. As she walked through the great room, she saw Roman and Jennifer coming back into the manor. She didn't stop to talk to them; they looked preoccupied with something.

Chapter Fifteen
For Sale

Angela was on her daily walk before starting to work on her next project when Jeff met her from the other direction. She smiled and shook her head.

"Why didn't you tell me you were going to walk this morning? I would have waited for you," she said as they met and kissed.

"I wanted to surprise you at your house, but you are already up and out walking," Jeff replied as he took her hand and turned around to walk with her.

"You don't need to repeat your steps if you don't want to."

"Oh, I want to. I want to show you what I found this morning."

"What could be that important at this hour?"

"You know how you said you wanted to buy a house here in this area?"

"Yes. When I was ready and when I found what suited my needs."

"I found it!"

"Here?"

"Close enough, yes. It's at the end of the pathway."

"That big house on the hill? Are you kidding me?"

"Nope. I was there yesterday, and the sign was not there. Today there is a for sale sign posted! It's perfect for us."

Angela stopped in her tracks. "Us? Who said anything about 'us' buying a house?"

"I know we have not discussed it yet. But think about it. Well, wait until you see the house and hear my idea."

"Your idea? What if I do not like or agree with your idea?"

"But this place is perfect!"

Angela shook her head and took her hand out of Jeff's grasp. "We shall see." She walked with him but slowed her pace. She had some quick thinking to do.

When they turned the corner at the end of the path, she looked up at the house on the hill. She could not help the smile forming inside. Hoping Jeff did not notice, she lowered her head to hide the excitement in her eyes.

Jeff took her hand and raised it to his lips. Gently kissing it. "See, it's perfect."

"Perfect for what? That house is huge! I could only dream of living there and have no intention of finding out how much it would cost to buy!"

"That's just it. Together we could. Us and a few friends I know."

"A few friends? What are you talking about?" Angela was leery about his intentions.

"Listen. I know we cannot buy it on our own. I have had my eye on this house since I moved here. I have looked at the photos of it. I have researched its history. We, no, You, need this house."

"I Need no such thing."

"Hear me out. If a few of us went together to buy it, we could convert it into a bed and breakfast, and over a short amount of time, we could be making enough money to pay the mortgage and eventually buy out our partners and live well."

"You forget, I own a magazine business, and you are a medical helicopter pilot….. we already have jobs we love."

Jeff was feeling defeated. "Will you at least look at it with me? Maybe that will change your mind."

"I will look at it. I will admit I have always liked that house." She snickered.

"What? Why the snicker?"

"I have always wondered if this is one of the haunted houses."

Jeff looked at her. He had the same thoughts but did not want to scare Angela away from the house's potential. "See, we could market it as a haunted house and get more people who want to stay here."

"Or a Lot fewer people!" Angela took Jeff's hand and steered him away from the property, down the walking path back to her apartment.

~~~~~~

Sara awoke in the middle of the night. Her dream disturbed her. She lay there a while and listened to Randall sleeping soundly. She admired him for the way he could always sleep through the night. She imagined he would be awake half the night with all the court cases and the difficult situations he handled. Instead, he had found a way to turn his mind away from work when he closed his office door.

She slipped out of bed and walked to the kitchen. After pouring herself a glass of water from the tap, she walked outside and stood on their deck. She loved to watch the sky full of stars on clear nights. She sipped her water and gazed at the sky. The mountains were not quite visible in the darkness. She wondered how people could hike them and spend the night in the wilderness. She loved to hike, but she was not a tent camper. She preferred a hotel or cabin.

She swallowed the last of the water and thought back to her dream. It did not make sense. Who was the man in her vision?

Randall opened the door to the deck to find Sara lost in thought.

"What is on your mind, my beautiful lady?"

"I am not sure," she whispered without moving.

He stood beside her without saying another word. He knew she needed to stay in that trance until whatever it was faded.

After several moments she shook her head. There was no way she would forget what she saw in her mind. No one could forget a man of that description. The sign was what bothered her even more.

Sara smiled up at her husband. He reached for her hand as they walked back inside the house. The aroma of freshly brewed coffee awaited them.

~~~~~~

Jeff called the Realtor he knew to schedule a time to tour the house he wanted Angela to see. He already saw the potential in it. His hope was for his girl to see it too. If nothing else, he did have a plan. One that he and Angela had briefly discussed in the past. One he hoped she was ready for.

A week later, Angela and Jeff walked inside the main doors of the beautiful home on the hill. She had thought about it and did some research on the specifics of the property. In doing so, she had read the long history behind it.

She already knew it was built in Nineteen Hundred. It was family-owned for three generations before being sold to an outsider. The outsider had only lived there for five years while remodeling the inside. During the remodel, several unfortunate things happened to his family, and when it was complete, he was forced to sell it to take care of his family members. At least, that was the written story. Angela had spoken to a few of the area's long-time residents and heard a different story. She tended to believe the stories she heard more than the ones written.

Jeff watched Angela's reaction to the vastness and beauty of each room. He did not comment much in the beginning. He wanted her to absorb it all on her own before he voiced his opinion and discussed his plan. The Realtor spoke briefly about each room, pointing out the highlights without revealing his opinion.

After the tour, Jeff took Angela to the backyard to talk. She followed him with her mind made up.

"So, how do you like the house?"

"I love it. It's just not something I want to take on. It is way beyond our means."

Jeff frowned. He knew she was probably correct. He had to give his speech anyway. "What do you think about a few of us going together and turning it into a bed and breakfast?"

"Are you kidding me? There is no way I want to take that much work on. Besides, the town already has the Bella Rose Estate. I will not take business away from Sara and her family."

"You don't think the town could handle two of them? The town is growing. Look at how many people visit each year."

"I know it gets busy during the year, but I am not willing to invest all my money into such a major task."

"How about we turn it into a haunted museum?"

"Oh, so you do know this place is haunted? I was not sure you were aware. I do not want any part of it for that reason alone." Angela turned away from him and walked back inside.

Jeff was left speechless. He had not had the chance to bring up his third plan. He reached inside his pocket and shook his head. That plan would have to wait for another special moment.

Chapter Sixteen
The Missing–Found

There were two days remaining of Storytelling in town. The local businesses had stayed busy, as did the food trucks and other vendors who had paid for spots throughout the town to set up and sell their merchandise.

Terri had been concerned about the food trucks in town taking business away. By the second day, she knew she had nothing to worry about. So many people attended this event that the food trucks were needed to help handle the crowds.

Barbara was once again helping Terri at the end of the evening. While clearing the tables, Barbara noticed the lady with mesmerizing eyes again. She decided she was going to talk to Steven more about her. He must know something about her. She had not had the time to talk with Steven about her the morning before. Barbara had almost put her out of her mind until seeing her again.

Barbara watched as the blonde-haired lady walked with determination to the far end of the bar. Soon after she sat down, Steven walked over to her, and she whispered something to him as he leaned closer to hear her. Steven shook his head, then turned and mixed a drink for her. She smiled and then took a sip of the drink he handed her. She raised her glass to him, nodded, then stood and walked into the crowd on the dance floor.

That was when Barbara noticed the other lady from town. Barbara gasped. Terri heard Barbara's gasp and asked if she was alright.

"I'm fine. I think." Terri followed Barbara's eyes and did a double take. She had been right. Those two ladies had the same startling eyes. "Who are those two?"

"I don't know. But watch the two of them. The red-haired one is not paying attention to the blonde. It's like she didn't even notice her. How can you not notice the resemblance in the eyes?"

Barbara had been watching and noticed the same thing. "Do you think I should talk to them and tell them how much they look alike? Everyone has a twin in this world, right? Maybe that is what these two are, and they don't even notice it."

"I would wait. Did you talk to Steven yet?"

"No, it was too late last night, and I forgot about it this morning."

"How? How could you forget those eyes?" Terri laughed as she and Barbara returned to the work they had been doing.

Steven took a break and went to the café to talk to his wife.

" Hi, Babe. Barbara turned to face Steven and the dance floor. "Care to dance?"

"Not at the moment. That song is about over, and Adam is playing the next few for me so I can talk with you. We hardly see each other during busy events like this one."

"You certainly stay busy. You even have strange, beautiful women whispering in your ear. Yes, I saw her whisper something to you."

"Oh, her. She is nothing to worry about."

"I would not say that. What did she say to you?"

"That, I cannot say. I am a bartender with confidential information I am forbidden to share."

"Now that sounds mysterious. Who is she?"

Steven looked out onto the dance floor. He was not a good dancer and rarely danced. But his wife was asking. "Ok, let's go dance to this next song. He took his wife by her hands and led her to the middle of the floor.

Barbara noticed how close they were to the blonde lady. "Are we here for a particular reason?"

"Yes." Let me introduce the two of you."

"Don't you mean the three of us?" Barbara had turned them around. Steven looked up and stopped dancing.

"What's going on, Babe? Who are these ladies?"

Steven took a deep breath and led his wife off the dance floor. Barbara was confused.

When Steven found a quiet spot outside on the one bench, he and Barbara sat down. She did not understand and felt almost like she was being disciplined and getting ready to be lectured.

"I guess it cannot be avoided now." He shrugged his shoulders and shook his head. "How can she expect me to keep a secret?"

"Who and what secret?"

"I was just talking to myself. It's ok. Now let me explain. Steven took her hands and began to speak. "The older lady is Suzanne. The younger one is her daughter. The daughter does not know her mother is here."

"What? Why not? They look so much alike I figured they had come together or with family."

"Nope. Suzanne is here on her own. Her daughter is here with her husband but has no idea she is here for more than the research she and her husband are doing."

"What sort of research?" Barbara temporarily forgot where she was going with her story and questions.

"I am not sure. Suzanne would not say. She may not even know."

"But why are they here?"

"Suzanne wants to connect with her daughter. You see, she has not seen her daughter since she was a baby."

Barbara's eyes opened wide. She loved to know the story behind why a parent gave up a child. She wondered, in this case, if her connection with foster families played a part in any of their lives.

"Why not?"

"I do not know the full story. Suzanne told me she was here to connect again after all these years."

"And they have not connected yet? This event is almost over. They may never get another chance."

"I agree with you. It is up to me to at least get the two ladies to see each other."

"I can help. Let me help. I can bring two people together easily."

"I know you can. This is a different circumstance."

"Not really. Instead of introducing people to their foster family, I could introduce her to her biological mother! How awesome an experience."

Steven shrugged his shoulders and shook his head. "Let's go inside and see what we can do." Barbara followed her husband inside. Once inside Steven looked at Suzanne and raised his eyebrows. He pointed to his wife and waited for the lady's reaction.

Suzanne raised her eyebrows and looked in the direction of her daughter. Then she looked back at Steven and nodded.

"Well, my dear loving wife, it seems you have silent approval to go do your thing." Steven let go of his wife in the middle of their dance.

Barbara took a step away from him and looked at the mother, who nodded to her. Barbara turned and nearly ran into the redhead with the same eyes.

"Oh, excuse me." She said to the young lady. The young lady looked at Barbara and hesitated before reacting. She sensed something. She stopped dancing with her husband and looked at Barbara without saying a word.

"Hi, I'm Barbara. I could not help but notice the resemblance between you and the blonde lady over there." Barbara pointed in the direction she wanted her to look.

The young lady glanced over. Her husband looked as well. The two ladies locked eyes.

Chapter Seventeen
Anguish in Memories

Jennifer grabbed Roman's arm as her knees buckled under her. She could not breathe. Roman pulled a chair out from the bar and helped his wife sit down.

Suzanne stepped closer. Roman shook his head at her, raised his hand, and said, "Don't. Don't take another step closer."

Suzanne stopped and stepped back a step. She maintained her gaze on her daughter.

Barbara and Terri stood beside Steven a distance away, waiting to see what would transpire between the two women. They each were prepared to step in if they were needed.

"What is she doing here?" Jennifer whispered to Roman. "Did you know she would be here? How in God's name did she find me?" Jennifer began to cry. Her childhood dream was to have her mother back in her life. Now, there she stood, but Jennifer was full of anger instead of love. At the moment, she hated the woman standing near her.

"Jennifer, I am sorry. I know I am the last person you want to see right now, but I needed to find you to explain what happened when you were a little girl." Suzanne said quietly.

"Explain? What is there to explain? You left me alone with that man!"

Suzanne heard the anger in her daughter's voice. She wished she could take back all those years they had missed with each other. It had not all been her fault for not being there for her. She wanted her marriage to work, and when it didn't, she at least wanted her daughter to have a happy life. She had eased her way closer to Roman and her daughter. Roman held his wife's shoulders but allowed the woman to step close enough to speak.

"What do you mean? I wanted to be there for you too. Your father would not let me. He made it so that people thought I was crazy. When that wasn't enough, he had me committed. 'Lock her up and throw away the key' had been his idea of keeping me away from you. He knew I loved you. But I had a meltdown soon after you were born. No one knew what it was at the time. Now they call it postpartum depression."

Jennifer had stopped her tears and calmed down while she listened to the woman speak. She had wiped her eyes and looked at the woman who had left her as an infant. The stories she had been told as a child suddenly were dispersed into a new reality. She listened as her mother spoke.

Suzanne pulled up a stool and sat closer to her daughter. Roman looked at his wife and raised his eyes. She waved him away. He looked at Barbara, Terri, and Steven, shrugging their shoulders and stepping away. Roman walked a few steps away from Jennifer and joined the trio.

This was mother and daughter time. Steven mixed a couple of drinks and quietly set them beside each of the women as they began their conversation.

"Jennifer, I am so sorry for what happened to you after you were born. I had no control over what I was doing. I simply lost it. I could not take care of you or anyone else. Including myself, according to your father. He sent me away to get better. Instead, I got worse. They did not even know how to deal with my depression."

"But why did you never come back? Why did you not contact me as I got older?"

"The way they had to drug me up all those years kept me in the institution until you were married. I never knew if your father tried to get me out or not. I remember being half out of it most of the time until a new doctor took over the place. He required all new up-to-date testing on all the patients. I was not the only one who got weaned off the drugs and has been able to leave and finally start a life on their own."

"Please tell me you sued them." Jennifer hated hearing this truth.

"I did better than that. I had the place shut down. The medical personnel investigated, and some are in prison."

"Why? Why would my father do that to you and do what he did to me?" Jennifer was ready to cry again. Her father had ruined her life. That was why she had run off when she was so young and gotten married.

"Why did the man I loved do that to you? I do not know. I thought he was sending me away to get better and would send for me as soon as I was healed. I would have traveled all over the country to find you if I had known you were in danger or unhappy."

Jennifer sat in silence. How could she tell the truth about what she had been through? This was not the time nor the place.

The music had stopped playing, and suddenly they were engulfed in silence. They had both blocked out the world while they began their conversation. Now there was nothing to muffle their words to the world. They both stopped talking.

Barbara stepped over to them and suggested they come to her and Steven's house to continue getting to know each other. Steven was standing with his wife and agreed that they could come, along with Roman, to talk. They would give them all the room and all the time they needed in private.

Jennifer hesitated and shook her head. Suzanne looked into her daughter's eyes, and Jennifer understood without her mother saying a word. Her mother needed to talk.

"Okay. If you are sure, you don't mind."

"We certainly do not mind." Steven took his wife's hand in his. "We love to help people in any way we can."

Roman stood by his wife and said he would give them all the time they needed to talk. He would go to the manor to their room to give his wife time alone with the woman who had given her birth. He could not imagine the emotions they each felt.

"Thank you, love," Jennifer said as she stood down from the stool. "I have no idea when I will be back in our room. This could take all night." She realized how tired she was, but as much as her mother needed to talk, she needed to hear her mother's side of what destroyed her life.

Twenty minutes later, mother and daughter sat facing each other in the living room of Steven and Barbara's home. Their hosts provided sweet tea and water and told them to make themselves at home, including spending the night if needed. It was already past midnight, so it was a possibility. Then they retreated to their bedroom to get some sleep.

Suzanne began to speak. "I know you may not understand everything I am about to tell you, but it is the truth."

"That is all I want from you. I want to know your side of my life."

"Well, after I was in the institution a while, I got word that your father wanted a divorce. He found a 'normal' person he wanted to marry and raise you. He sent word that he wanted nothing to do with me and for me to have no contact with you. He sent word that you were doing great and did not need me in your life. I was devastated but in no condition to fight for you. I had no home, no job, and no income. I was still being drugged to keep me as sane as possible. After I signed the divorce papers, I lost it again, and the drugs were increased."

Jennifer felt for her mother. She wanted to hug her and tell her everything was alright. But it wasn't. Suzanne needed to hear the truth. The truth, according to the grown woman who lived the nightmare of an unloving father.

"I hate that about your life. I wish you had been there for me. My life was horrible from day one."

Suzanne listened.

"As a young child, I didn't know better. I thought every child had a father like I did. No one told me any different. As a young teenager, I made a few new friends and found out their fathers were not like mine. By the time I was fifteen, I had left home. I had met Roman, and we ran away together. He has been the best thing to happen to me."

"My sweet child, I am so sorry."

Jennifer shook her head. "I hated you for years. My father told me you abandoned me right after I was born because you didn't want me. He told me he was forced to raise me but didn't want me either after a while."

Suzanne didn't say a word, so Jennifer continued.

"When he found the lady he married, my life worsened. They would go away on short trips and leave me at home alone for days on end. I would go days without food. I never told anyone. I was afraid they would take him away, and I'd be forced to live with her." Jennifer never looked up as she spoke. This time she didn't wait for any response.

"She was worse than he was in some ways. She never wanted me to be there. She ignored me. She cooked enough food for her and my father and then gave me a little plate of food to eat. She would send me to my room right after dinner and tell me not to come out until morning when it was time to go to school. In the summertime, she told me to go outside and play, then locked the doors so I could not get back in until she wanted me to. When I would get back inside, she would tell me to clean up the house because I had made it dirty."

A tear fell from Suzanne's eye. If she had only known. If she had not been so comatose from the drugs and been able to live a normal life. None of this would have happened to her baby girl. She reached out to hug Jennifer.

Jennifer moved away. She was not ready. Not yet. She had more to say.

"It got to the point that my father knew he had to get rid of his wife or me. He could not deal with the tension in the house all the time. He started working later and later into the night. Then I realized he was drunk when he came home. I heard him hit her. I crawled into my bed and covered my head. That night she left and never came back. The next night he came home drunk again. This time he came into my room."

Jennifer stopped talking. Tears were falling, and her hands were shaking. She could not see nor speak. The memory she had suppressed for years was back. Suzanne reached over, not taking resistance. She hugged her daughter. She held her in her arms as they both cried.

Jennifer cried out the memory and the fear. Suzanne cried out the sorrow and love that had blended as her lost daughter spoke. How could she have allowed this? How could the man she had once loved do this to her and to their daughter?

Their only solace was that he had died a few years earlier. His drinking had killed him.

Suzanne knew there was more to her daughter's life story. In time she hoped to hear it. She hoped she would be forgiven for her part in her troubled life. She held on to Jennifer until they both stopped crying.

Holding each other on the sofa in Barbara and Steven's home, they fell asleep. Peace had started to rest in their hearts. But it was only the beginning.

Suzanne dreamed that night about the pain her daughter must have suffered. She envisioned things no person should endure.

The next morning when they awoke, Jennifer could tell she needed to finish telling about that night.

"Suzanne, good morning," she whispered.

"Good morning, child. We both fell asleep to our tears last night. Are you okay?"

"Yes, I'm fine. I need to tell you about the rest of the night."

"Only when you are ready. I can only imagine."

"That's just it. I don't want you to imagine what could have happened. I fear you are seeing something more than is real. When my father walked into my room that night, he was drunk. I could tell by the way he walked, acted, and smelled. I was fourteen at the time. I was strong for my size and age. He reached my bed and started to pull the covers off me. I knew what would come next if I didn't act fast. So I raised my legs and kicked him in the chest with both feet. He fell backward and landed on the floor. I rushed out of the house in my nightclothes and went to a neighbor's house. I told them what happened, and they let me stay with them that night."

"Did they call the police?"

"No. I am not sure why they didn't, but they didn't. The next morning I went outside and sat on the porch to watch my house. It wasn't long before he came out of the house, got in his car, and drove to work. We never spoke of that night. I am not sure he even remembers it. But that never happened again."

"You were so brave. The neighbors should have called the police. Or you could have called them."

"I should have. But I still feared I would have to live with his wife, even though she had left. I knew I had to leave, so I started a plan in my head."

"You said you were fifteen when you met Roman and left?"

"Yes, Roman is my lifesaver. I literally owe him my life."

"I will have to thank him when I see him later. We need to get up and see about getting out of here."

They both smelled coffee brewing. Jennifer and her mom walked into the kitchen to find Barbara making breakfast.

Chapter Eighteen
Compelled

Roman woke up early and felt the loneliness of missing Jennifer. He wondered if she and Suzanne had stayed up all night talking or if they had gotten some sleep. He knew his wife did not function well with little to no sleep.

He also wondered how much of her story she told the woman who had left her when she was born. He knew her story. He was part of it. He had been honored when Jennifer agreed to run off with him. A few years later, he had the privilege of calling her his wife. He never wanted to lose that feeling. He loved her with all his heart and soul. He hoped she understood how much.

Jennifer walked into their room as Roman was opening the door to go to the dining area for breakfast

"Good morning, Love. How are you?" He asked as he took her into his arms and kissed her.

"I'm weak. I feel like I lifted so much off my shoulders by telling Suzanne the beginning of my story."

"How did she take it?"

"She was devastated that she had caused it all. I told her it was not her fault. She had serious postpartum depression and spent years in an institution receiving drugs she did not need. My father made sure she stayed away. My tragic life was more my father's fault. You know what he did to me. I cannot imagine my mother allowing such behavior if she had been there."

"I couldn't either, even without knowing who your mother is. How do you feel about her?"

"I'm still processing that. I am not ready to call her Mom yet, but she is easy to talk to. She seems genuinely sorry for what she put me through. She had not been

married long enough to know what my father was like."
She was already defending her mother and smiled as soon
as she realized it.

"What are you smiling about?"

"Never mind. My private secret. There are some things
you cannot ask me. I learned things I'm not ready to share
with anyone yet. And I thought of other things that bring
smiles."

"Okay, but you will need to tell me later."

"We shall see." Jennifer teased as they walked down the
hallway together.

"Welcome to breakfast!" Andy greeted them. He poured
two cups of coffee and set them on the table where the
couple sat.

"Good morning," Jennifer mumbled. "Sorry, I'm not
awake yet. I was up most of the night."

"Unable to sleep? Or is something going on?" Andy
knew it was none of his business, but he never missed a
chance to learn about people.

"Something is going on," Jennifer responded. I was busy
talking with Suzanne most of the night.

"Who is Suzanne? I don't think I know her."

"Probably not. She is only here visiting." Roman
offered.

"She is my birth mother, who I never knew," Jennifer
added.

"Whoa. Your birth mother?" Andy asked. He was
putting Danish on a plate and almost dropped them.

"Long story, but yes." She hoped that was the end of
the questions. She was not sure if she was ready to relate
any more details.

"I'm glad you finally were able to meet. I hope the
connection is a pleasant one." Andy did not press for more
details. He knew about family secrets. He did not need to
get involved with hers.

After Jennifer and Roman finished breakfast, they returned to their room before heading to town. Jennifer had forgotten that Roman would tell his story later that day until he picked up his notes.

"Are you prepared?" Jennifer asked Roman.

"I am. I was able to plan more of it last night while you were talking with your… Suzanne."

"My mother. You can say it. I am not ready to call her Mom yet, but she is my mother. I am finally learning the truth. I never did believe my father, you know that."

"I do. You always told me there must have been another side to the story. You could not imagine a mother leaving her child and staying away."

"I still can't, and now I know it was not her choice. That makes me happy yet even more angry at my father. I hope she and I can get to know each other better."

"I am too." Roman agreed. "If we need to stay in the area longer for you to do that, I will arrange for that."

"Are you sure? I don't want to take you away from your work."

"Don't worry about me. I can work from just about anywhere. Or I can arrange for you to stay here while I return home."

"I am not sure I like that idea. I've never been on my own."

"You will be just fine. If you stay here, you will be with people you have gotten to know. Plus, you will be spending time with Suzanne. I am confident it will work out."

"Thank you. You have always been so kind and generous to me. I would be lost without you."

Roman smiled a half smile. "I know," he said half-jokingly.

"What are we going to do before it is your time to tell your story tonight?"

"I want to go back to the cemetery for a while this morning. I need to get lost in thought for a while. And if you don't mind, I need to do that alone."

"I don't mind. I need some extra rest to give me a chance to catch up on some sleep."

"For now, let's just go for a walk." Roman opened the door and let Jennifer out ahead of him. He was always being a gentleman with her. She deserved the best he could give her. As they walked down the hall and into the great room, Sara walked to her office.

"Good morning, you two. How did you sleep?"

"I slept well; she only got a little bit of sleep. But we are fine. Don't forget storytelling tonight. I'll be telling my sec... story."

"Oh, I won't forget. I have it on my calendar. We will be there. I think most of the family will be there."

"Perfect," Roman said as they walked beyond Sara and reached the front door. "See you all there."

"You were a little short with her, don't you think?"

"Sorry. I have things on my mind. I did not mean to be. Let's go for that walk."

They followed the hiking path along the creek and to the little bridge. There they stopped and looked at the water and the view. This truly was a beautiful location. Roman's mind was miles and years away. He gazed toward the cemetery. Would he be able to tell his story the way he needed to? He had to. They all needed to know. He knew he should make it a private matter, but a force inside him compelled him to reveal the secrets to the world, not just the family it affected. He had done his best to fight it, but it was wearing him down, and he could not resist the push.

"What are you thinking about?" his wife asked. Roman never heard her. And she never repeated it. She knew something was eating at him, and although she had attempted to find out what it was from the time they arrived at Bella Rose, she knew it was futile to keep trying.

Tonight he would tell the world what he could not even tell her.

After a small lunch, Roman headed to the cemetery. His wife went to their room and laid down to rest. Sleep quickly overtook her.

Roman walked to the cemetery on the Bella Rose property. He walked to the gravesite in a daze. The world around him disappeared. His mind was filled with visions. An hour passed by without him moving. He knew what his story needed to be. He knew it would change lives. He shook his head when he heard a crow. He looked up and saw the crow sitting on a tree limb, looking straight at him. He turned and walked out through the opened gate. Slowly he walked back to the manor.

Jennifer slept soundly. When she awoke, she felt lost. The room felt wrong. Momentarily she had no idea where she was. Her dream had taken her to a place deep in her past. A moment in time that she had forgotten –to her mother. She sat up on the bed. Her eyes looked back into her dream. She wanted to feel real. Her former reality. Something was not right about her life story that she had known.

Roman entered the room and noticed the look on his wife's face. He started to say something, then knew better. He imagined her look was similar to his look while in the cemetery. He wondered what was on her mind. What had she seen? He watched as she stood and walked to the window. She never said a word as she gazed outside. She felt the glass, slowly moving her hand across the pane. In silence, motionless, she stood. Roman stood still and watched. A few moments later, she shook her head and returned to the present time.

"Hello, love. How was your time at the cemetery?" She asked. Giving no indication of what he had just witnessed her doing.

"It was okay. How was your nap?"

"It was amazing. I feel well-rested. Are we going to get something to eat before the event tonight?"

"I thought we should. Are you ready to go?"

"Give me a few minutes to redo my hair and make-up. Then I'll be ready. I may need to take a jacket. Can you grab mine from the closet?"

"Sure. Yes, it will get chilly tonight." He was not only talking about the weather.

Chapter Nineteen
Options

Sara finished getting ready to attend the last night of Storytelling in town. She had missed most of the events this year but was told to be sure and attend this last night. She had spoken with her siblings, and they all were going. They had babysitters for all the kids as the last night's show was normally not for children.

Randall watched as his wife got ready. Something was on her mind. He debated asking her, then thought better of it. He had learned to be quiet and let her think for a while. If it was something important, she would voice her thoughts.

Ben had been talking with his sister and was glad she and Steven were also attending the last night. He knew she had been in town for most of the week helping Terri at the café and did not have time to talk with her like he normally had. He loved having a sister to share things with. They had missed so much as children, not being raised together.

Andy finished preparing breakfast for the next day so he would not have to get up so early after being out late. Karen was busy talking with the babysitter when Andy walked in and still wanted to get changed. She smiled at him as he kissed her in passing. They still acted young and in love, making her feel good.

When Roman and Jennifer walked inside the large event tent, there was haunting music. The lights hanging from the cross beams were dim, adding to the mystery and suspense of the night. The event always took place in October with an air of Halloween and ghosts. The final night was usually reserved for ghost stories told after dark. Roman would be part of that.

Jennifer picked out her seat but moved when she saw everyone from Bella Rose arrive. She asked if she could join them. Of course, she was welcomed.

The tent was full, and the lights got dimmer. A tall man stood at the microphone. The music stopped. Silence. A wind picked up outside and sent a chill through the opened sides of the tent, sweeping over the crowd. Many pulled their jackets tighter as they prepared for the unknown.

The man thanked everyone for coming who had been there all week. He acknowledged the storytellers who had been there that week and then introduced the first one for the night.

"Our first storyteller tonight is new to this venue. He came to me at the beginning of this year's event and asked to be included. I told him it was highly unusual to find a spot at the last minute. Then he told me a little of his story. There was only one thing to do. So let us all welcome newcomer Roman Watson.

The crowd applauded, and a few even whistled even though they knew nothing about him. Roman stepped on stage and took the microphone from the gentleman.

"Thank you, Sir. I appreciate you allowing me to tell my story tonight." Roman then turned and faced his audience. He scanned the tent looking for Sara and her family. He spotted them and Jennifer sitting with them. He smiled and nodded his head.

"Good evening, ladies and gentlemen. I am honored to be standing before you tonight to share my story. As most of you know from your years of hearing the stories or telling some of your own, some stories are fact, some are fiction, and all will hit you one way or another. I have two stories to tell, but don't worry, I will only tell you one of them. The other one needs to be told in private to the family it involves. They may know some of it, but I am sure they do not know what I know. Or, maybe what I know is not fact. I will let them decide that. I will also let you all decide if the story I will share tonight is a fact, fiction, or a mixture. They say fact is scarier than fiction. Right?"

Roman looked over the crowd as he formulated his thoughts. He had decided to change the story he wanted to tell at the last minute. The family deserved to hear the truth on a personal level.

"My last name is Watson. To most of you, that means nothing. To those who live in this town, it should mean I have a connection to this place. True, I have never been here before in my life, until last week. So those trying to recognize me, you can relax. You don't know me personally. The older folks may know my great-grandfather. Or may have heard of him. Raymond Watson. Ring a bell with anyone? If not, that is okay too. He was only here for a short time. Well, that is not true. I know for a fact he is still here. He walks among you every day. He has told his son all about this town. His son is my grandfather. As I said, Raymond Watson used to live here. He used to work here. Now he closely watches. He pays attention. He remembers. In some ways, he still has control. A control he began when he was alive. You wonder how a dead man can have control? I will tell you."

Everyone was listening. Some were trying to remember the man about whom Roman spoke. Some were anticipating the figure of this man to show up in the air above them. Another chilly wisp of night air moved across the people. Many listeners developed chill bumps and rubbed their arms.

Roman smiled. He had their attention.

"You see, Raymond was only here for a short time. He worked here. He fell in love here. He is buried here. Yet, his work has been forgotten, and his love never materialized. His life has been forgotten. Yet, when he died, he requested to be buried here. And the lady he loved made sure he was returned here. She loved him, but they

99

could not openly share their love then. So, in secret, they connected. They shared life for a short time. Then fate stepped in, and he was forced to leave town. If he had stayed, a lot about this town would have changed. Instead, he now hangs around and lives."

"Have any of you ever been visited by a ghost? Have any of you ever wondered why this town is so haunted? This town is one of the most haunted cities in the nation. Do you know who caused it? He may not have caused it all, but Raymond is a part of the hauntings. Raymond could not stay here and marry the lady he loved, so he went on with life with the self-understanding that he would be back one day and the town would never be the same. He did tell the love of his life that she and her family would always know he was present."

"Raymond went on with his life. He stayed away from here for many years. He met and married a lady named Veronica. Together they had a son. Their son grew up, married, and they had a son. Raymond's son was killed in the war. His young wife died soon afterward from a broken heart. Their young child was sent to be raised by his grandfather. I am that son. The one raised by my grandfather. My grandfather spoke to me not long ago about the story of his father. And about a key." Roman pulled the antique key from his pocket and held it up. "This key and others like it."

Sara gasped. Heather's mouth dropped open. Andy looked at his sisters, then back at this man who dared talk about an antique key.

"This key was found among Raymond's belongings when he died. Attached to it was a locket with a photo inside. When my grandfather opened the locket, he expected to see a photo of his mother. Instead, it was of a stranger he had never seen. This key with the locket is for the private story I have to share with a particular family. I want to share the story of the land, a few homes, and other keys here in town."

"Raymond was a builder. He was contracted out by many of the town residents when he was here. He also made furniture for people and always included at least one secret cabinet or drawer that required a special key similar to this one." He held up another key. This one had no other key or locket attached.

"After Raymond was forced to leave this town, he decided that someday, somehow, he would haunt the buildings he had been a part of. Whether he helped build the actual building or a piece of furniture used inside, he would let his presence be known. He would cause issues with the people who lived there and their descendants or the future owners of the properties. His voice can be heard in many of the homes. Floors creak as you walk on them. Doors will open on their own. Lights will blink in the middle of the night. A man can be heard singing in one of the homes. All are related to things he made for the homes. The owners of the furniture pieces have never been able to open some of them without calling a locksmith. The reason? This key." He held the key above his head. Raymond kept the key. He also hid something inside each piece he created. Something that could only be found when you could open the locked cabinet drawer."

People were looking at each other. The locals were looking at the town leaders seated to the upper left of the seating space. Roman knew why. He had been in town long enough to know about the town's secret storage area. Inside were several pieces of furniture that people had donated to the 'locked pieces of history' kept in storage. No one over the years had been able to open any of them.

Sara was glaring at Roman. What did he know about Bella Rose? Was this the reason they were in town? Was this the real reason they had come to check out the town? What was it about the cemetery? Was Raymond one of the men buried in the Bella Rose Cemetery? If so, why? What was his connection to the manor? What was his connection to the whole town? Was he simply a builder? Or was there more to him and the mysteries of Bella Rose and the town?

Roman continued to tell his story. Sara had blocked some of it out while thinking about how it connected to her family.

"So, I ask you all. Believe in ghosts? Does this answer the mystic of the town?"

The town leaders were busy whispering to each other. A few local homeowners were talking with their spouses. The guests from out of town were skeptical that one man could haunt an entire town. How could he be in so many places at once? What were his motives for so many different people? Why the hidden treasure in all his pieces? Had anyone found a treasure?

Roman watched the crowd. They were spellbound. They wanted to hear more of the story.

"I have no idea what was hidden inside the pieces of furniture. He never told my grandfather. That part of the story could all be a lie. Although it was written in the journal that my grandfather found."

"I have been to Raymond's grave. I have sensed him. I could almost hear him trying to talk to me. He is the reason I am here to tell this story. He wanted it told. I am not sure why. Maybe someone here has a connection I don't know about. Maybe someone here knows something else about his story. Maybe by telling his story, his hauntings will stop. I have a list of the homes he helped build. I have an inventory of the furniture he built, which house it was placed in, and the family it originally belonged to. He documented everything. When he was sent away because of his love for a young woman, he wrote in his journal that he would always let the area know he was there. So when you hear a ghost or see the evidence of one, or see one, it could be my great-grandfather, Raymond."

As Roman ended his story, another chill blew through the tent. The dim lights went out. A shrill was heard outside. The haunting music began to play again. Sara tried to stay focused on where Roman went. She wanted to talk to him. She needed to hear how Raymond was connected to the manor and her family. She knew he had made some of the furniture. But who was the lady he loved? Whose photo was in the locket?

A moment later, the lights came back on. No one had moved inside the tent. Except - Roman was nowhere to be seen. Sara turned her head. Jennifer was missing.

Chapter Twenty
Bella Rose Connection

Sara and her family returned to the manor after storytelling. They had not stayed after Roman told his story. There was no need. None of the other stories would affect them like Roman's had.

Sara walked to Roman and Jennifer's room and knocked on the door. There was no answer. Normally she would have left them alone and knew she would see them in the morning. This time she was concerned. Jennifer had disappeared into the darkness. Roman had left right after he finished his story.

She went to the office to get the key to their room. The spare key was missing from the key holder in her office. She opened her desk drawer and reached for the key to the safe. It was not in the usual place. She moved her hand around and found it. Walking to the safe, she prayed the master key would be in the safe. The safe door opened when Sara turned the key. Sara jumped when she heard her office door open. Heather walked in.

"What are you doing?" Heather asked.

"I am trying to get into the Carpenter's Star room."

"Where Roman and Jennifer are staying? Why?"

"Because they are not answering their door. They both disappeared when the lights went out in the tent. I don't trust Roman."

Sara reached into the safe for the box holding the master keys. The master key was still there. She pulled it out, closed the safe, and walked past her sister.

Heather followed her with her phone in her hand. She did not like the feeling she was having. Sara was right—

something was wrong. Sara turned the key to the room and pushed the door open.

Roman and Jennifer were not inside. Sara and Heather entered and opened the top dresser drawer and the closet door. Their things were still there. So unless they left with nothing, they would be back at some point. Sara breathed a sigh of relief. At least her biggest fear was not real.

The sisters walked out of the room and relocked the door. Roman and Jennifer walked in through the manor's front door as the sisters returned to the office.

"There you two are," Sara said. "I wondered where you went after your story tonight. The lights went out, and you were both gone."

"I know. I am sorry about that occurrence. I did not want to be pursued by anyone in the crowd. Too many of the town's people may be affected by my truth."

"That would include us, in case you forgot."

"Oh, I remember. And you are affected more than you know."

"What do you mean by that?"

"I mean, let me just say I think it is time for one of your family meetings with just your family." She looked at Heather before adding, "You know about our family meetings?" Sara didn't realize any of their guests knew about them.

"As much as I want it now so I can get some answers, I will call for one tomorrow after breakfast with the guests."

"That will be perfect. And I assure you, we are not going anywhere until after we tell you the story involving your family."

"In fact, I may want to stay on a little longer. But we will talk about that later. It is late, and we know everyone is tired. It's been a long, eventful week." Jennifer added.

"Okay. Let's let everyone get a good night's sleep. We will discuss everything in the morning."

Sara did not sleep well that night. Her imagination was going wild. She tried to ease her mind. She realized every scenario she came up with was probably not close to the truth. Finally, sleep overtook her, and when she opened her eyes, Randall had a fresh cup of coffee waiting for her.

Andy served the breakfast he had prepared the night before for the guests. Most everyone was leaving later that day. The ending of storytelling always left them empty for a few days. It was a relief to have the quiet after all the chaos.

Rachelle took care of all the checkouts so the family could have their meeting.

Roman and Jennifer met them in the dining room. He had the key and the locket in his hand. When everyone was there, Sara let him start his story.

"I know you all became curious last night at the storytelling. Let me start by saying I knew nothing about this when we arrived. It was my grandfather who told me all I now know. He sent me the keys while we were here. Along with the journal and the details he knew. All he knew, in the beginning, was that Raymond had a connection to Bella Rose and this town. When we found the locket, we searched for the truth of his love and heartache and vow to always be present somehow."

He handed the key and locket to Sara. She took it from him, intending to open the locket as soon as she got it. Instead, she hesitated. Heather looked at her. She sensed something from her sister. Their eyes met. Without opening it, Sara knew whose photo was inside. She handed the locket to Heather, who took it and slowly opened it.

Andy looked at his sisters. Sara and Heather had the same look even though Sara had not looked inside the locket yet. He reached for the locket. Roman and Jennifer remained silent.

Looking back at them, as they all looked at the photo together, was—Rose. Their grandmother.

They looked up at Roman. All with the same questioning look. What was his great-grandfather doing with a locket with a photo of their grandmother? A quick calculation of ages would put them at the same age. Raymond had been the one who built the furniture for the secret room. They knew that already. They already knew about the keys and how he had a different one for each piece. They even knew about the hidden treasures, although they had never found any. They assumed their grandmother or mother had gotten those. They never suspected a love affair between Rose and anyone, and certainly not this Raymond!

"I know. You have a million questions. So did I. It boils down to Rose and Raymond liking each other, and we can only assume, but there is no proof, of them having an affair. When Rose called it off, Raymond got angry. He told Rose that somehow she and her family would always know he was around."

"That makes no sense. I have never read anything about Rose having another man in her life. She was with Robert from the time they were in their early twenties. They had the perfect relationship. They devoted themselves to this place and helping those girls from when the first girl showed up on their steps. I am not ready to accept what you are trying to tell us."

"But why would he have her photo?"

"I don't know. Maybe she was his fantasy!" Sara was getting angry. She stood up and started to pace the floor.

Heather looked at her older sister. She had not expected her to react that way. She wasn't sure of her feelings about this strange man having a photo of their Grandmama, but she wasn't angry about it.

Andy sat in silence. Their lives were being turned upside down if what Roman suggested was true. They had no proof. How could they prove or disprove any of what he was saying?

"What makes you suspect an affair? Simply because he threatened to haunt the place?"

"Isn't that good enough, considering how your place and much of the town are known for being haunted?"

"What makes you say the Manor is haunted?"

Roman hesitated before speaking. "Didn't I hear you all talking about the keys being moved and gone missing for a while?"

Sara looked at Roman. When had he heard about that? Who had told him? When had she or her family talked about the keys while they were around? She stayed silent while she processed his words.

No one said anything for a moment. Each had thoughts of their own to deal with. Roman found it fascinating that there could have been something going on or that his great-grandfather had been jilted and then was the ghost haunting this old town.

Sara, Heather, and Andy were trying to wrap their minds around everything. Jennifer's thoughts were miles away, thinking about her mother.

"I think we need to keep this quiet, just between those here. We have no proof of anything from just Roman's story. None of us have read anything in all the journals we have already been through. I won't believe anything until I have proof somehow."

"I agree. We have no proof. This town is known to be haunted, but no historical documentation exists. In all the stories, this Raymond person has never been mentioned."

"I agree. I can see no connection of anything about the keys either." Sara added. She was about done with the conversation. Here was a stranger attempting to mess with her family. She was done. They had to go.

Heather looked at her sister. Somehow she read her mind. "I think the two of you need to leave Bella Rose in the morning. We will give you another day to finish whatever work you need to, but you must leave our family alone."

"You may be right. We have caused your family trouble. We may have caused issues with the whole town." Roman felt bad. He was beginning to doubt what his grandfather had told him and the so-called evidence he had to show the connection. What did his grandfather have to gain by digging this up? Was there something to gain? Or was it all a part of his imagination? Roman began to doubt his own story. So much for a good storyteller.

Chapter Twenty-One
On the Move

The next morning before most of the world was awake, Roman and Jennifer walked out the front door of Bella Rose Manor. Suzanne met them at the bottom of the lane, where Roman transferred Jennifer's luggage. Roman turned and headed home while his wife climbed into her mother's car. This was mother-daughter time.

Terri's phone rang as she walked into the café the day after the Storytelling festival ended. She had a lot of cleaning to do, as did the town. Keeping the streets and area clean was hard with so many people in attendance. She picked up the phone after hoping they would give up and leave a message.

"Good morning, Downtown Café. How may I help you?"

No one said anything on the other end. Terri said hello again, and when she heard nothing, she hung up the phone. She turned to go into the kitchen area just in time to see a figure walk past the door. A shiver ran down her spine. She kept walking into the back and brushed off the feeling she had.

An hour later, the phone rang again. This time it was Jay. He and Carrie were loading up their things for the last part of their trip to Tennessee. They had found a house they liked, and closing was in a week. They would stay in a hotel for the time being until they had the keys to the house they bought.

Terri told Jay to stay in touch and let her and Adam know when they arrived in town. She knew Jay, Carrie, and Tamara would spend a few days with Angela and Jeff until closing on the purchase of their place. Terri was glad she and Jay had been able to become and stay friends after their history together. She was sure the six of them would have some fun times together.

Steven arrived at the Café a short time later to help clean up inside and the outside areas. He noticed Terri was in her own little world when he spoke, and she did not respond.

"Hello? Anyone home in there?" he spoke again.

"Oh! Hi. Sorry. I had something on my mind and didn't hear you."

"I could tell. What's got your attention?"

Terri laughed. "Would you believe Jay and Carrie?"

"Yes, I would. What's the latest? Have they found a place?"

"They sure have. Now that you mention it, I'm not sure they have seen the place, but they bought it!" Terri shook her head. "How can anyone buy a house without physically looking at it and inspecting it?"

"That is a good question. I can see moving to an area and renting a place for a while, but not making such a major purchase as a house. Are you sure they have not seen it?"

"No, I'm not sure. But you would think they would have told Adam or me if they had been in the area. Angela never said anything about them being around either."

"Maybe they had Jeff find them a house. I have heard he is pretty good at that."

"True. He found that condo for Angela to rent, and it has been an amazing place. Maybe you're right. Anyway, they are headed this way. Jay said they are staying with Angela and Jeff until closing on the house."

"It will be nice to have new people in the area."

"He's not new to me." Terri shook her head. "Far from new."

"I know. It is amazing that you and Adam can be friends with him and Carrie. I mean, after I broke up with an old girlfriend, the last thing I wanted to do was stay friends with her."

"Jay and I always did have a unique relationship. Even when we were dating, people did not understand how we were. But it worked for us. Until it didn't, of course."

"What happened anyway? If I may ask?"

"We just fell apart. Nothing major happened. We were away on vacation and decided to become close and might have gotten married, but when we came home, we drifted apart. We let life get in our way. Before we knew it, there were no more of us. He went his way. I went mine. Then I moved here and met Adam a year or so later. Jay met Carrie."

"What a story. You could write a book."

"Not me. I don't have the gene in me." Her mind drifted away again.

"Something else is on your mind. I can tell. You are not focused."

"I had a strange phone call earlier."

"Stranger than Jay calling you? Who else called?"

"That's just it, I don't know. When I said hello, no one was there. I even repeated myself, but there was nothing. That was when I noticed a figure outside."

"A figure? What do you mean? A ghost?" Steven laughed.

"You laugh, but yes, a ghostly figure."

"Whoa. I was only joking. Maybe you listened to too many ghost stories at storytelling last night."

"Yea, maybe." Terri let the topic end and went back to cleaning.

Three hours later, Jay called her back to tell her they had arrived at Angela's.

"Thanks for letting me know. When are you moving into your home?"

"Another week. We have the closing in a few days. The movers will be here next week with everything. You and Adam are welcome to help us move in and set it up."

"We may do that. What are you all doing for dinner tonight? Why don't you come to the lounge and enjoy the music? You know, relax for a while?"

"Relaxing would be wonderful, but our late nights out have been limited since Tamara was born. We are on her schedule for a while. We may stop out tomorrow at the café. I know you'd love to see our little one."

Terri rolled her eyes. She would love to see the baby. Yet part of her could not help but think that if things had been different, that little girl could have been hers and Jay's. Instead, he had a beautiful baby girl with Carrie, and she had adopted a precious little one with Adam. She smiled when she realized she would not have it any other way.

"You all are welcome here anytime," Terri replied after a few minutes of silence.

Jay ignored the silence and smiled. He seemed to understand even though no words had been spoken. "I know." He said. Then added, "we will be over sometime tomorrow."

"See you then." Terri hung up her phone and got back to work.

A week later found the six of them and the movers at Jay and Carrie's new home. They had chosen well for never seeing it in person before buying it. They were lucky to have Jeff they could trust.

It took all day, and they were not done with everything, but they were all exhausted. The women had set up the kitchen and bedrooms, including the nursery. The men had set up the rest of the house with several boxes remaining unopened and stored in the garage. Those could wait, Jay told everyone.

Terri and Jay had some alone time when everyone had taken a break earlier. They talked about how fortunate they were to still be friends. Jay told Terri that he would always love her but knew things were perfect the way they were. Terri agreed. She loved Adam and Jay loved Carrie. They each had a family started. Life was good –for everyone.

When they had finished for the day, Jeff told everyone that he and Angela had found a house to buy. Everyone's attention focused on him with many questions for them both.

Angela held up her hand. "One at a time. First, nothing definite; we looked at it and put in a bid. We are waiting for a reply and will go from there. Second." She stopped talking.

"Second, yes, we have decided to move in together," Jeff said with a gleam in his eye as he looked at Angela. She smiled back and looked at her sister. Terri nodded her head, giving her approval. She knew love when she saw it.

Chapter Twenty-Two
A Step Forward

Angela lay in bed that night after helping Jay and Carrie move into their new home. She was exhausted but excited. She was excited that her boyfriend would have his brother living nearby. They had had a whirlwind courtship. She laughed at the thought. She didn't know if anyone her age still used that word. Most people she knew called it dating. She felt she and Jeff had something deeper than dating. It had not taken her very long to feel love for him. She held back her feelings at first because of what her sister said about him. He had been married before, and Terri knew him during that time. Angela listened to her sister at first. Then realized that it was her life to live. Jeff had changed since his divorce, and things were great between them. She did not hesitate to say yes the second time he suggested they move in together.

Angela rolled over and hugged her extra pillow. The pillow Jeff would be using soon. Her smile hung on as she fell asleep.

The phone rang, waking Jeff up from his sound sleep. He glanced at the clock and sat up in bed as he answered the phone. He had not meant to sleep as late as he did. The lady on the other end of the phone was obviously more awake than he was. He listened as she spoke.

The conversation had been short, but it left Jeff with quick energy and a desire to get busy with his day. First, he needed to call Angela. He looked at the clock again and wondered if she would even be home. She may have been in her office and working already. At least she would be up. Even if he interrupted her, he dialed her cell phone.

"Hello," Angela whispered.

"Good morning, Beautiful. Are you at work?"

"Work? I just woke up. What time is it?" Angela sat up in bed and looked at the clock. Then she nearly jumped out of bed.

"Later than either of us thought, I take it. I was woken up by a phone call."

"Who would call so early? Oh, wait, it's not that early. Anyway, who called?"

"Our Realtor," he hesitated to build her anxiety.

"And? What did she say?"

"Are you sitting down? The sellers accepted our offer!"

Angela squealed! "Are you sure? They accepted our low offer?"

"Yes. They accepted it. I guess they were anxious to sell it." I don't care why they accepted it. I'm just thrilled that they did."

"So, what do we do now?"

"She said she would call me later today to let me know the next step. I think it is just to set a time for the closing. Once we all sign the papers and the mortgage company pays them, we can move!"

"I am so not ready!"

"Angela, you don't need to be ready. Closings usually take a couple of weeks or a month. Plus, we don't need to move the day we take possession. We can do repairs, painting, or whatever before we move in. Neither of us has a house to sell first. That is one advantage of renting for a while."

"Yes. If I remember correctly, we did want to change a few things."

"Yes, you did." Jeff laughed. It was more Angela who wanted the changes. He just wanted to move in with her. It could be into a tent, and he'd be happy.

"You did too. I know I wanted more changes, though. Get used to it, Babe."

"Oh, I know. Women always want things changed."

"I will let that one slide. I need to get ready for work. We will talk tonight about the house. I am so excited! Wait until I tell Terri!"

"We will talk later. Go call Terri and then get to work. I love you."

"Love you too, Babe. I am excited." She hung up her phone before Jeff had time to say anything else.

Jeff looked at his cell phone and smiled. He loved Angela. He knew they had a connection the moment he met her. Life was going to be amazing with her by his side.

Angela made coffee and took a quick shower before she called her sister. The news was exciting, but it could wait until she was more awake. She knew they would talk for a while once she had Terri on the phone. They always did, even when they were busy.

"Good morning, Sis. How are you?" Terri said when she answered her sister's call.

"I am great! Running late, so I can't talk long, but I have news! The sellers accepted our offer on that house!"

"That's awesome! Weren't you afraid they would reject it because Jeff gave them a low bid on it?"

"I was afraid of that. And we were prepared to offer more, but now we can use the extra money we thought we would need just to buy it to make the changes we want."

"I am happy for you, Sis! Your life is changing quickly."

"Yes, it is. And it is all your fault."

"My fault? What did I do?"

"You said goodbye to Jay, met Adam, got married, and because of that, I had to come here to help with the wedding and met Jeff. It is all your fault."

"That is a bit of a stretch, but I will take the blame. If that is what it took to get you to move here, I will accept the responsibility. Just don't screw it up."

"Never. My life is finally moving forward to a good place. One step at a time, but moving."

"So is mine, Sis. So is mine. When Jay and I broke up, I was unsure how life could be good again. But it has become even better."

"And you still have Jay as a good friend. To you and to Adam. That does not happen very often with relationships."

"We are blessed, that is for sure. Now, you said you were running late. I will let you go. You and Jeff need to come over tonight to celebrate at our house! I'll take a bottle of champagne home for us."

"Thanks, Sis. Let me talk to Jeff later, and I will let you know if we can make it tonight. We will celebrate as soon as we can."

"Perfect. Congratulations again!" Terri hung up her phone and smiled. Life was good for them, finally.

Later that afternoon, Jeff called Angela to talk about the house. She mentioned going to Terri's, and he said they could as soon as they talked to the realtor after work.

~~~~~~

"Cheers!" Terri, Adam, Angela, and Jeff raised their glasses to toast the new house purchase.

"Our lives are about to change like never before."

"That they will. We are thrilled with owning our place. It takes some work, but it will be all yours, and you can do with it what you want. It is so much better than renting."

"And do we ever have plans!" Jeff said as he looked at Angela and smiled.

"If you need help, you know my company can make it happen." Adam offered. "Just let me know. Even if you want to do the work yourself, I'd be happy to be a consultant and offer suggestions."

"Thanks. We will call on you. It is a small home, but with such a view, we could not resist. We have room for an addition built on, which I think we want to do early."

" I'd like a larger deck on the back, too," Angela added.

"Yes, babe, we will get that deck enlarged to entertain. I agree."

The two couples continued talking about the new house and the needed work. Terri took a few breaks to prepare Makenna for bed, including time to read a bedtime story to her. Terri did her best to show her foster child the love she deserved. She knew that as an infant, she would not remember this time in her life, but Terri hoped it would somehow make a difference as she grew older.

Angela stood at the doorway to the nursery while Terri read the short bedtime story and could not help but smile. Her sister had become an amazing mother.

"I hope one day to be half the mother you are to Makenna," Angela said as Terri rejoined the others in the living room.

"When it is your turn to be a mother, you will be as good if not better than I am."

"It will be a while before I become a mother, don't rush me."

Terri put her arm around her sister's shoulder. "Not about to rush you. First, we need to get you moved into your new house."

"That's right. First, we need to get moved," Jeff said. He had no idea what the sisters were discussing, but he agreed with the part he heard.

Angela sat down next to Jeff. She was finally happy with her life. She had thought she was happy being single and just living her life. Now that she had Jeff in her life, she could not imagine ever being alone again. This life was amazing. People needed a special person to spend their life with. She had found hers.

Chapter Twenty-Three
Truth Unseen

The music played on the radio as Sara sat in her office with the newest journal she had found. She had no idea why none of them had noticed it before. It was not where the others had been in the attic, but it was very visible.

It had been a while since anyone was in the attic or the secret room of the manor. They had seen no need to go. After Sara talked with Roman, she returned to the attic, trying to feel any vibes from her grandmama. Anything about her past that she had not read about or felt before.

She remembered feeling the presence of her mama a few times when they had been in the attic or as they left, but she never thought to try to feel more. She had not tried to feel the sensations she and Heather had before. They were just there.

While she was alone in the attic, she heard muffled voices. She looked around, knowing full well that no one else was there. That was when she noticed the journal. Seeing it caused a wave of shivers to run down her spine. She immediately knew it held the answers she was searching for.

Now that Sara sat alone in her office, she hesitated before opening the writings of Rose. She walked to the office door and locked it. She did not want to be disturbed. This time was between her and her grandmama. The words she was about to read were a message directed to her. There was something about the impending truth Sara was about to discover. Whether Roman was telling the truth or it was something he or his family created, Sara would only believe Rose and her written story.

Sitting at her desk with hot coffee waiting in the carafe, she began to think she would need a glass of wine before she was finished. Her mind ran through the possibilities of truth or what she wanted the truth to be. Was she ready to find out? Taking a deep breath, she gently moved the cover to reveal the front page of her grandmama's journal.

Sara knew what she was looking for and began to skim through the pages until she found what she thought would give her the needed answer. She would read the entirety of the journal later. For now, she just needed the truth. Several pages in, she stopped and began to read.

> *Life has not always been easy for me here at Bella Rose. Robert and I began taking in the girls soon after we married. We soon realized we needed more for them. More space if possible. More places for their things and their infant's things while they were here. Robert contacted a man who had recently moved to the area and was looking for work. We later found out he had a connection to the town far beyond what we had.*
>
> *Raymond was an amazing carpenter.*

Sara gasped. She realized she was unprepared for what she may be about to read. How could something like this be part of her family? Were her family dynamics about to change?

> *Robert and I talked details at length with Raymond about what we needed. More security in the upstairs attic and secret room. Pieces of furniture for the girls that could be locked. He also suggested each piece have individual keys so no one but the*

girl it was meant for could open them. He said he had a thing about keeping secrets and staying private.

We accepted his work offer with a friendly handshake.

Robert had to go on a business trip while Raymond worked on the pieces. Raymond assured Robert that he would look out for the girls and me and take care of things for me. Robert appreciated that and told Raymond to feel at home while he was gone.

Robert's trip took longer than expected, but Raymond stayed true to his word. He took care of us to keep us safe. As much as the girls distrusted most males, they loved Robert and quickly loved Raymond and all he was doing for them.

Raymond had a place in town where he lived, but one night at the manor, I had an angry man at my door who refused to leave until I threatened to call the sheriff. The next day I told Raymond about it, and he insisted he move in while Robert was gone. At first, I said no, but the few girls staying there at the time pleaded with me to let him stay. So I told Raymond he could sleep in the one spare bedroom we had vacant.

Robert returned from his trip and thanked Raymond for caring for all his 'girls." We all had a good laugh about how Robert called all of us his 'girls." Robert then offered Raymond to stay with us until his work there was complete.

I was uncomfortable with the arrangement, but I never went against what my husband said, so I allowed it.

A month later, Robert got called away again. He was working on getting better help for unwed mothers, so he could not say no. And the girls were more comfortable with me being there, so Robert always made those trips.

Again, Raymond stayed.

When Robert returned that last time he knew something was different.

Sara did not want to read anything further. The truth was about to come out. What Roman had told her must have been the truth. Sara had mixed emotions. She wanted to cry. She felt a little angry. She hated this Raymond man. In turn, she also hated Roman at that moment, even though it was not Roman's fault. Telling her was his fault, but she supposed it needed to be revealed if it was true.

Or did it? Why did it?

I know whoever reads this may be shocked if I do not destroy it first. Your image of our family may be pure and simple. Believe me. Life, in general, is not pure and simple. Things happen. Mistakes happen as much as we want to control them and always be that image of perfection. And we pay the consequences. I have paid dearly. I have also been blessed with an understanding man who continued to love me.

You see, or by now, maybe you know, have heard, or suspect what happened. I won't deny the facts. Truth is key to any relationship and any family. Forgiveness and grace play a major part in life as well. If you are fortunate to give or receive it.

It took a while, but Robert had more grace than anyone I have ever met. No, not at first. We battled it. We went down a road we thought would end Bella Rose and what it stood for. And temporarily, it did just that.

One night one of the girls went into early labor. It was the first time Robert was not there for the event, but Raymond was, and I put him to work. It was a long and complicated delivery, but we all survived. The little boy was born healthy and perfect. Once mom and baby were settled in for a few hours, Raymond and I sat and talked. He was more amazed at our work than he had been. Before either of us knew it, things happened between us. We made a connection that night.

We tried to hide what had happened, but when Robert returned a few days later, he sensed something had changed. I could not keep it a secret from Robert. When I told him about that night, he told Raymond to move out. Robert was angry. I did not blame him. We spent days trying to talk. Trying to pretend things were normal for the girls' sake and our mission.

Two weeks later, when we had no girls there to take care of, Robert and I separated. He put our home up for sale. He wanted nothing to do with me, our mission, or our home.

I moved into an apartment in town. Unfortunately, it put me closer to Raymond. Raymond wanted to take up where things left off with me, but I refused. I wanted

Robert back in my life. I knew my chances were slim, but I refused to give up.

It took over a month of Robert and I talking, crying, arguing, and spending time together, but he agreed to give me another chance. His trust in me would take time to build back, but our love was stronger than my one-night mistake.

And there you have it. The truth. Yes, I screwed up. I hurt the man I loved with all my heart. I damaged our relationship. I hated myself for it.

Robert took Bella Rose off the market. We hired a different man to do the carpentry work for us only when Robert and I were both there. We took in more girls for another year.

Raymond? He moved away. Last I knew, he had married, and they had a little boy. I never saw him again.

Sara turned the page. The next page was missing. Someone had torn it out. She wondered why. Rose had completed her story. Her life was back to normal. She and Robert lived happily ever after, as all fairy tales end.

The next two pages were blank. On the third page, her grandmama continued to write.

Yes, I tore out that page. And I left the other two blank. It was my hesitation to keep telling my story. And I have concluded that for me, some things will go to my grave.

There is no reason to tell all. What took place in my life during that time is of no concern to anyone but me. It is what I chose to do. It was my life.

All that anyone needs to know is that Robert and I lived a full life after that. We had a child and changed what Bella Rose was all about. Our time taking in the unwed mothers and dealing secretly to care for them ended. It was no longer needed, plus we did not want our child or children to be involved with the illegal life we led. It was needed while it was needed. God had somehow and for some reason chosen us to care for all those girls. Chosen us to welcome those new little humans into this world. He chose Robert to gently care for those babies that did not make it.

The hardship we survived taught us that truth is key and honest communication is a must. Trust is earned. And love is constant and from the soul.

Sara smiled. Truth – at least one page was missing. Two pages were blank. She knew there was more to her grandmama's story and life. She would never know what that was.

Sara had learned the truth. Roman had been correct, although she suspected his version and the story he had heard was exaggerated from the truth.

Sara shook her head. Or maybe his was the full story, and her grandmama was holding back. Rose was holding something back. Sara admitted to herself that love endured. Sometimes, the truth should be kept silent. The key to bringing smiles to yourself and your family is to give love, forgiveness, grace, and a chance. In the end, to accept what is known and not push for more. Yet, when in doubt, search for the truth. No matter what it was.

129

Sara flipped to the back cover, but it opened to the last page of the journal. There, written in Rose's handwriting, were the words.

" R & R – Always a part of my heart."

Sara closed the journal. She let the words simmer over the flames in her mind, cooled by reality and grace.

There were no more questions.

Chapter Twenty-Four
Secrets Held

Sara placed the journal in her secret hiding place on the bookshelf in the office. No one knew about it. As she placed it there, she noticed a paper fall from the journal. She bent to pick it up.

She carefully unfolded the paper. It was the obituary of Raymond Watson. She sat at her desk as she read it.

She skipped the dates he was born or that he died. She wanted to know who had been in his life and who he had left behind. Mr. Watson is survived by his wife, Veronica, his son, Jeremiah (Helen), his great-grandson Roman and his forever love, Rose Fairchild.

Sara stared at the paper. After all those years, he had the gall to mention her grandmama? What did his wife think? Who wrote the obituary? They had to have known what to write unless Raymond wrote it before he died. No one questioned it?

She jumped around on the rest of the details. He was born in 1914 and died in 1995. He was a carpenter specializing in unique furniture requiring custom made keys. He enjoyed traveling, time with his wife and son, and many lifelong friends.

Sara folded the paper, placed it between the pages in the middle of the journal, and placed it in the bookcase. Then she carefully closed the hidden door and secured it with the custom made key.

As she left the office, she held the key in her hand. Her mind was afloat with all the secrets within her family for as far back as she knew. Now there were more.

A call to Roman was needed. She also needed to talk to her siblings. Which one should she do first? Of course, it should be Roman. She needed more facts he seemed privy to that she could only accept as truth.

She got home before Randall and Gayle and made a phone call.

"Hello, Sara, how are you?" Roman answered graciously.

"Hello, Roman. How am I? Maybe more confused than before today, but I need to humble myself and admit you were right."

"I was right? About what?" he had other things on his mind and momentarily was lost in what she was referring to.

"About your great-grandfather and my grandmother. However, from what I can tell, it was not as detailed, nor did it continue as long as your family thinks it did."

"At least you discovered that they had an affair."

"No, I discovered they had a one-night stand. That was all."

"I beg to differ, but that is fine. Is that what you called about?"

"Yes, and no. I have decided I need more information. More details."

"Are you sure you can handle the details we have about your family?"

"About my family? I am talking about details between Raymond and Rose. There is no more to know about my family. We are an open book."

"So you thought or obviously still think. Your family is not the innocent family they perceived to be."

"Oh, I know illegal things were going on. I know there were a lot of secrets that are only now coming out after my parents died a few years ago."

"I am glad you realize that. Shall we get together sometime to discuss the secrets my family knows?"

"Yes, I think we need to. When can you return to do just that?"

"Well, Jennifer is away with her mother for a couple of weeks, so I can come any time."

"Good; I will reserve a room for you starting this weekend."

"I will be there. Goodbye, Sara."

"Goodbye, Roman." Sara hung up her phone. Something about the way he spoke and what he said bothered her. He had something up his sleeve. He was still hiding something.

Randall walked in from work while Sara was still lost in thought. When he closed the door, she jumped.

"Hello, Babe. I didn't mean to startle you. Your mind must have been out in no man's land."

"It's ok. Not sure about no man's land, but it was certainly out there." She let it go and hoped her husband would not inquire further.

"Okay. I won't dig. I know you will tell me if and when you want to. I learned that about you many years ago." He kissed her on her forehead and set his briefcase on the counter.

"Thank you. Yes, I will tell you when the time is right. I am so glad you understand me. Sometimes you know me better than I do."

"That is not easy, trust me. But I do my best."

"I have a room reserved for Roman starting this weekend."

"Why are they coming back so soon?"

"Jennifer will not be with him. She is spending time getting to know her mother or something. Roman will be on his own. I need to talk with him more."

Randall looked at Sara. He wanted to ask so many questions but kept quiet. He would hear the details later. "Okay. Not a problem. We don't have anything going on that I know of."

<hr />

133

Roman arrived early Friday morning at the manor and met Sara in her office. He carried a small satchel in with him.

"Good morning Roman. Welcome back to Bella Rose. Have a seat."

"Thank you. It's good to be back. I like it in this town. Just something about it draws me here."

"Has nothing to do with your family history being here in this town, does it?" Sara grinned.

"That may have a little to do with it. Do you want to get right to all your questions, or are we stuck in chit-chat?"

Sara looked at him and hesitated. She tried to be friendly but sensed he had a hidden agenda. "We might as well get down to family business."

Roman opened his satchel, pulled out a paper file, and handed the entire file to Sara. "You will find all the writings Raymond wrote about that time in his life in this file. I have read them, and believe me, his story is a true love story."

"I gathered that when I read his obituary. No one I ever knew added an ex-girlfriend to their survivor's list. To have someone know that about another person meant that they talked about that person enough that others knew about that love."

"I agree. When my grandfather told me about Raymond's love affair, I wanted to deny it as much as you do now. But there was something about the story that made it beautiful."

"I am not sure about beautiful. And my grandmother did not say that her love for him was even there, let alone continued after their one-night stand. According to her journal, there was nothing between them after that night."

"But, did you not tell me that there was at least one page torn from her journal and then a few blank pages before she added the very end?"

"I will admit that Rose left things wide open to speculation of her feelings."

"So, read Raymond's story and tell me what you think."

"I will. As much as I hate him for making Rose do what she did, I admire him for loving her for the rest of his life. However, she chose to remain with my grandfather and make a life for them and my family. This place is because of them and their love for each other. They persevered and won. My family will always know about their dedication and love for each other."

"But, they will not know about her secret love?" Roman smiled. He understood. Family was important to him too.

"I have not decided that yet. I may tell them and even write about it in my book about my family.

Roman left the office and returned to his room before going to the café downtown. He wanted a good drink.

Sara closed her office door as soon as Roman walked out. She locked it. She wanted to read his side of the story and draw her own conclusions. Either Rose was right, and Raymond held a one-sided love, or Rose hid something Sara was about to discover. If she found out there was more to their story than she wanted to know, she would do her best to set it aside, say enough was enough, and leave her family alone. After all, they had been through enough with what they already knew.

Sara sat down with the file.

Chapter Twenty- Five
Two Sided Truth

Randall called Sara's cell phone from his office. Sara always made an effort to have dinner ready to prepare, if not already cooked, when everyone got home, and he wanted to let her know he would be a little late. When she did not answer her phone, he left a simple message and returned to work with his client.

Sara was still in the office when she heard her phone ring. She was engrossed in the papers she was reading and easily ignored her phone. She never looked up to see what time it was.

The next thing she knew, there was a knock on her office door. She jumped when she heard the loud knock. She looked up and noticed how dark it was outside and panicked.

She stood and rushed to the door, stumbling as she went. She held on to the edge of her bookcase when she opened the door. Randall was standing there and saw her sway when the door opened. He reached out to hold her up.

"Are you alright?" He asked while guiding her to the easy chair in her office.

"I'm good, I think," Sara looked around the room, squinting her eyes. Her mind was not focusing.

"Babe, what's going on? I called you an hour ago, and you never answered or called me back. Then you were not at home when I arrived. Gayle said she had not seen you either. Why are you still here in the office? Why do you look like you are lost?" Randall held her cold hand in his. He rubbed it in an attempt to get the circulation going inside her.

"I'm fine. I'm," she didn't continue.

"Sara, what is wrong?"

Sara pointed to her desk and the opened file on top of the other papers. Randall did not understand it until he read a few words.

"Is this what I think it is? Is this why Roman returned?"

Sara nodded her head. Then she raised her head and rubbed her arms, which suddenly felt cold. It took her another moment to bring herself back to reality.

"And, what have you discovered?"

"This is Raymond's truth about him and Rose."

"Okay." Randall dragged out the word changing it to a question as he ended it. "You say Raymond's truth as if it differs from Rose's."

"That is because it is different," Sara said with her confidence back. She reached over to pull out the paper. This one says their affair lasted more than that one-night stand. He indicated they dated a while and that he wanted to marry her."

"Wow. That would have been interesting. I wonder if you would have still been born who you are if it had been him as your grandfather?"

"I doubt it. I would have been here but as someone else. I could have been born a boy instead of a girl."

"That would have been interesting." Randall laughed. I am not sure I would have liked you the way I do if you were a boy."

"You never know. Maybe you would have been changed."

"What have you discovered so far from his journal? You seemed lost in what you were reading."

"I have discovered that Raymond had some major feelings for Grandmama."

"How so?"

"She is included in his obituary as one of his survivors."

"Really? I never heard of an ex-girlfriend being listed in anyone's obit."

"They were not even boyfriend/girlfriend. Rose's journal states they had a one-night stand, other than an ongoing friendship."

"Maybe he wished it was more, or maybe there was more to it that Rose just did not want anyone to know."

"Randall! That is my grandmama you are talking about."

"Hey, we are all human. We all make mistakes. We all have things in our past we would rather not share with the world."

"Oh? What is your big bad secret?"

"I cannot tell you. I will take it to the grave with me," Randall laughed. He put his hand on Sara's shoulder. "You have nothing to worry about. I have no lifelong secrets to keep."

"Okay. If you say so. I don't want to read about something in your journal after you die."

"No fear of that; I don't write a journal." He shook his head. Sara thought everyone wrote a journal about their life. It was in her family to do so. Obviously, not in his.

Sara closed the file and stood up. "Let's make supper and end this nightmare of a day. "How was your late client, by the way? Anything serious going on?"

"You know I cannot tell you anything about my clients."

"I know. I'm just testing you. I don't want you to break any rules and be kicked out of your firm."

"Funny, considering my firm consists of me, myself, and I. I don't think me is going to fire myself." He laughed at the thought.

Sara smiled. Deciding it was time to call it a day, she closed the file and turned to be with her husband. Hand in hand, they walked from the manor to their home. Gayle met them at the door. "Where were the two of you?" She shook her head against her thoughts and tried to block out the picture she had in her head. It was not a pretty sight for a teenager.

Sara hugged her daughter and held her for a few moments longer than normal. Gayle looked at Randall with raised eyes. She silently wanted to know if everything was alright.

"Okay, you two. Enough mother/daughter time; I'm starving."

"You are always hungry." Randall smiled at her. He would not have her any other way.

Together, the three made a simple meal and sat around the table to eat. Gayle was glad her family believed in family time. She heard horrible stories at school. She hated hearing about some of her classmates' lives at home. She was one of the few fortunate ones.

After dinner, Sara told Randall she wanted to go for a walk alone. He looked at her and knew exactly where she was going. She was not done with the writings from Raymond yet. Randall knew that Sara would not sleep until she read the truth. Or at least one side of the truth. He nodded his approval and said he would leave a light on for her, but if she was too late, he would be asleep when she got home.

Sara hugged her husband and daughter and returned to the manor and her office.

Three hours later, Sara's eyes were so bloodshot she doubted she'd be able to take her contacts out. She had learned a lot. She put the papers back inside the file folder and the whole file inside her secret place on the bookshelf. Her family was asleep when she returned home. She poured herself a glass of wine and sat on the window seat, staring out into the darkness. Life had changed again. Rather, her view of family and life had changed.

Sara awoke, still sitting at the window seat. She laughed at herself for her behavior. So determined to find answers, she had lost sleep, worried her family, and refused to accept that there were more secrets to her family than they first realized. Life certainly was interesting. But facts were facts, and the papers held the evidence.

She would call for a family meeting the next night. She would talk to Roman first and send him on his way home. He had provided enough damage, even if it was the truth.

When she spoke with Roman, he said he would stay in touch if they had any other questions or discovered anything else. Sara asked him what the purpose was of opening this family history. He told her he did not know except that his grandfather seemed to think it was important. He said he suspected there was still more to the story and Raymond's connection to her family.

～～～～～～～～～～～～～～～～～～～～～～～～～～～～～～

The siblings gathered once again around the island for a family meeting. Their spouses joined them while all the kids were playing or napping in the great room.

"I know you all wondered why Roman was here again so soon after his last visit during Storytelling. I won't keep you in suspense about it. It involves his great-grandfather, Raymond, and our grandmama, Rose."

Everyone was silent as they let her continue.

"When Roman and Jennifer were here, you may or may not know that he met with me privately after telling his story in town. The one he told in town was not his main story. He saved our family from embarrassment by telling the public one story and telling me another one. One, mind you, that I refused to believe. Until I had him return with proof. Yesterday morning he presented the truth." She held the file up for all to see.

"What are you talking about?" Heather asked.

"We all know the secrets in this family. Well, there are more. Seems that Rose and Robert hired Raymond to do some carpentry work on the manor and to make some of the furniture for the attic and secret room upstairs. We all know about the keys made for getting into them. Raymond was the one who insisted that each piece have a custom key designed specifically for that piece. He did the same for several people in town."

"Okay, something tells me there is more. That is not much of a secret." Andy stated.

"Hang on, little brother. Believe me, there is more. Roman told me that Rose and Raymond had an affair while he worked here. I refused to believe him. Then I went back to the attic."

"We found everything there was to find up there." Heather protested.

"That is what I thought. However, I found another journal when I entered the attic the other day. One that should have been easy to find when we looked before but somehow missed."

"Or that someone planted there on purpose," Karen suggested.

"I thought of that but cannot prove it. Anyway, the journal I found was written by Rose. It was only a few pages, but it was about the time when Raymond was here."

Sara told them what Rose had written about the torn and blank pages. And then the final page with the initials written. She handed the journal to them for proof when she ended that part of her story.

"Wow. That is interesting. So glad she and Robert reconnected, and we can be here today." Ben said.

"Okay, but what is Raymond's side of the story? Does it match hers?"

"I was hoping it did. Roman insisted there was more to it. So I had him bring what he had to show us. The one thing about Rose's journal that caused me to call Roman is this." She held up Raymond's obituary and pointed to the survivors listed. Everyone read it and glared at Sara.

"There's more," Sara lightly laughed." It seems the affair continued for a while. Raymond did finally get married to a lady and had a child. They moved away, but he never stopped loving her. When Rose finally cut him off and ended their relationship, he vowed to always be a part of her and her family's life. I didn't know what he meant, but listing her in his obit could have been his way of doing that."

"You would think that would affect his own family more than ours. Do you think he had more in mind?"

Sara gathered up the papers and returned them to the file folder. Then walked over to the wine cabinet. Wine glasses for each of them and a bottle of wine indicated there was more. But was it a celebration or such a theory that they all needed a drink to digest? Sara poured each of them a drink, including Andy.

Chapter Twenty-Six
Theory or Possibility

Sara raised her glass in a toast in preparation to tell her family the rest of her discoveries.

Before she had time to say anything more, her cell phone rang. She looked at it and excused herself to take the call.

"Roman, what is it? You know I was going to talk to my family tonight. I'm still talking with them."

"I know. I just had to talk to someone."

Sara thought it odd that he would call her of all people. She barely knew him.

"Okay, I'm listening, but can it be brief? I've left my family hanging with a glass of wine to drink." She laughed when she realized how silly that sounded.

"I will keep it short." Roman took a deep breath. "We found more."

"More what?"

"More hints, I guess you could say, about what Raymond wanted to do after Rose broke up with him."

"Oh?"

"I will take a photo of it and send it to your email. You can view it whenever you want if you want to. Seems his wife got pulled into his plans."

"Plans for what?" Sara sat down in her office. Suddenly this conversation sounded serious.

"Plans to cause issues with Rose and your family."

"How?"

"Let me send you the information. You won't believe me if I just tell you. I am having a hard time believing it. But, from what you have told me, I think their plan worked."

"It worked? This will show how they have been messing with Rose?"

"And your family. Longer than you would think."

"Okay, send me what you have. I have to see this. Until then, I need to talk to my family."

"You may want to wait and add this to your discussions. I will add my thoughts to the message I send you."

"You are talking in riddles, you know this?"

"Not on purpose. Trust me."

"I would laugh at that, but I hate to admit it, but you have been right so far."

"I wish I wasn't. It puts my family into the position of being the bad guys against your family."

"You have no control over what Raymond did."

"I hope not. Let me send this. You should get it in a minute."

"Thank you. In all honesty, you don't have to do any of this for my family."

"Yes. I do. Trust me."

"You keep saying that. I guess I will until I don't."

Roman was silent for a moment while he wrote his message and sent the photo to her email. 'Okay, I just sent it. You may want to check it on your computer, not just your phone, so you can read it all."

"I can print it out from my phone. Not a problem."

"Okay. Call me if you have any questions. Good night."

"I will. Do not turn your phone off tonight. It may be late when we call you."

"For you, I will keep my phone on."

Sara hung up without saying another word. She immediately opened her email app to see what he had sent.

Before returning to the kitchen where her family waited, she opened the email, read what he wrote, and pulled up the photo. It was a print of writing, not a picture photograph. A picture of writing. She pushed to print it on her main printer in the office before reading it.

Pulling the copy from the printer's paper tray, she skimmed over it and immediately sat down in her chair.

Heather knocked on Sara's office door and walked in. She took one look at her sister and knew something was wrong.

"What is going on, Sis? We are worried about you. You are acting strange."

"I will explain as best as I can when we return to the others." Sara stood up and put her arm through Heather's, and they walked into the kitchen together.

"Sorry for the delay. But I promise the hold-up was well worth the time it took."

"So what is this all about?" Andy asked. His patience seemed to be wavering and getting thin.

"The phone call was from Roman. At first, I thought nothing of it, just him checking on us for some reason. But he had more information about his Great grandfather, Raymond."

"Now what would he have us believe about him and Grandmama?"

"Well, he had told us, and the papers we have tell us that Raymond was angry when Rose broke up with him, and he was going out for revenge of some sort. He never really did any damage to her at the time. He married, and his wife convinced him to move away from here. They had a son, Jeremiah. That son is the one who wanted Roman to come here in the first place to see what he could dig up about us. That is why he and Jennifer were here in the beginning. Once he found the connection, more details began to appear."

"I still can't believe Grandmama would do such a thing and risk losing it all for a stranger. What was she thinking?"

"People do crazy things at times. I am glad she came to her senses and held on to her marriage and Bella Rose."

"We all are. Now, on to Raymond, who was unhappy that she held onto her family. He threatened Rose that he would haunt her even after he died."

"How can a person predict that? That's ludicrous."

"I agree. But everything else he has said or written has been true."

"So we are supposed to believe he could come back as a ghost and haunt us? Has anyone ever seen a ghost here? Or suspected anything being from a ghost?"

"I will add that according to this writing, his wife, Veronica, joined in that threat because she had never had all of his love. She knew he always loved Rose. So Veronica wrote that she would do whatever she could in her power to haunt us after she died. She added that it was safer to do that after she died so she would not be put in jail. But that things would not always be great for Bella Rose."

"Again, I ask, has anyone had a ghost encounter?" Andy did not believe in such things and thought the whole story was stupid.

"No, not in person."

"I have. Well, maybe. I didn't see anything, but I have felt things." Heather admitted.

"I have also," Sara said, looking at her sister.

"Where? When?" Andy asked.

"When we were beginning to search for things in the attic and again when we discovered the secret room. I remember feeling a slight brushing of something on my arm as we climbed the stairs."

"That is when I felt it too. Both times I was alone, so I never said a word. I attributed it to my imagination and the feelings of being there where our mother and grandmother and, as we discovered, so many others spent time."

"I wasn't alone the first time, but I was the last one to walk down the steps. It was almost like someone wanting me to stop searching."

"Okay, now you both are giving me goosebumps," Karen said, rubbing her arms.

"You both have wild imaginations," Andy said. He stood up and walked to the window in the kitchen. Facing the backyard, he stared into the evening twilight.

Ben had been quiet during most of the conversation. He was part of the family but a distant part. "Knowing what we know now, what are you two ladies thinking? Could it have been Raymond or Veronica fulfilling their threats? Their attempt to keep things secret?"

"I don't know what to think," Sara said. She picked up the paper she had brought from the printer. "According to this, both Raymond and Veronica vowed to destroy Rose's family in any way they could. Dead or alive."

"You all are crazy," Andy said. Then he made a sound no one had heard before. Everyone looked at him.

Andy stood frozen. He wanted to turn around and deny what he had just witnessed, but nothing moved except his eyes, which were blinking, trying to focus on what obviously was nothing.

"Andy?"

"Babe? What's wrong?" Karen walked to her husband and rested her hand on his shoulder. He brushed it off and shivered. "Andy, what is it?"

Heather and Sara joined Andy at the window. They watched as fallen leaves rose from the ground and swirled into the air. The large solar panel ground light in the largest flower bed flickered. Everyone watched, spellbound. It was a calm day. There had been no wind and none in the forecast.

Chapter Twenty-Seven
Mother-Daughter Reunion

Jennifer rang the doorbell and stepped away from the door. She heard music through an open window that stopped when the doorbell sounded.

Suzanne opened the door and smiled. "Come in, Jennifer. I am so glad you agreed to come to see me."

"Hi, Suzanne. It was not an easy decision until Roman decided to take off again. That helped make up my mind." Jennifer stepped inside, walking past her mother. She was not ready to call her Mom even though she had accepted the facts.

Suzanne peered outside before she closed the door. She wanted to assure no one was watching. She hated nosey neighbors.

"What do you mean, Roman took off again? Does he make a habit of leaving you?" The two ladies entered the living room and sat on the sofa.

"Oh, no. I didn't mean for it to sound that way. Sorry if I gave you that impression. He said he had to return to Bella Rose to take care of something, that's all. He told me it was a good time for me to come see you."

"Okay. I don't want my daughter married to a man who runs around on her."

"Oh, heavens no. He has been my lifesaver since I was a teenager. He got me safely away from Dad. It was no fun living there all those years after you disappeared."

"I told you before that my leaving was not my idea. Your father took advantage of my mental condition and set it up so I could never return. He was a horrible man."

"Yes, he was. I learned to manage my life around him, but it was not easy. As soon as I met Roman and told him my story, I got out and never looked back."

"I am so sorry for what happened to me and thus to you all those years ago. If I could have changed any of it, I would have."

"I know that – now. It took me years to forgive you without you asking for forgiveness. The stories Dad told me were easy to believe. I had heard them all my life. I didn't know anything different. I didn't know enough to ask questions. As I got older, he got more abusive. I thought it was how all families lived."

Suzanne sat and listened as her long, lost daughter spoke. Her words were painful to hear. The reality of her childhood that could never be erased pained her. She could only tell her side of the truth and let the two begin healing and moving forward together. The trouble was she was not sure she was ready to tell her complete story. Like her daughter, she had been lied to for so long that it was hard to decipher the full truth.

"I am so glad you found Roman. He seems to have helped you escape into a better life."

"He is wonderful. We do everything together. I don't think I've even gone anywhere until now without him by my side." Jennifer had to think. No, she had always had Roman by her side. He controlled where they went and all the things they did. It made her life so much easier.

"You have never been anywhere without him? How is that possible? Does he go to the store with you, shopping with you, the hairdresser? Everywhere?" Suzanne was not liking what she was assuming.

"Of course. We shop together and cook together. You'd love him and his cooking," she smiled, thinking of how well they coordinated their movements at home. It was like a dance. "He takes me to have my hair done when I need it."

"Need it? Verses want it?"

"I would probably just let it grow long and not mess with it much. Like when I was little and just wore it in a ponytail most of the time. Roman pays more attention to things like that." Jennifer wondered why all the questions about Roman's behavior. She loved how he took care of everything.

Suzanne stood up and invited her daughter to join her in the kitchen for coffee. The two ladies walked together. They had the same height, build, features, and of course, those eyes. There was no denying they were mother and daughter.

The coffee maker beeped when the coffee finished dripping. Suzanne poured them each a cup, never asking how Jennifer took hers. She already knew how much they were alike and assumed the coffee taste was the same. The smile from her younger self said she was right.

The two ladies spent the afternoon talking about everything they had missed in their years apart. Suzanne's life didn't begin until she was off the meds and out of the institution, but she had spent her time searching for her baby. She would have never given up her search. Finding her took a couple of years, but now she had an indication of why. Roman may have saved her from her ex-husband, but he was a monster of his own. Her daughter just did not know any better.

The phone rang as the day was ending. They had decided to go out to eat and were headed for the door when the landline phone rang. They looked at each other and laughed. People rarely used a landline number anymore. Suzanne picked up the receiver.

"Hello. Hold on, Roman, I will get her," she handed the phone to Jennifer.

"Hello, Love. How did it go at Bella Rose?" She listened for a few minutes. "I hope you don't mind. May I spend the night here? It's getting late, and I prefer not to drive in the dark. You know how I am. Yes, I know. But, we will survive apart for one night. I promise to head home first thing in the morning. Thank you. I love you too." She hung up the phone and joined her mother at the front door. "Roman says it's okay for me to stay the night."

"I'm glad. We can have a slumber party. We'll buy a bottle of wine on the way home. Party time tonight."

Jennifer looked at her mother. Who was this person? She liked her and her free spirit way of life from all she had learned that day. She was proud of her mom.

"Mom, thank you," Jennifer said quietly. She was testing the sound of that word and acceptance more than anything.

Suzanne turned and smiled. She put her arm around her daughter's shoulders. "That is the most beautiful word I have ever heard."

During dinner, they discussed Roman. By the end of the meal, they had a plan. Life was going to change for both of them. It would take commitment and determination. Their goal was set. Getting there would not be easy.

~~~~~~

Roman sat alone in their bedroom. He looked around at the emptiness and listened to the quiet. It was not the first night he had not had his wife by his side. He was determined that it would be the last. He needed her.

He did not sleep well that night. Instead, he had plans. Plans for his marriage and their future. Life was about to change. Now that he had taken care of his family secrets and what his grandfather wanted from him, he was finally free to live the life he dreamed of. One with Jennifer by his side everywhere they traveled. And traveling is what they were about to start doing. Life was too short, as he realized in dealing with the troubled life his Great-grandfather had lived.

He made coffee and ate breakfast while waiting for the love of his life to return home. Love was a shallow word for how his heart felt.

Chapter Twenty-Eight
Haunting Threats

Sara had not slept well the night of the family meeting. The talk about Bella Rose being haunted bothered her. It was true she and Heather had felt brushed by something they could not explain when they first began to look through the attic and then the secret room. Could those brushes have been more than a sensation? Were there more secrets with a sinister past in her family's lives?

When Randall got up for the day, Sara was sitting on her window seat in the living room.

"You didn't sleep well, did you?" He asked his wife.

"Not at all. I can't get rid of the idea that our property is haunted. Can someone actually threaten to haunt a place and then have it happen? I've never heard of such a thing."

"That I don't know. From what you told me, though, that is what happened. I doubt there is any way to prove it."

"I know. I am worried about it. When I think about the first times we looked for things in the attic and Heather and I both felt those sensations walking down the steps, it still gives me chills. Could there be more going on, or was it just those touches? And why?"

"Well, we know why now. Raymond was a jilted lover who took out his revenge. True, it was only after becoming a ghost, as far as we can tell. He still managed to be a part of Rose's life well after she was gone."

Sara shook her head and upper body to rid her feelings and thoughts. She twisted around to stand up.

"Are you okay? What was that shaking about?" Randall asked. He had gone to pour each a cup of coffee and noticed her movements when he walked back with fresh coffee for each of them.

"I need to clear my head. Time to start the day and not think about the manor or our family being haunted." She accepted the mug and took a sip of coffee. She walked with Randall into their bedroom so they could get ready for the day.

"I will work in the office today and work more on my book writing. This new development changes a few things. I think this story needs to be part of the book. I feel that things will come to light as I write."

"I am sure they will. Please do not get bogged down into any darkness over this."

"I won't. I find it interesting as well as frightening."

"Make it more interesting, and don't dwell on the frightening potential."

"Oh, so you agree it is scary?"

"It can be if you let it." Randall held Sara for several minutes before kissing her forehead and letting go. "I don't want the love of my life dreaming up anything that isn't truly there."

"I am a writer, but the truth tends to be more fun to write about than fiction at the moment."

"That's my girl. Call me if you need anything, think of anything, or if anything more happens. I'll be in my office all day."

"I will. Have a great day, my love." Sara kissed him as he left the house.

~~~~~~

The door to the office in the manor opened without someone knocking. Sara did not look up because she assumed it was Heather, who never knocked. Instead, she heard a man's voice.

"Good morning, Sara."

Sara turned in her chair to see who had walked in unannounced. She saw no one. She shrugged her shoulders and turned back around. Her imagination was playing tricks on her. She was so enthralled with the latest events it was getting the best of her. She continued to write on her laptop.

"Sara," This time a female voice. Again, Sara turned around, and no one was there. She stood up and walked to the office door. She pulled it fully open, looked out into the great room, and saw it was empty. She retreated into her office and closed and locked the door. Sitting back at her desk, she mentally closed out all distractions.

Heather knocked on the office door, and when no one answered, she left and returned to cleaning the empty rooms in the manor. Later that day, she saw Sara leave the manor and wondered why her sister had not answered the door. Heather walked to the front window and watched Sara walk down the steps and down the lane. She picked up her phone and called her sister. There was no answer. Shrugging her shoulders, she returned to the kitchen for a drink of water. Her sister was acting strange. She wondered if it had anything to do with Raymond and his threats to the family.

Sara returned to her office an hour later and began to write. This time about the ghost in the family.

A knock at the door made Sara jump. Fully aware of her surroundings, she yelled for whomever to come in. Heather walked in and sat down in front of the office desk so she could talk with Sara. Sara turned around after she finished writing a sentence.

"Good afternoon, Sis. How are you?" Sara asked.

"I am fine. The real question is, how are you? You have been acting strange today."

"What do you mean? I've been in the office all day and have not heard from you."

Heather raised her eyebrows. "You don't remember me knocking earlier? You didn't notice me watching you walk down the lane?"

"When did I walk down the lane? I've been shut in my office writing all day."

"No, you left for an hour."

The two sisters looked at each other and didn't say a word. A chill swept through the room. Sara glanced at her desk. She had printed out a few pages of the book she was writing and wanted to show Heather what she had written that day. The pages were not there.

A key was.

Sara and Heather stared at each other. A cold chill filled the room.

Sara took a deep breath, opened the top desk drawer, and reached into the back, where she had all the antique keys. Heather sat, breathless, waiting. The color of Sara's face changed, and Heather knew—the keys were gone.

Sara refused to be afraid. She tried to think who may have them or where she may have moved them.

"Do you remember where I put the keys?" Sara asked her sister.

"I only knew you kept them inside the desk drawer. Did you put them in the safe for some reason?"

Sara smiled. "The safe!" She took a deep breath. Yes, she had put them in the safe when they started hearing about Raymond and when she was unsure about Roman and Jennifer's motives for being there. She stood and went to the hidden safe. She knew they would be in her secret hiding place if they were not there. How would she get them out without revealing the location to Heather?

She opened the safe and saw the box she had kept them in. Pulling the box out, she smiled. "That's better! Let me put it back there and be over this with the keys. We are overthinking things." She closed and locked the safe. She had kept the one key on the desk where she had found it.

"So glad they are still there. I was getting spooked."

"As was I. I am writing about Raymond in the book I'm working on, so his threats are fresh in my mind. I talked with Randall this morning, wondering how someone could threaten to haunt someone or someplace and years later to actually pull it off. We don't recall it ever happening."

I don't recall that either. I hope we are just overreacting to all of this. We don't need any more drama in our lives. Things were settling down until Roman and Jennifer showed up."

I think it was the mysterious couple before them that started it all. Remember the couple none of us saw while they were here?"

"Yes, what about them?"

"I don't want to scare you, but I think it was Raymond and Veronica."

"What??" Heather's eyes grew big, and she backed away from her sister.

"I think..."

"I heard you. I just don't believe it."

"I didn't want to, but the more I think about it, the more it makes sense. No one saw them. They never ate breakfast here. No one in town really saw them. And when they left, what did you find in the room? Hints that led us to investigate, and then Roman and Jennifer showed up and brought us all the other evidence and stories."

"Wow. You have a vivid imagination, sis."

"Maybe. Or maybe it's all true. We are being haunted."

"How do we stop it?"

"Why should we? I am just now trying to figure it all out. It makes for a great story to add to the history of the estate and our family."

"Do you think so?"

"I know so. This last bit," she lifted the stray key, "This key has a link to something. I intend to find out what it is."

"Okay. You do that. I am going home to my normal family." Heather stood to leave.

"I hate to tell you, but you are a part of this haunted family as much as I am."

"I know. I am not ready to face it yet. Give me time to sleep on it."

"Okay. I will keep you and everyone updated. Love you, Sis."

"I love you, too. No matter if we are normal or not." Heather left the office.

~~~~~~

Sara opened the safe again after Heather left and removed the empty box.

Chapter Twenty-Nine
Good Intentions

Roman looked around the house he shared with his wife. They had lived in a simple home since he rescued her from her father. Before they married, he had brought her to live with him. He made her feel safe and, within a short time, feel loved. He felt her love from the day she agreed to live with him. Although he was not sure if it was love or just a need to have a safe place to live. She was young. He wondered if she understood what love was. She certainly had not received it from her parents.

He smiled as he walked around while cleaning the house in preparation for her return. Her little touches had made his house a home. Without her there, it seemed empty. Almost to the point that it echoed when he talked out loud to himself. He needed her in his life. He also knew that things needed to change. He spent so much time engrossed with his grandfather and the story of his great-grandfather that he neglected Jennifer and the things that made her happy.

That would change when she returned later that day. Their life and love needed attention.

Suzanne and Jennifer spent the night talking. It was their last night together before Jennifer went home. Suzanne knew she had to do something to keep her daughter with her. Anything that would make Jennifer rethink her life. She needed her daughter. All the years she had been in the institution had given her plenty of time to plan her moves when she was eventually released.

The last year she lived there, Suzanne pretended to take the medications the doctors wanted her to take. Her depression subsided. Her anxiety and paranoia left. Her mind became clear. Clear enough to plot her revenge against her ex-husband. She would do anything to get her daughter back.

When Suzanne found out that Jennifer was married and no longer under the rule of her father, it temporarily bothered her. There was no longer the need to plot the way she was. Now her goal was to investigate Roman. That is what she had spent the last couple of years doing. That was what led her to find them where she did.

She was thrilled that her daughter had found someone to love and that loved her. Then she learned about Roman's family history and felt she needed to get Jennifer away from him.

Jennifer smiled as she listened to her mother. She was so glad to have her birth mother in her life. She loved sharing about her life with her husband. Their love was pure, or so she thought. After listening to her mother, she began to wonder.

"How can you say those things about all men in general, Mom? Not all men are like my father was."

"Yes, they are. Every single man has an ulterior motive when it comes to their woman. They want her solely for themselves. No contact with family or friends. By their side at all times. Taking care of them. Being and doing everything they want them to."

"Mom, Roman is nothing like that!" Jennifer tried to understand why her mother thought that way. And did to a point. She thought her mother had gotten past that after she left the institution and made something of herself.

"How many friends do you have?"

"We have a lot of friends."

"That was not my question. How many friends do you have? Friends that only you spend time with?"

"I have a few. Roman and I do everything together; we always have."

"That's my point. Do you always do what he says and go where he says to go? Or do you have a say in those things?"

"I have a say in everything we do. Sometimes we do what Roman wants. Other times we do what I want to do. We discuss everything about our lives."

Suzanne was quiet. This was not going the way she had hoped. She wanted Jennifer to find fault with Roman to the degree that she would leave him. She shrugged her shoulders.

"Why are you drilling me about my relationship so much? Don't you believe a person can be happy in a marriage?"

"No, I don't. There is always something to complain about."

"From time to time, yes. But Roman and I discovered a long time ago that we discussed everything. We are there for each other if we have a complaint, suggestion, idea, or want to talk. We listen. We work together in life and in everything we do. And we are good at it."

"How did you manage to find such a person? I never knew those people existed."

"I agree they are few and far between, but I found one."

"I am happy for you." Suzanne was defeated. Her daughter had found the life she deserved, a life she wanted more for herself. She felt cheated. Both out of the true love of a husband and now so many missing years with her daughter.

Jennifer sensed what her mother was feeling. "Mom, why don't you come to live near us?" You could get to know Roman and maybe one day be nearby when we start having children."

"Are you planning a family?"

"Maybe, one day. We are not ready yet. Too much life to live and places we want to go first."

"I will give it some thought." Suzanne looked at the clock. It was three in the morning, and Jennifer planned to leave before seven. "Right now, you need to get a few hours of sleep.

Jennifer looked at the clock. "You are right. Mom, I love you. I want you to know that I am happy. Yes, Roman and I may have an issue from time to time, but our love is strong. He spoils me. We give ourselves one hundred percent to each other and work fifty/fifty on everything in our lives."

Suzanne smiled. She guessed that was all she could hope for. Her years of plotting revenge may have been erased, seeing how much love there was in her daughter.

~~~~~~

Roman sat in their living room, enjoying a cup of hot coffee. Dinner was in the oven. The house was clean. Roses were in a vase on the kitchen table. Empty wine glasses sat ready to be filled. His home was waiting for the final addition that made it complete. His heart was filled with joy and love he had not felt in a while.

His dreams were fresh. Life was going to be better for him and Jennifer. He was done dealing with his grandfather's antics about his great-grandfather and thoughts of him being a haunting force back in his past. It was time to live in the present and plan for the future in his life with his bride.

He smiled when he thought of her being his bride after all these years together. That was still how he felt. She would always be that beautiful young woman he married.

Three hours later, he heard a car pull up to the house. He walked to the door to greet Jennifer. He stood and watched her get out of the car. She wasn't smiling. His smile faded as he understood her somber expression.

166

Suzanne stepped out of the car's passenger side and waved at Roman.

Roman met Jennifer's eyes. She shrugged her shoulders slightly, hoping her mother did not notice. Together the women walked up to meet Roman.

"Hello, ladies. It is good to see you. Both." He added the last word after an intentional pause.

"Good to see you too, Roman. So glad to be invited to stay with the two of you for a while."

Roman's heart sank. He glared at Jennifer.

"I invited her to stay with us for a few days while she decides if she wants to live nearby. She has no other place to really go where she feels welcome. This will give her a fresh start and time for us to be a family like families should be.

"Okay. That is good to know. I will help get your things from the car, and we will prepare the spare room for you." Roman walked to the car, silently angered. This was not part of his plan for a happy present and a wonderful future.

When everyone entered the house, Jennifer could smell the aroma of dinner baking. She noticed the roses and candles and wine glasses. Her heart sank. She realized the look on her husband's face was more than a blank look of surprise. She had ruined his surprise for her. She wanted to cry. She hoped they could salvage the dinner and their time together. Her mother was only planning to stay for a short visit.

The evening went well for the three of them. The tension eased as they continued to enjoy the wine after dinner and talk. Suzanne apologized a few times during the conversation, but Roman told her not to worry about it. Family time was important, and plans could be changed.

The next morning the phone rang. Roman answered it and listened without saying much. He got off the phone and shook his head. So much for not wanting to deal with the issues of his great-grandfather. Would it ever stop?

Jennifer poured everyone coffee and was preparing breakfast when she heard the phone ring and the front door slam shut a few minutes later. She glanced beyond the kitchen half wall and saw that it was Roman who had walked out. At the same moment, Suzanne walked in and picked up a mug of coffee waiting for her.

"What was that door slam about? Does he do that often?"

"Mom. Stop. I know what you are trying to do, and you need to stop--now. Or I will put you on a bus back to the institution. You will not ruin my marriage and my life."

"I simply asked a question."

"Your tone gave away the true meaning behind your question. No, he is not always like that. It is the first time I have witnessed that reaction in him. He is so laid back people think I am the strong one most of the time."

"Okay, sorry. I didn't mean."

"Mom—stop." Jennifer raised her spatula into the air. She didn't like being that way, but she also was not going to stand still and take things from her mother that she did not have to. And nothing she said was anything Jennifer had to take. She had lived her whole life not taking things from her. Now was not the time she was going to start. She was her own woman. And she had Roman to thank for that. She looked toward the front door, still wondering what had set him off to act that way.

Several minutes later, Roman walked back into the house and apologized to the ladies. Then he excused himself from breakfast as he had no appetite and had to make a phone call.

When he returned, he overheard the two women in his life discussing the upcoming holiday. He stopped to listen and discovered that his mother-in-law was staying through Thanksgiving. He had hoped she would not stay that long, then realized it was not that far away, and maybe she would leave before Christmas.

He walked into the kitchen with a more positive attitude. At least he hoped his disguise of happiness would prevail for a while to keep peace in his otherwise perfect life aspirations.

Chapter Thirty
Thankful

Sara was sitting in her office writing when she looked at the calendar on the wall. She knew the fall festivals were over, then realized Thanksgiving was six weeks away. She needed to talk to Andy about hosting a special family dinner.

As she sat there thinking about family, she smiled. Their family had grown over the years. Her parents would be proud of them. Not only did they have a blood family, they now had adopted family members, foster family, and friends who felt like family.

She picked up her phone and called Andy. This would be a task for all of them. Her idea quickly grew into excitement, and when Andy answered, she spoke so fast he had to tell her to slow down.

"Slow down, Sis. What are you trying to say?"

"Sorry. I just came up with an amazing idea. It will take all of us working together, but I think we can do it!"

"Okay. I have not heard you this excited since, I don't know, you adopted Gayle, maybe? What's your idea?"

"Thanksgiving!"

"Yes, it is coming up. What about it?" He had told her to slow down, but he didn't mean for her to drag out her thoughts this far.

"A large Thanksgiving dinner for the family. I am talking about blood family and extended family. Our friends we consider family."

"Some may have other plans as they have other families."

"I understand that, but not everyone does. We are the only family some of them have here."

"This is true. Some won't be traveling this year. I guess we could get everyone together and work out the details." Andy laughed.

"What?"

"You are talking reception hall large meal and gathering, not Bella Rose Manor dining room large."

"Now you understand my thinking!" Sara was still full of excitement.

"Gotcha, Sis. Yes, we've done weddings, Christmas, and other events for Heather; we can do Thanksgiving this year.

"Good. I'll start working on the guest list. You start thinking about the food."

"I will need an estimation of people coming, but I can work up a list of food to prepare. We will need Heather to help plan and decorate."

"Of course. This is a family affair."

"And by family, you mean everyone we know." Andy smiled. He could visualize his sister's smile. He could tell she was pacing the room as she talked and thought. She would not sit still until she had at least one thing organized about it.

"Of course! You know me well. I will start my list. You start yours. Thanks, little brother! Love you!" Sara hung up and almost missed Andy saying he loved her too. She knew he did. They had a history. One that was more than the fact they were related by blood. Secrets shared in the past held them close over the years.

Sara grabbed a fresh legal pad from her supply closet in the office and sat at her desk. The first name written was Randall. From there, she went down the list. Before she finished, she had thirty people to invite. She knew she would think of more before she was done.

They had closed the manor in the past at Thanksgiving until the New Year. They had not discussed that this year. She quickly checked the future reservations and found a couple of the rooms were already rented out for Thanksgiving. There was nothing after that.

She opened her other software program, created a viral sign, and was about to post it on their website when her phone rang.

"Hello, Sara speaking."

"Hey, sis, just me. Are we closing for the holidays this year?"

"Andy, I am about to post the viral sign to say we are closed right after Thanksgiving. I missed putting it up in time, so we have a few rooms already rented out over Thanksgiving weekend. Do you think we should close this year or stay open?"

"I say we close for December like we usually do. Few people come in January either, so we can stay closed while we do what we normally do around here."

"Clean!"

"Yes, clean and get recharged for the year."

"Okay, let me call Heather and Rachelle and let them know."

"Okay. Should we include those staying here over the holiday in our family meal?"

"Let me email them and see if they have plans, which may be why they are staying here to be close to family."

"Sounds good. You seem energized, Sis. It sounds good on you."

"Thanks. I think I am. Something new to do and take my mind off.. things."

"I agree. You, we all, need a break. Talk to you later. I have work to do." Andy hung up the phone. His oldest sister did sound good. It was a positive change.

Sara called Heather and Rachelle to let them know the plans. They were all in agreement. Both ladies offered to help as much as possible with the large dinner gathering.

That evening she took her legal pad home with her. Three pages of notes and lists were the beginning, and she knew she could think of something at any moment. Her legal pad would be by her side at all times for a while.

Randall arrived home in time to see her set the pad on the counter along with her pen.

"What are you planning to do now?" He recognized her method.

"Oh, just a small gathering," Sara said with a wink.

"How small?"

"Thirty or so people." She tried to hide her face.

"And this event is when?"

"Thanksgiving. I talked with Andy, Heather, and Rachelle this afternoon, and we will host the family thanksgiving dinner in the reception hall."

"We have thirty people in our immediate family?"

"Well, not exactly. But we do when I extend it out some."

"Okay. I know you and your siblings have it all under control. Let me know what you need me to do, and you know I will help. And, of course, I will be there to eat. I am invited, aren't I?"

"You are the first person on my list, my love."

"That's where I belong. The top of your list." Randall hugged his wife, then sat down to enjoy the dinner she had made.

~~~~~~

The following three weeks were busy for everyone. The fall leaves had peaked in the mountains, and people came from miles around to see them. They stayed at the manor, had breakfast there, traveled the mountain tops, hiked on the warmer days, and ended their days at the lounge in town.

Sara worked up her guest list, designed professional-looking invitations, and emailed or texted them to everyone.

In the first week, all except one couple had responded affirmative and asked what they could bring. She had not thought about it being a potluck meal but talked to Andy about it. A few plans changed, and they agreed to make it easier for him to have everyone bring something. So, Sara made a new list. She loved making lists. A few days later, they had covered everything anyone could think of having for a Thanksgiving meal. As long as everyone could make it, they would be fine. If someone could not make it, there would be enough food, and no one would notice something missing. Andy was making the turkey and ham. All other food was being brought by others. It would be an interesting gathering.

A week before Thanksgiving, Sara finally heard from the last couple. Jay and Carrie would also be able to make it. They had held off making their decision until after talking with Terri and Adam and after Carrie spoke with her family. Her parents were going away, so she was free to be with Jay and what had become his extended family. Carrie had become used to him being such good friends with Terri. The bond between her husband and his ex-girlfriend was unheard of, but it worked for everyone.

Even Joe and Nicole were going to be there. Nicole said they could not stay long but would love to stop by for a while to visit.

~~~~~~

Andy was up well before dawn. He made a full pot of fresh dark roast coffee. Glad to have the kitchen to himself, he prepared the turkey and the ham for dinner. He was thankful that the guests had offered to bring other dishes to complete the meal. While he waited for the oven to heat up, he heard the kitchen door open. Sara walked in, picked up a coffee mug, and poured herself a cup before she hugged Andy.

"Good morning, little brother."

"Good morning. Happy Thanksgiving." He raised his mug to meet hers in a toast to the day. "May today bring joy and happiness and create wonderful memories."

"Cheers to that!" Sara said. They each sipped their coffee before Sara spoke again.

"You have recently changed. What caused the change?"

"I never did talk about that, did I? I shared it with Karen. I guess I can share it with you and everyone. Are you sure you want to know?"

"Believe me, I can take just about anything with all that has happened over the last month or so. Don't tell me some doctor has you on strange medication that alters your mind."

"No, nothing like that. It did alter my mind, but no drugs were used. I was shocked. Not literally." He laughed. "I had an experience few people will ever have. I was visited by a man named Harry."

"Okay. That does not sound shocking."

Andy stood up and refreshed their mugs. "On the first day of my week of solitude a couple of months ago, I found a trail to hike in a small town I stopped in to eat lunch. I talked to the waitress, and she suggested I hike the trail. I needed to stretch my legs, and off I went. Backpack on my back and a five-mile hike ahead of me. I had to stop halfway through due to being so out of shape."

"That's what is different. You got in shape."

"That is part of it. The real change was mental. While I sat there resting, this man came and sat with me. We talked for a few minutes, and he told me I needed to go home and let go of the past. And that I was blessed to have the family

I have. He told me other things too, but when he told me to go home, that stuck."

"You stayed away the full week."

"Yes, I did. I spent that time hiking, traveling, and thinking. I stopped at the restaurant where I had met the waitress on my way home. We sat and talked, and I told her about the man I met on the hike. She told me it was her grandfather."

"That's awesome."

"No, it's spooky. Her grandfather, Harry, was killed on the trail in the nineties. She said Harry has been talking with hikers on that trail ever since. He doesn't talk to everyone but chooses who he thinks needs to hear his wisdom."

Sara almost stopped breathing. Not another ghost connected to their family. She looked at Andy and shook her head.

"Oh, it gets more interesting."

"How?"

"The waitress's name.. was Susan."

Sara wiped the goosebumps from her arm.

"Now you see why I don't tell everyone. I just changed and let it go at that."

"Wow. I am thankful someone was able to reach you. Even if it was a dead man named Harry."

They were interrupted by Randall coming in from the side door.

"There you are. I don't like waking up alone." Randall reached over and kissed Sara on her forehead. "Are we ready for today?"

"We are ready for whatever the day brings. Help yourself to coffee."

Dinner was laid out on the tables on the side by the kitchen in the reception hall. Guests were arriving quickly, and conversations were flowing. Sara watched everyone from a far corner. Family. Her family. The entire family was together again. Her attention was directed to the front when Randall rang a bell to get everyone's attention. When that did not work, Rachelle whistled. That sound echoed even in a full room. With everyone's attention, Randall thanked everyone for their help and for being there to celebrate Thanksgiving and how grateful he was to be a part of the amazing family for all these years. Then he told everyone to dig in and eat.

Sara joined her husband in line once everyone else filled their plates and sat down. Sara felt a tear falling and tried to hide it.

"I saw that. Let them flow, my love. You have worked hard for this family since your parents died. Seeing all these people together when it was just you, Andy, Heather, Ben, and Mark less than ten years ago. This is quite an accomplishment. No one can deny the love in this room.

Chapter Thirty-One
For the Kids

The week after Thanksgiving, the manor was empty. When the last guests left, the family cleaned the rooms, and Heather began to gather the Christmas decorations for the manor. Even without guests, she liked to decorate the great room. It had become the gathering place for family Christmas.

Sara was in her office when Heather came down from the storage room with the first box of decorations. Sara smiled and closed the computer program she was working on. The financial reports could wait. She wanted to help her sister.

It did not take long to get all the boxes down from storage. Heather appreciated the help. They talked and laughed while they worked. It had been a while since the two of them had worked together without other people around them. They didn't know if it was that or the fact of the joys of the Christmas season. Christmas was always a special time for them.

While they worked and talked, they discussed how the family could celebrate Christmas Day. By the end of their time together, they had the great room decorated except for the Christmas tree that Ben would bring later that day. They also decided to have Christmas morning in the great room as they had in the past.

Later that day, Sara received a phone call from Barbara.

"Hello, Barbara, how are you?"

"I am doing fine. I have been thinking about Christmas and was wondering if I could use the reception hall for a children's event for the foster children."

"That sounds like an amazing idea. What do you have in mind, and how can we help you besides opening the hall for you?"

"I wanted to ask if you know anyone who could play Santa."

"I know Bob played Santa for us one year. You could ask him if he would do it again. Are you sure that is all you need? Do you need food, decorations, or any other help?"

"I will let you know. I have talked with Terri about doing the food. That is if you don't mind me using the hall but not Andy for the food."

"I am sure Andy appreciates the break. But if we can help with anything, just let me know."

"I will. Thank you so much. I am looking forward to this for the kids. They don't get much most of the time."

"Glad to help. I will reserve whichever day you want. No one else has reserved it for anything."

'I will let you know. Thank you, Sara."

"Anytime. As long as there is an opening, you are welcome to use it for the kids."

After Sara hung up her phone, she called Heather. Barbara's request had given her an idea.

"Hi, Sis. What's up?"

"I just spoke with Barbara, and it gave me an idea. She is going to use the reception hall for a Christmas party for the foster kids and their families. A mixture of those waiting for families and those living with their foster families. This would include Terri and Adam, too, come to think of it. Anyway, what can we do special for them? Barbara plans to ask Bob if he wants to play Santa again this year. What else can we do?"

"Does she have a source for gifts for the children? We could talk to the people in town to donate gifts or money for gifts. Or we have funds we could use and do it on our own. Getting the town involved would help spread the word about the need for more foster families."

"That is a promising idea. Let me talk to Randall about getting the town involved. Maybe call Terri to see what she could do with the help of the people who eat and party at the café."

"I am sure the town's people will be glad to help. We don't have much time, so if you need me to help, let me know."

"Thanks, Sis. I will." She hung up and called Randall. This required immediate attention instead of waiting for him to come home from work.

When Randall heard Sara's idea, he fully agreed to get the town and community involved. That night the two sat down and made a list of the other businesses. Sara worked on a flyer to give the merchants to hand out to the general public. Randall contacted a few of the other attorneys and got them on board.

~~~~~~

Snow fell gently during the night before the Christmas party for the foster children. Excitement filled the air as the adults attended to the final touches before everyone arrived.

Bob was preparing for his entrance later in the day but helped with the decorations and set up. When he heard the first car pull up, he went into the back room and changed. Playing Santa had always been a joy. He loved seeing the children's excitement and even smiled at the little ones who cried. He loved them all. The fact that he and Rachelle had no children gave it special meaning. He would have loved to have his own, but it was not in the cards.

Rachelle helped her husband fix his beard and Santa suit before they walked to the reception hall to greet the children as they arrived. She had surprised everyone by dressing up as Mrs. Santa.

The town and the local community had outdone themselves with donations of toys for the children and basic necessities for the families. Gift certificates for families to buy what they needed. Large and small toys arrived almost immediately after the fliers went up. Sara, Heather, Rachelle, and Karen helped Barbara by wrapping all the gifts.

The looks on the children's faces were priceless. Some of them had never celebrated Christmas. A few of the youngest ones cried when they first saw Santa Clause.

Adam had joined them to play the music and even set up the karaoke system so the kids could sing along. Some sang beautifully, and others were tone-deaf but gave their best attempt. It was all in good fun.

After everyone had food to eat and had played the games for a while, Santa sat in the front, and kids lined up as he and Mrs. Claus handed out gifts. The little children sat on his lap and told him what they wanted for Christmas. The older children stood by his side and talked with him. Some did not say anything as they took their gift and just walked back to their seat.

The joy on their faces as they opened their gifts brought smiles to the adults. Bob sat back after the last child had visited him. His eyes showed his somber expression hidden behind his beard.

Rachelle leaned over to her husband, knowing what he was feeling. She had heard some of the requests.

"It is so sad to listen to what they want for Christmas."

"I know. I expected a list of gifts a mile long. Instead, I heard more tell me they wanted a family to love them. Some wanted to live with their parents. Only a few asked for toys."

"To think they want what most of us have taken for granted all of our lives."

"I almost understand their desire for a family."

Bob/Santa reached over and held her hand. I know, Baby. I am so glad you finally got the family you wanted. Even if you were an adult by the time you felt that love."

Rachelle bent down and kissed him. "And that love and connection grew when I met you."

"Mrs. Claus, I think we have a decision to make after the holidays." Santa looked out over the room. So many children without a family. Maybe it was time they provided a home for one or more.

"I think you are right. I don't think we have much to decide." She smiled and helped Santa up. They walked around the room, mingling with the children and talking with them.

~~~~~~

Barbara was exhausted the next day when she first woke up. The Christmas party for the foster children and the families was a success. In her hand were three applications from couples wanting to become foster parents. One was from Bob and Rachelle. Barbara smiled when she remembered what Rachelle had told her. "We want at least one child to foster. What do we have to do?"

Barbara told her she would be in touch as soon as she could. It would have to wait a day or two. Exhaustion took over, and Barbara fell back to sleep.

Chapter Thirty-Two
Fresh Start

It was dark outside when Sara sat in the manor's great room with a fresh cup of coffee. The only light was the burning embers that remained from the fire in the fireplace the previous night when her family gathered to celebrate the end of one year and then welcomed the new year. When she made a cup of coffee, she smiled at the empty champagne glasses on the counter. They had washed them but not put them away. She raised her full coffee mug to them as she walked out of the kitchen.

She loved the quiet mornings when she could sit alone to think. She rarely had those anymore. Life continued to change; every year, something new occupied their lives, and Bella Rose.

This year would be the same. Unless she found a way to change things. She shrugged her shoulders. What would she change? She loved her growth and expanding family. The close friends who were more like family than she could have imagined.

She was interrupted by Andy, who walked in with his mug of coffee. He had taken the time to make a full pot of coffee instead of Sara's single cup. She smiled up at him. She loved her baby brother. They sipped their coffee in silence. They shared an understanding that was added to so many other things over the years. A special bond few siblings shared.

"What is on your mind, Sis?" Andy broke their silence.

"Enjoying the quiet." She teased.

"As usual, I had to break that. So what are you thinking about the new year? Changes to the Manor?"

"I have not figured that out yet. I know I want to finish writing the book about our estate and the family. I would like a year without new drama."

"Ha. Good luck with that. Have we ever had a year with no drama?"

"No. I think it is time we had one. No ghosts, no new people with, let's say, interesting backstories. Kids are all doing well in school and growing. A calm, easy-going year. That is all I ask."

"That would be nice."

"Oh, and no one running away." She stared at Andy.

"I cannot promise that."

"I know. I can't promise a no-drama year either." Sara swallowed the last of her coffee and stood up. Andy joined her as they walked into the kitchen. As they entered the room, the main landline phone rang. They looked at each other and laughed. So much for quiet and no drama.

"Hello, Bella Rose Manor, Sara speaking."

Sara looked at Andy as she listened. He stopped what he was planning to do and watched her.

"Yes, I understand. That is not a problem. We are closed for the month but have openings for that weekend. I will put you down for it." Sara shook her head. Then added. "Yes, you may have the same room."

Andy's eyes opened a little wider.

Sara hung up the phone and wrote a note on the notepad. She was not in her office but would add that reservation to Valentine's weekend when she got there.

"And who is making reservations already?"

Sara laughed. "A couple who wanted to celebrate a renewal of their vows here at the manor."

"Oh, that sounds like fun. Do they need a special dinner, use of the reception hall, or a cake?" Andy rattled on.

"All they asked for was the room."

"Okay. At least no drama yet."

Sara had not told him who had made the reservation. She poured herself a fresh cup of coffee and went to her office. She had work to do and her book to work on.

Andy began cleaning the kitchen. It was that time of year to thoroughly clean and purge things he did not use or need anymore.

~~~~~~

Roman and Jennifer celebrated the new year alone. Suzanne had spent Thanksgiving with them but decided to move back home after watching her daughter and son-in-law interact with each other and with her. Roman may not have been enthused about her staying there, but he did his best to make her feel welcome. He loved his wife enough to do the best for her and her mother. Once Suzanne realized her goal of breaking them up would not work, she went home to settle her life. She quickly found a new place to move to that better suited her. Suzanne wanted to live near Jennifer. And if she was being honest, she wanted to live with her daughter. Her time with her and Roman proved she was not needed there and that her daughter had found her soulmate. It was time to start fresh and make something of her life.

Christmas day, Roman proposed to Jennifer to renew their vows. He explained that his love for her had grown, and he understood life and love better. He wanted her to be a part of the new person he was becoming. Jennifer accepted immediately. She loved him with all her heart. He was her soulmate.

They waited until the new year to make reservations at their favorite place. The place that had transformed them both. They agreed that Bella Rose Estate and the community would always be their special place.

Jennifer had enjoyed most of her time with her mother and learning the truth about what happened. She loved sharing her story. She also was glad Roman had gotten to know her mother. As much as she loved her mother, she was thankful for her mother's decision to move on. She called Suzanne on Christmas day to share her news of redoing their vows. She invited her to the ceremony, but Suzanne declined. She said she had plans that weekend. Jennifer was disappointed but would not force her mother to be there.

~~~~~~

Rachelle and Bob had celebrated the new year by receiving word that they had been accepted into the foster system and would be considered for any child that met their requirements. Their only requirement was for the child to need a home. They were willing and able to take in any child that needed placement. Any time of day or night, for a day for a year or longer. They had love to give and a home to share.

Rachelle was so glad she had agreed to move out of the manor into Bob's house after getting married. He could have easily lived in her little apartment, but since he already had a larger house, it only made sense for her to move to his house. Together they had made it into a home. One they hoped to share with children in need.

It was not long before Barbara called them. She had a young teenage boy who needed placement. An hour later, they were in Barbara's office learning about the young man. He had been acting up in school, so the teacher contacted the parents. This led to the police being called to the home due to illegal drugs and weapons. The young teen knew it was his fault that his parents were taken from him and acted out at the foster holding home. Barbara knew just where he needed to be placed and called Bob.

"I know this is not your ideal child, as most want infants, but I think you will be a good match for him. You have the control and compassion he needs. I think he will do good with the two of you."

After Bob and Rachelle arrived at Barbara's office they continued their discussion. They soon would meet the young man.

"Thank you for your confidence in us. We will do the best we can. Anything else we need to know that you have not told us?"

"Not that I know of. We are still searching for any other family he may have, but his parents are not talking. It is as if they don't want their son to be with their relatives. And that is if they do have other family members. They don't have to live in this area; they just need to be family. Some foster children never realize they have other family members they can stay with."

"That is so difficult to understand," Bob said.

"Not for me. Although, in my case, I knew I had other family members. The heartbreaker was that they did not want me. Or they did not love me."

"That is sad. And that is what will make you a good foster parent. You have felt some of what these kids feel. You may not have gone through the foster system, but you easily could have if your uncle had not taken you in."

"I wished for most of my life that he had not been there, and I had other people who wanted me and loved me."

"Let me go get Daniel and have you meet him. He can be difficult, but I hope the three of you have a connection."

"Let's meet our boy," Bob said. He smiled and reached for Rachelle's hand. "Are you ready?"

"Ready as ever," Rachelle answered with a smile.

Barbara left the office and was gone for almost thirty minutes. When she returned, a tall young man followed her.

"Daniel, I would like you to meet Bob and Rachelle. They will give you a home to live in for as long as you need it."

Daniel raised his head and looked at them through the top of his eyes. He noticed they were holding hands.

"Hello, Daniel. We want to be your foster family and give you a safe place to live. We hope you will let us."

"Hi." Daniel lowered his head and shrugged his shoulders. "I don't have any choice in the matter, do I?" He looked up at Barbara.

"Daniel, you and I discussed this. For now, no, you don't. I have chosen this couple because I think you will have a good connection."

"Okay," Daniel spoke in short words.

Rachelle reached out to shake his hand, but he pulled away. This may be harder than she thought. She and Bob would do everything they could to give Daniel a new start to a good life.

When they arrived home, they showed Daniel his room. He had it all to himself. Until more foster children came their way.

"All this is for me?" Daniel asked when he looked inside the room.

"All yours. If we get another boy, you may need to share the room. For now, it is all yours.

Daniel walked over to the bed and lay on top of the covers. He smiled.

"Make yourself comfortable. We will be in the kitchen making dinner. Come join us if you want. If not, we will get you when it is ready."

"Okay," again with a short answer.

But it was a start.

Chapter Thirty-Three
Family Truths

Sara knew it was early when she placed the call to Roman, but she wanted answers, and the sooner, the better. She had been writing and hoped to make major progress but needed more answers.

When he did not answer, she left a message, hung up the phone, and waited for him to call her back. She sat at her desk and began to type out the newest developments in her family history. She never dreamed she would be writing about a ghost.

Roman returned her call and answered her questions about Raymond and Veronica. Sara noticed the frustration in his voice and asked what was going on. After he explained his desire to rid himself of his family history and then the intrusion of his mother-in-law, Sara apologized for adding to his troubles. He added that he and Jennifer would be there in a couple of weeks to renew their vows and that he wanted nothing to do with his ancestors while he was there.

When they hung up, she laughed. She knew all about family history, secrets, and surprises. The trouble now was that the two of them and their families were affected by them.

Sara spent most of the day writing. She was intrigued by the keys. With the introduction of Raymond wanting revenge, Rose not wanting some secrets known, and finding the truth in writing, she began to put two and two together.

The keys.

She called Heather and Andy and asked them to come to the office.

An hour later, she had formed her opinion, written down some notes, and opened the safe for the empty box.

Heather was the first to enter the office and noticed her sister's facial expression. Then she noticed the box on the desk. She didn't say anything. She didn't have to. She somehow knew.

Andy walked in, already talking about something but fell silent when he felt the air in the room and looked at his older sisters.

"Now that you are both here, I need to let you know what I have been working on and what I have discovered. I was hoping what I found would not be true, but I am afraid it is the only thing that makes sense."

"I know you've been writing the family book. Please don't tell us you found more secrets."

"After spending time with Roman and talking with him, getting his great-grandfather's journal, and finding another journal that our grandmother wrote, yes. There were more secrets. Then I started putting two and two together."

"About what?"

"The keys." Sara lifted the box. Her siblings noticed how light it was.

"That seems light. It was full when you showed it to me the last time," Heather said.

Sara shook her head. "No, I pretended it was full. After you left, I removed it from the safe and opened it. I knew it was empty when I picked it up in the safe, but I didn't want to talk about my fears."

"And now? What are we thinking?

"We all learned that Raymond was a carpenter and made the furniture that we found in the attic and secret room. We found out that each piece had a distinct key. And that sometimes the key or keys were missing."

Please don't let it be what I think it is."

"I think we all know the truth about the keys," Sara said as she opened the box. Again it was empty.

192

"Raymond."

Sara nodded her head.

"But how? He's been dead for years. And why?" Heather asked.

"The how is simple if you are willing to believe. He is a ghost. No one sees him. The other question is the one most people will ask. I think I know why."

"Revenge," Heather said with a sigh.

"Revenge and fulfilling a promise to haunt not only Rose, if he could, but also her family. She probably never thought it would be generations later before he was found out."

'So you think he was the one moving the keys and only making certain keys available at certain times?"

"That is the only thing that makes sense. Somehow, Raymond knew what journals and photos were in the attic and which key fit where they were kept. When he was ready for us to find specific things, he ensured that a particular key was easily found. The rest of them he hid. Do you remember when the keys were together, and then there would only be one next time? Remember how no keys are alike, so we could not accidentally open the wrong thing? He knew which journal he wanted us to read or photos to see."

"But the last journal from Rose did not show itself until the other day? Why?" Heather asked, but sensed she knew the answer.

"Because he was ready for his truth to be learned, and he knew or sensed that hers would also tell the truth. He hoped hers would confirm their affair and how they loved each other even after all those years of being married and raising families with other loves they were married to."

"He never stopped loving her. She went back to Robert, but I have a feeling she never stopped loving Raymond. That is the secret she took to the grave."

193

"Do you think the whole truth has come out now? The truth about our family history and the mystery about the keys?" Andy asked.

"I am not sure. I have not finished reading either one's journal. Rose tried to keep it all hushed. Raymond wanted the world to know about them, and when that didn't happen, he vowed to her that he would haunt the area."

"And now he has. The question for us is, how do we stop it?"

"Do you think we should? Isn't there an appeal that goes with haunted places around here?"

"Sara!" Andy protested. "I can't believe you want to keep them in the family."

"I don't. Not really. But I am close to realizing we may need them. Or at least the stigma of being haunted. What do you think?" Sara laughed a ghostly laugh.

"Stop that!" Heather said. "I am not ready to see a ghost."

"Maybe that is why we have felt one but never seen one. They know we are not ready."

"They?" Andy asked, feeling left out of something, although he didn't know what and maybe should not have asked.

"Yes, they,
Raymond and his wife Veronica, who he convinced to join him in his revenge."

"Okay, we have two ghosts flying around." Andy ducked as if feeling one.

"Very funny, brother. But, yes, we have two. I do not know where they live and am not sure they will stay longer."

"Is that why the meetings with Roman and the phone calls?"

"Yes, I needed his family history and his grandfather's knowledge about him being a ghost. From what Roman

194

says, they do not know much about him other than what they have read in his journals."

"So, how do we get all the keys returned to us? How do we find them to start with? And what do we do to stay sane?"

Sara laughed. "There is not much we can do about the keys. Raymond will return them when and if he wants to. We have been able to open everything we needed to. As for keeping our sanity? We add them to the history of Bella Rose Estate and enjoy the truth about love, the things people do for love, and what they will do in the loss of love."

The three siblings sat in silence. Each tried to wrap their mind around the latest facts about their family. Would the mysteries ever stop?

"So, what do you think? Should I add all of our assumptions to the book? As far as we can tell, Roman and his grandfather, Jeremiah, believe that Raymond plays a big part in our family history. More than anyone knew. Certainly more than we knew about."

"If the book you write is meant to be the truth about our family and Bella Rose Estate and its history, then those facts need to be included," Andy said.

"I hate to say it because I would rather not believe in ghosts, but I think Andy is right. Truth is truth. And this truth is key."

"Okay. I will include it. I hope Raymond presents himself and the keys sometime along the way."

"I do not want to be here when that happens."

"You already were."

"When?" Heather asked.

"First, when we were brushed by something as we left the attic the first couple of times. Then, those clues were left in the Carpenter's Star room after the mysterious guests had stayed there. Right before Roman and Jennifer reserved

195

that same room. Raymond and Veronica were the previous guests. No one saw them because."

"They are ghosts." Andy completed his sister's sentence.

A shiver ran down Heather's arm, and she brushed it off.

"Yes." Sara nodded her head.

A chill swept through the office.

Chapter Thirty-Four
Vows

Roman and Jennifer arrived early on the day of their reservation. Sara greeted them and invited them to her office after they had settled into their room.

"I told you I did not want anything to do with my family while I was here," Roman said sternly. His instant anger rose and came out in his words. Jennifer touched his arm to calm him.

"No, nothing to do with Raymond or Rose. You will like what I have for you."

"We will be there shortly." Jennifer smiled at Sara and directed her husband down the hallway to their room.

When Roman opened the door, he pushed it open and stepped back to let Jennifer enter first.

"Wow! Look at this."

Roman was behind her and saw the white roses in a vase on the dresser. They looked at the bed and noticed a box of chocolates and an envelope on the pillows. Jennifer picked up the envelope and opened it. A card fell out. She picked it up and shook her head.

"What is it?"

"It is a gift card for a meal at the local Italian restaurant."

Jennifer read the card out loud and then read the note. "They have gone beyond what they needed to do for us considering."

"Considering what?" Roman asked and immediately wished he had not responded. He knew the answer.

"Raymond."

"Don't. Don't even mention his name or Jeremiah's name this weekend. I am done with that part of my life. I want this weekend to be solely about us. Just the two of us."

"I am sorry. I forgot. I am so used to that being the topic of conversation when we are here; it was an automatic thought."

"I know. I hope this family does not bring it up while we are here."

"Well, let's go see what Sara wants. She promised that it was not about your family."

A few minutes later, Roman knocked on Sara's office door.

"Enter," Sara said a little louder than she normally spoke. With the door shut, she wanted to make sure they heard her.

Jennifer opened the door and walked in with the confidence of being a lady on her own. It was a feeling she had not always possessed. The feeling made her smile.

"Hello, you two. I hope you found your room to your satisfaction."

"More than we expected, that is for sure."

"That is just the beginning of what we have planned for you if you will accept our help."

"What do you have up your sleeve?"

Sara smiled and handed them a piece of paper. Jennifer reached out to take it. She held it up so Roman could read it over her shoulder.

"You are cordially invited to attend the renewing of vows between Roman and Jennifer Wilson on Saturday, February thirteen, at two o'clock, followed by a small reception in the reception hall at Bella Rose Estate."

"We didn't ask you to do this. What do we owe you for all of it?"

"Not a thing. Andy and Karen are making the food and the cake. Our family, a few of our friends, and those who got to know you while you were here will be there. Nothing too big. We just wanted it to be a special day to remember.

We have a minister lined up. Adam will bring the music and sing if you want him to."

"This is all so much. After what my family did to yours."

"Stop. You said you did not want to discuss anything regarding your family. That is what we are avoiding. This weekend is all about the two of you."

Jennifer wiped a tear as it escaped. "Thank you so much. We planned to find a minister or someone to stand before us as we said our vows to each other."

"Now, you are having a mini wedding," Heather said as she walked in at the end of their conversation. I would not have it any other way. That is if you will let us do this for you."

Roman looked at Jennifer. His eyes showed he had an idea. Jennifer smiled and nodded. She knew him well enough to know what was on his mind. "I agree." She smiled.

"On one condition." They said simultaneously.

"What condition?" Sara asked.

"If you, Heather, and Andy join us in renewing your vows with us."

"This is your day. Not any of ours." Heather answered.

"We would not want it any other way. All or none of us."

Sara and Heather looked at each other. "Okay. Let us talk to our brother and our spouses." Sara answered. She looked at Heather and shrugged her shoulders. "Why not?"

"Sounds like fun to me. Heather agreed. She could not imagine any of the rest of them objecting.

~~~~~~~~~~~~~~~~~~~~~~~~~~~~~~~~~~~~~

The day was perfect—beyond perfect for February. An unusually warm front had drifted in, and the temperature and the brilliant sunshine created more beauty than they could have asked for.

What was originally meant for one couple to renew their vows became a major event, with eight couples standing before a few friends and family. The local minister that conducted the occasional church service at the chapel was performing the ceremony for them. She was well-known and loved by all in town.

Adam set the music up and played a snippet of each couple's wedding song as they walked down the aisle. There was no common formal dress worked out, and each couple wore what they wanted.

They ensured that Roman and Jennifer stood in the middle of the group since it was their initial idea.

Following the ceremony, everyone gathered in the reception hall for food, dancing, and a good time.

While everyone was preoccupied with the party atmosphere, Jeff asked Angela to go for a walk with him to see the sunset from the gazebo. They had only been at the manor a few times and never spent much time exploring what was to see. Angela put a sweater across her shoulders and walked outside with him. They held hands as they walked.

When they reached the gazebo, Angela stood looking out over the mountains. The stars were shining brightly. The moon was bright, and there was no need for extra light. Angela felt Jeff move away from her. She looked and saw him bending down onto one knee. She shook her head but smiled.

"Angela, my love, I fell in love with you when I spotted you at the airport. Sitting next to you on the plane ride was an added bonus for me. I could not have planned it any better. Little did we know what our future would be. I just knew how I felt. Waiting for this moment has been difficult. I knew the time was right tonight. Seeing all those couples' love helped me know, without a doubt, that I want to spend the rest of my life with you. Angela, Will you marry me?" Jeff opened the little box he had taken from his pocket as he spoke and directed the contents toward Angela.

Angela had watched him and listened to every word he spoke. The love of her life felt the same way she did. How could she say no? The ring she was staring at was much more than she expected.

"Yes! Of course, I will marry you!" Angela said and reached down to kiss him. He kissed her and reached for her hand, placing the ring on her finger as he stood, embracing her in his arms.

As he stood, she saw the flash of lights. To her, it was an explosion of fireworks in celebration of their love. Instead, it was the flashes of cameras.

Angela and Jeff turned towards the cameras. Angela smiled when she saw that it was Terri and Jay. Together. Taking photos.

Chapter Thirty-Five
Love's Reality

Terri and Jay had been informed of the proposal and knew they had to work together to capture the event. They laughed when they saw Angela's reaction.

"Your sister seems happy."

"Her? Have you looked at your brother? We couldn't wipe that smile off his face if we used sandpaper."

"Ouch." Jay looked at Terri and shook his head. He smiled at her. She had not changed much since their summer of dating. She was still beautiful, carefree, full of life, and a wonderful lady. She just was not his.

"What are you thinking about?" Terri noticed his face and him staring at her.

"Nothing," he lied.

Terri looked at him as they both continued to stay in the gazebo, sitting on the bench. The engaged love birds had gone for a walk and left them alone. Terri noticed Angela looking back at her as Jeff led her away. She could not read what was on her sister's mind but wondered what she was thinking.

"You are full of it. I know there is something on your mind. Are you and Carrie okay? I know you just renewed your vows with the rest of us, but she seemed a little distant."

"We are fine. She had some sad news yesterday and hasn't been able to deal with it yet."

"Oh, I am so sorry. Is there anything we can do for her?"

"No. She will be alright. One of her best friends called her yesterday with bad news. She and I are fine."

"That is good to hear. I worry about you sometimes."

"About me? Why? No need to worry."

"Well, maybe worry isn't the right word. I think about you from time to time. And more now that Angela is engaged to your brother. Doesn't that make us related somehow?"

"Humm, it makes me your sister's brother-in-law or will when they marry. And you will be my brother's sister-in-law."

"Oh, that sounds so confusing." Terri laughed. Her eyes looked up into her head, trying to think. "Somehow, I think that should make us related like brother and sister-in-laws once removed or something. Like cousins are when they are not directly across the genealogy board cousins."

"You always did have a weird ability to create connections between people."

"I know. It's a curse."

"So what have you been up to besides the café and Makenna?

"That is about all. Helping out here at the manor when they can use it."

"You say you think about me every once in a while. Do you ever wonder 'what if' about us?"

Terri looked at him. She had not thought much about what if regarding him in a long time. Life had gone on. She was in love with Adam. She still had a spot in her heart for him but knew that going their separate ways was the right thing to do. "No. Not anymore."

"That hurts. Just kidding. I know what you mean. I wasn't happy when we broke up, but it was the right thing to do. I'm glad we have remained friends over the years."

"Me too. Hard to believe how long ago we were a couple. Life gave us an amazing summer."

"Yes, it did." Terri stood up. She knew if she stayed there much longer, she might say the wrong thing. When they lived farther apart, it was easy to move on. Adam had filled the void left by Jay. Filled it to overflowing most days. But there was an occasional strong pull in a direction she did not trust herself to go. Stepping away was needed.

"I will never forget our travels and shared time together," Jay said as he stood to join Terri.

"Me either. I think we need to get back to our spouses. They will wonder where we ran off to."

"I agree. I told Carrie we did not have to stay longer than she wanted, so I need to see if she wants to leave."

"Okay. Please have Carrie call me if I can help her in any way."

"I will. You have always been the best female friend a man could have."

"I think the same about you. You are the best male friend this girl could ask for. Right after Adam, that is." Terri smiled when she mentioned Adam, the love of her life.

Angela and Jeff joined them just before they all entered the reception hall.

"Everything okay with you two?" Angela asked.

"Of course. Why do you ask?"

"Just a vibe I thought I was getting at the gazebo. If all is well, we are happy. After all, I think we will somehow be related when we get married."

Terri and Jay laughed.

"We've already discussed that one. Terri created our new relationship. All is good." Jay said. He opened the door for everyone to walk inside.

"Good. We are glad our relationship would not cause issues with the two of you."

"No. We are fine. The reality is we agree we could not be happier the way our lives have turned out." Terri said. She looked at Jay, who was nodding in agreement.

The four of them entered the reception hall. Adam saw them and invited Angela and Jeff to where he stood. He had placed two chairs there and had them sit down. They looked confused. This event was not for them. Angela looked at Jeff, who shrugged his shoulders.

Adam then adjusted the mic and began to play his guitar and sing a love song he had written just for them.

Angela shook her head. Everyone seemed to know about her engagement ahead of time but her.

Soon after Adam began the song, Jeff reached for Angela's hand. He pulled her to her feet, and they began to dance. The other couples soon joined. Terri stood next to her husband and smiled. He was her soulmate. She watched her sister dance and hoped she had found hers as well. A glance at Jay and Carrie dancing assured her they were truly in love.

Following one last song and dancing, the celebration of love ended. Everyone helped clean the reception hall before leaving for their homes.

Sara and Randall were the last ones to leave. After they locked the door, Randall reached for her hand.

"Do you know how much I love you?"

"Only about half as much as I love you."

"No, I love you more."

"I don't think so. I love you most."

"That is not how it goes." They reached their house, and Randall bent down, scooped Sara up, and carried her over the threshold of their home."

"Well, that was a surprise," Sara said as he set her down. She balanced herself and turned to kiss him. She was so happy to have him in her life. Love was real. She was glad she opened her heart again when she started dating Randall.

That night several couples fell asleep with smiles and a new feeling of love in their hearts.

Chapter Thirty-Six
Waiting on the Return

Spring was around the corner. Ben was busy preparing the land and gardens around the estate. He wanted to feature more rose beds and a larger vegetable garden.

Terri had spoken with Ben about raising a few things she would use in the café. They had reached an agreement on which vegetables and spices to plant. Once they grew, they would work out the price. Ben had spoken with Andy about some food that would also be used at the manor.

Sara had spent time writing her book about their family history. All the secrets, all the mystery, all the discoveries. There were days when she would go home with tears in her eyes. On other days she would be laughing.

"How far have you come with the book?" Gayle asked her mother when she got home from school the day before her Spring break.

"I believe I am nearing the end. I know I could continue since we continue with Bella Rose, but I think it needs to end. I just wish the keys would be returned. That would make the perfect ending." Sara was excited that her daughter was so interested in the book and the history of her adoptive family. Most days, Sara forgot Gayle was adopted. She fit in with the family so easily and fully. She seemed more like a biological daughter.

"Maybe I can help locate the keys over my Spring break."

"I don't think they can be located. I think it is a matter of Raymond bringing them back and placing them where he wants them. For whatever reason, he will have a purpose to where we eventually find them. And to make matters

207

more intriguing, they will be in plain sight where we look daily."

"You really do believe in the ghosts, don't you, Mama?"

"It took me a long time, but I do now."

"I think that is so cool. I would love to see one someday.

"You want to see a ghost? Why?"

"I think it would be cool. Can you talk to a ghost?"

"Most people do. They tell it to GET OUT?" Sara laughed. She agreed with her daughter. She would love to talk to Raymond. She'd even talk with Veronica if they showed themselves. Her question to Veronica would be why she had gone along with her husband to play the revenge. Sara thought she knew the answer. She assumed that Raymond could never love her the way she wanted because his heart still belonged to Rose.

"What are you thinking about? You were drifting far away." Gayle got her mother's attention.

"Sorry, I was trying to imagine talking to Raymond or his wife. It would be interesting. However, I doubt we will ever get that chance."

"One never knows. Maybe when he returns the keys, he will stick around long enough to hold a conversation with one of us."

Sara smiled and tilted her head. Her eyes had a gleam to them.

"Now, what is on your mind? You are full of expressions today, Mama."

"Oh, just imagining how strong his love was for Rose. Wishing and hoping it would last, only to be heartbroken. Then spending the rest of his life moving on, having a wife and a family, but feeling the pangs of love that lingered for his lost love."

"Such a romantic, Mama." Gayle was old enough to see what love looked like. She hoped she would have that one day. She saw how her parents shared their love. And hearing about Raymond and Rose helped her know that true, lasting love was out there. It took finding the right person. She was not ready for anything close to that. She wanted to finish high school and go to college first. She knew what she wanted to do with her life. Chase ghosts! She laughed out loud.

"What is that laugh about?" Sara looked at Gayle.

"Oh, just thinking more of what I want to be when I grow up."

"You will soon be grown up. At least college is not too far away. What do you want to be?"

"A ghost chaser."

"A what? I don't think there is such a thing."

"I am sure there is. If not, I want to be a detective."

"Now I can support you on that. That is a good field to be in."

Sara's phone rang, interrupting her mother/daughter time.

"Hello." She listened to the caller.

When she hung up the phone, she turned to talk to Gayle, but her daughter was gone.

Sara smiled and got busy making dinner for her family. The phone call got put at the back of her mind. She would deal with that conversation later.

Gayle was extra talkative at dinner that night. All she wanted to talk about was the ghosts that could be living on the property. They fascinated her. Randall reminded her that few people believed in them, and she may want to be careful about who she talked to about them. She could lose a few friends.

"If my friends do not understand what I believe or want to pursue in my life, then they are not true friends."

"That is one way to look at it. You will need to be aware of how others will react to you. Some people, especially the boys, may not like that you are smarter than they are."

"Well, they can just get over it and move on. I will be as smart as I need to be to succeed." Gayle said as she took her last bite and set her fork down.

"That's my girl," Randall said and smiled at Sara. They had chosen well when they adopted their daughter.

After dinner, Sara sat with Randall and told him about the phone call. She told him Roman called to warn her that Raymond may be around this week.

"What is the significance of this week?"

"According to him, this is the week Rose called off their relationship. I have not read the date they split up in any of the journals, but I still have a little left to read. So I believe him."

"We will keep an eye out for indoor breezes, a brush on our arm as we've had in the past, or an unexpected chill in the air."

"I think there may be more this time. Raymond knows we know about him. This is when he may show his face, so to speak. And he may return the keys at some point."

"Any idea where he will put them?"

"In the attic is my guess. Or they could go into what used to be Rose and Robert's bedroom."

"Whoa. That would mean he may place them someplace in this house."

"Yes, I am letting you know what the phone call was. We need to be vigilant."

"Did you tell Gayle?"

"Are you serious? She would refuse to sleep if she thought he would return while she was home on Spring Break."

"Who would return?" Gayle asked as she entered the living room to say goodnight to her parents.

"Have a seat, dear," Randall motioned for his daughter to sit next to him.

Gayle sat down without a word.

"Roman called Mama today and told her that Raymond might show up this week."

"Why?"

"From what Roman says, this is the anniversary of the week Rose told him their relationship was over. He was heartbroken. And this week is when he told her he would haunt her."

True to Sara's suspicion, Gayle asked if she could stay up all night and wait. When her parents said no, she stood up and said she would stay awake in her room and let them know if she saw anything.

They said goodnight to her and knew she would stay awake as long as she could waiting for the return. The return of Raymond and the keys.

Chapter Thirty-Seven

Seen

Reservations were pouring in from people across the country to rent rooms at Bella Rose Manor. Sara wondered why business had picked up so much since the previous year. She didn't think anything had changed enough to warrant the influx of guests. None of the changes they made in January and early spring were known or significant to the outsiders.

The vegetable gardens would provide fresh food for Andy's recipes. Ben had planted more roses and refreshed all the gardens. That was all that had changed as much as she knew.

Until one of the guests who called let it be known why they wanted to stay there. They had been at Storytelling the year before and heard about the place possibly being haunted.

Sara shook her head. She knew they had to let Raymond and Veronica be there as much as they wanted. If they ever decided to return. She also knew there was no way to stop them anyway.

Gayle was disappointed when Raymond did not show up during her Spring Break. Sara was also surprised because she believed Roman's assumption that he would. Something else significant must have happened that they did not know about yet. She was certain he or Veronica would return sometime. She hoped the keys were returned. She could not imagine why they wouldn't be.

Sara laughed at herself when she thought about the keys being returned. Raymond and Veronica were both ghosts. As ghosts, there was no way that they could possess the keys. In the real world, the keys were somewhere at the manor or the estate. And someone alive and real had been the one who moved them.

She shook her head. How could a rational person believe in ghosts? True, she and Heather had felt the gentle touch of something years ago. And now they were to believe there were two ghosts in the area? She started pacing the floor.

Gayle returned home from school to find her mother pacing.

"Are you okay? Why are you pacing?" Gayle said as she set her books on the kitchen counter. She went to the refrigerator to get a drink.

Sara didn't say a word at first. When the refrigerator door closed, she came out of her trance. "Sorry, what did you say?"

"I asked why you were pacing. What is on your mind."

"I have decided the keys are on the estate somewhere. There is no such thing as ghosts, and someone alive has been the one who has continued to move them and play tricks on our family."

"Mom, calm down. Didn't you and Aunt Heather agree that a ghost had touched you?"

"We felt air on our arms. Just air. Unexplained air." Sara replied. There was no explanation for it, but she was doing her best to dispel the occurrence of a ghost.

"Well then, we need to start a thorough investigation."

Sara smiled. Her daughter, the detective. "You are correct. We must search long and hard, high and low, deep and wide." She walked over to her daughter and gave her a hug. Gayle was becoming a mature young lady. Emotion overtook her for a moment. Her little girl was growing up so fast. Too fast.

"Let me finish my homework, and we can begin the search."

"You got it, Detective Gayle." Sara saluted her and walked away.

An hour later, Randall called to say he had to work late and would not be home for dinner on time. Sara said that it was okay that she and Gayle were on a mission. He was smart enough not to ask for details. He said he would get something to eat in town.

Sara and Gayle each took a deep breath as they began their search. Knowing that their house was the property's original building, they thought it best to start there. That was until Sara realized that the manor was built when Raymond was involved with the estate and Rose. So they changed their course and walked to the manor.

The manor was empty when they arrived. The guests were all out for dinner in town. Andy was at his home. Sara loved being there where it was quiet. Until now. Now she was searching for keys. Or, if she wanted to be honest with herself, she was hunting a ghost.

Gayle walked into the great room and stood in the middle of the room. The silence allowed her to hear what most people would not pay attention to since they were normally talking. Her mind drifted into nothingness. Her senses were keen on what might be around her.

Sara stopped in her track as she noticed her daughter's stance. She watched as Gayle's body never moved. Then she saw what might be the reason.

A figure stood behind her daughter. He was tall and muscular, with dark hair. He had a fierce but gentle look on his face. His movements were slow but deliberate. Sara could not react. She didn't know if Gayle saw the man or not. She knew her daughter didn't budge. Was it fear? Was it her way of searching? Was she allowing the unknown to reach her being?

The figure must have noticed Sara because he quickly moved away and could no longer be seen. Sara walked to Gayle and touched her arm to bring her back to reality.

Gayle shook her head and, empty-eyed, looked at Sara. She seemed a million miles away. Her breathing was so shallow Sara could not detect it. She snapped her fingers. Gayle took a deep breath and shook her head.

"There you are."

"Yes, I've always been here. Why are you looking at me that way?"

"Do you know what just happened?"

"Yea. I walked in here and stood in the middle of the floor, trying to think like a ghost would. Nothing came to me, and then you snapped your fingers at me. That was rude."

Sara looked into her eyes. "You, Ms. Detective, were in a trance. You have no idea what happened, do you?"

"No, why? Did something weird happen?"

"Oh, yes, that is one way to say it. I walked toward you from the kitchen and stopped in my tracks. I could tell you were lost in no man's land and did not want to disturb you. Then."

"Then, what? What did you see? You saw something. I can tell. Tell me, what was it? Did you see Raymond?"

Sara simply nodded her head. She could not bring herself to describe the scene she had just witnessed. She was not ready to share what she had just seen. No one would believe her—including Gayle.

~~~~~~

Two days later, Sara was sitting in her office and heard a knock on her door. She answered it and invited the guest, directing them to the two armchairs.

"Good afternoon. What can I help you with? I hope your room is to your satisfaction."

"Oh, our room is perfect. This entire place is amazing. We are so glad we chose this place to start while we visit with his great-grandparents." The wife said.

"Yes, everything is perfect. The proximity to everything we could ask for is within driving distance of here. We could not have asked for a better location to vacation."

The lady reached into her pocket and handed Sara the object she had hidden.

"What's this?" Sara asked as she reached out her hand. No one brought her gifts. And certainly not hidden in her hand.

"We found these while we were walking the trail on the property. We thought you might need them. No one else we know would keep them. There must be a story behind them.

Sara accepted the gift. She pulled her arm back so she could look at whatever it was. Just feeling them in her hand brought a sensation of fear. Her hand shook as she opened her hand to look at what lay on her palm. Then her body shook.

The man reached over to steady her before she fell.

"Are you alright?" The man inquired.

Sara tried to speak but could only shake her head. Finally, she controlled herself and said she was fine. Then she took a closer look and asked them where they had found them.

"We were hiking behind the cemetery, and they were sitting on the top of the rail across the creek."

Sara smiled. "Yep, in clear sight."

"What?"

"Never mind. Sara smiled. "I need to call my daughter. Will you excuse me?"

"Of course. The couple said together. They excused themselves and went to their room - The Carpenter's Star room.

Sara walked to her desk and sat down. She opened her cell phone and speed-dialed Gayle.

Gayle saw that it was her mother calling and answered it immediately. She didn't even have time to say hello when she heard her mother's single word. She assumed she had missed the first few words, as all she heard was "Keys."

"What about the keys, mama?"

"In my hand," Sara replied.

"You have keys in your hand. Ok. What are you talking about?"

"The keys." Sara accentuated.

"OH! How, where, when, and where are you?"

"The office," was all Sara could say.

"I'm on my way over," Gayle said and hung up. She rushed out of the house and ran the path to the manor.

Sara was still sitting at her desk, staring at the keys, when her daughter rushed in. Gayle looked at her mother and then at the keys. They took up her whole hand.

"Where did you find them?"

"I didn't. A guest found them on the bridge railing behind the cemetery."

"Wow. So Raymond or Veronica decided it was time to return them."

"I guess. Or at least someone did. To put them in clear view seems too deliberate. And behind the cemetery, also seems directive."

"How do you mean directive?"

"To make us think a ghost is responsible for the mystery of the keys, it would make sense to put them near a cemetery."

"And maybe, just maybe, Mama, it has been a ghost."

"I am not so sure anymore. I know what we have felt and seen. My mind cannot accept it."

"So, we keep digging." Gayle sat back in the armchair opposite her mother. She smiled as she anticipated the work it would take as a detective to finally solve this mystery. She nodded her head. It was time to take notes.

Chapter Thirty-Eight
A Conversation

Angela held her hand up and looked at her ring as she sat on the bed in her hotel room. She hated being away from Jeff. She was thankful that he understood her business.

Her work often took her out of town, especially when the other photojournalists were working on other projects. Her magazine was growing in popularity, and with the inclusion of it being online, she was determined to make it even better for her readers. A recent poll indicated they wanted more stories about easy living. City life was fine for some, but she enjoyed the simple life and loved getting to know the people who were blessed to live such a life.

This assignment had taken her to Pennsylvania. When she first decided to head North, she asked around and found where she wanted to go. Karen told her about her hometown. A further conversation with Larry and Grace was her deciding factor. The lake seemed like the perfect story to write. Sure she assumed others had written about it. Her job was to find a different approach to feature the location and the people. That had always been her specialty.

She called home every day to talk with Jeff. One particular morning, Jeff seemed distant. When she asked him why he told her that he missed her.

"I miss you too, Babe."

"No, I really miss you. I miss what we are to become."

"How can you miss something we haven't become? And what is that anyway?"

"We need to plan our wedding. I want to call you my wife, not my girlfriend or fiancé."

"We will start planning as soon as I get home."

"Promise?"

"I promise."

Angela walked out of the hotel room and drove downtown. She had found the local diner the perfect place to talk to people and hear the stories about the old days. Those were the stories she loved to hear.

At the end of the day, she was satisfied that this last visit had finished her time. One more day of taking photos, and she would head home.

As she drove past the lake, she noticed a gentleman sitting on a bench in the park. Something told her to stop and talk with him. She pulled into the parking lot and walked over to him.

He was an older gentleman with the lines of many years of living on his face. His hands were rough from a lifetime of hard work. His clothes were a little ragged from wear. He looked up at her as she approached. His smile was inviting, and Angela sat beside him.

"Good afternoon, young lady. What can I do for you?"

"Good afternoon, Sir. How are you?"

"Oh, please don't call me sir. Call me Gregory. And I am fine, by the way."

"Hello, Gregory. My name is Angela. I am here writing a story about this area and its people."

"I have heard the locals talking about you." He looked at her and nodded his head.

"You have? I hope it has all been good. I don't want to leave a bad impression."

"It has all been good. No complaints from anyone, as far as I know. And I know a lot of people here."

"How long have you lived here?"

"All my life. Which means a long time." He laughed. He leaned forward and placed his elbows on his knees. He looked around the park and smiled as he watched the children playing on the recreational equipment. He watched the young mothers talking amongst themselves as they watched each other's children playing.

"You must know details about everyone and everything around here."

"No, not really. So many new people have moved into the area and built the place up. It's not the same anymore. I miss how it was. People are always saying that change is good. I don't agree. Not with all of it. Life used to be simple. Everyone knew everyone. We looked out for each other. If someone needed something, we were there for them. If my family needed something, people offered to help. No one had to ask; help was just there. Now, no one helps. And when someone asks for help, they get referred to one agency or another. People should help each other."

Angela sat silently and listened. She had heard several others say the same thing while she talked to the locals. The older generation missed the old days. She nodded her head as he continued to talk. She smiled when she realized she had not even asked more than two questions. This gentleman simply wanted to talk to someone who would listen.

Angela thanked Gregory for talking with her and asked if they could stay in touch. He smiled and gave her his phone number. "I don't have one of those Facebook accounts like everyone else. Maybe I should."

"It is a great way to stay in touch."

"No, it's a good way to avoid face-to-face conversation. You learn more when you have a personal connection and spend physical time together. A person's body language often says more than their words."

"You are correct. We get too busy with life. We forget how to live."

He turned to face her as she moved to get off the bench. "Thank you for your time today. You are a special lady. Don't let anyone tell you any different. Follow your dreams. Never quit going after what you want out of life.

Always be there for others, but don't let them take advantage of you. You are worth so much more than you think."

At the end of their conversation, Angela knew one thing. She wanted to go home to Jeff. She wanted to begin her married life. Gregory had such a loving story about his late wife and the family they raised. She knew that was what she wanted. Gregory was so full of wisdom. She knew she would stay in touch with him.

Before she walked away, she leaned over and kissed his cheek. "Thank you, Gregory. You have changed my life."

Before he could say anything, she walked away. He smiled as he watched her walk away. She had changed his life that day too. She would never know how much.

Chapter Thirty-Nine
Plans

Angela drove the long road home. Ten hours gave her a lot of time to think. A few stops and phone calls to Jeff along her way helped pass the time. She could not get Gregory's words and stories out of her mind. She hoped she could remember them all to include in her feature story. She hung her head when she realized she had never captured his photo to include in her article. Somehow she knew he would not want his photo there anyway. He was truly a humble man.

Jeff was waiting for her when she pulled into their driveway. He walked down the steps and opened her car door before she turned the engine off. She smiled as she stood up and felt the love of his arms around her. Yes, she was ready to marry this man. Jeff was her soulmate. He was her Gregory.

It was late when Angela arrived home, and she was tired after such a long drive. She sat down on the sofa and put her feet up. Jeff returned from the kitchen with a glass of white wine for her and another for himself. He sat next to her and put his arm around her shoulder. Her head automatically leaned on his shoulder. She took a sip of wine and smiled.

"I love you." She whispered.

"I love you, too. And I will come with you next time you go away for even a few days."

"Why? What about your work?"

"I can arrange my work somehow, but I missed you and don't want to spend another day or night without you."

Angela smiled and lifted her head to kiss him. "I missed you too. All I wanted to do was share my time there with you. You would have loved it there. You would have loved Gregory, too."

"You will need to tell me about him sometime."

"I will. Tonight, I am too tired for anything."

"I know you are. Tomorrow we start planning our wedding."

"Yes, it is past time for that. I want something simple and easy."

"We can always elope."

"Not that simple and easy," she shook her head. Her dreams in her childhood of a huge wedding were long gone. All she wanted now was to be Jeff's wife. It did not matter how big or small the wedding was. It was their marriage that would last a lifetime."

"We'll figure it out together. For now, you need sleep, young lady."

"I do." She sipped the last bit of wine from her glass. Jeff reached for her glass and took the empty glasses to the kitchen. He returned to walk with Angela to their bedroom. He smiled and shook his head. The love of his life was asleep on the sofa. He picked her up and carried her to the bedroom. Tomorrow was a new day.

~~~~~~

Angela and Jeff took less than a week to plan their wedding. Knowing the right people to rely on and to help was a benefit. They asked Heather to help organize everything. Karen to do their cake. Andy to make the food for the reception. Jeff asked Jay to be his best man. And, of course, Angela asked Terri to be her matron of honor. They made sure that the arrangement would be okay with Adam and Carrie. They both assured the couple that it was fine. Terri and Jay had a friendship that outsiders did not understand, but the family did, which is what mattered. They asked Adam to provide the music at the reception.

The wedding would take place in the chapel at Bella Rose. Only for the family and a few close friends. Jeff had a few special people he worked with that he wanted to invite.

One night as they were resting and enjoying a glass of wine Angela's phone rang. She did not recognize the number, but she answered it because she knew the area code. When she heard the voice, she smiled.

"Hello, Gregory. How are you?"

"I am well. How are you doing?"

"Jeff and I are enjoying a glass of wine. We just finished planning our wedding. Which reminds me. We were making our list of guests to invite. Will you be able to make the trip to join us?"

"Just name the day, and I will do my best to be there for you."

Angela stood up and walked away from Jeff to continue talking with the special man she had met at the lake.

"Gregory, I was going to call you in the morning to ask you something."

"Yes, what is it?"

"Will you walk me down the aisle at my wedding?"

Silence invaded their conversation.

"Gregory?"

"Yes, my dear. I am here. And I am honored that you asked. Of course, I will walk you down the aisle. I may need to bring my son with me on such a long trip. Is that okay?"

"Yes, of course. Bring whoever you need to. And thank you."

"You made quite the impression on me while we talked in the park. I will do whatever I can for you."

"You obviously made a lasting impression on me. I shared your wisdom with Jeff when I returned home. He is looking forward to meeting you."

"You tell that young man he had better treat you like a lady should be treated, or he will have me to deal with and make amends."

Angela laughed. Jeff entered the room to refill their wine glasses and asked why she was laughing.

"Because Gregory said you had better treat me right."

"Tell him, I would not have it any other way. You deserve the best. I plan to spoil you for the rest of your life."

"I heard that," Gregory said. "He is off to a good start. I will have a sit-down talk with him when I get there."

"I will warn him."

"I will let you go so you can spend time with your love. I just wanted to talk to you for a few minutes."

"Okay. You take care. We will talk soon."

"Yes, we will."

They each hung up their phones. Jeff looked at his fiancé and smiled. "He is coming to walk you down the aisle, isn't he?"

"He said, Yes." Angela smiled. "He is a special man. I am so glad I made that trip and happened to notice him. He looked like a lonely old man when I first spotted him. He is more than I imagined. It will be a pleasure to have him here."

~~~~~~

Two weeks later, all the invitations were mailed out or emailed. Everyone was working to make this wedding perfect for the two of them. Almost immediately, the RSVPs began arriving. Everyone they had invited so far was coming. Since they did not need much of anything, they had not done a wedding registry. Instead, they suggested donations to the foster care program or a charity of the guest's choice.

A week before the wedding, Angela received a call from Gregory. He was on his way with his son.

Everything was taken care of for their wedding. The last few days before the big day, everyone could relax.

Gregory arrived with his son and met the family. Everyone loved him. As promised, he sat down with Jeff and gave him sound advice on love and marriage. Jeff listened intently. When a man who has been married for over fifty years gives tips for making it work, you listen.

Chapter Forty
The Walk

The big day had finally arrived for Angela and Jeff. A chance meeting in an airport had led to more than either had been searching for at that time. All the obstacles they faced were overcome by love and determination. Their families grew to love and accept the two of them together. They would vow their lives and love for each other in front of family, friends, and even strangers.

Terri and Angela had time together while the sisters had their hair and makeup done. They had private time together while they dressed in the gowns Angela had chosen.

"I cannot believe you are getting married, Sis."

"It is hard to believe. Who knew that meeting a stranger at an airport would lead to a lifetime together?"

"Certainly not me. When I saw who you met, I warned you."

"Yes, you did. So if anything should happen to us in the coming years, you can tell me that you had warned me."

"I won't do that. All relationships take work. It takes both of you working together to make the life you want. Remember, communication is key."

"We have been told that by a few people. It must be true." Angela laughed. "We have no problem talking to each other. I don't think he has stopped talking since we met."

"I know what you mean. It must run in the family."

Angela knew what she meant. Jay had seemed the same way when he and Terri dated years before.

Sara knocked on the door of the dressing room of the chapel and told them the guests were all seated, and it was time to start. Angela asked if Gregory was with her.

"No, but let me go get him. Are you both ready?"

"Yes. You may come in if you want." Terri said.

"Let me find Gregory. He may want a few words before you walk down the aisle."

"Okay. Thank you, Sara."

Sara walked across the hall to the other spare room. She knocked and heard a male voice tell her to come in. She opened the door and saw Gregory, Jeff, and Jay standing there with big smiles.

"Are you gentlemen ready?"

"As we will ever be," Jeff replied. "Is my bride ready?"

"No, she isn't," Gregory replied.

"How do you know?" Jeff asked.

"Because I have not talked with her yet today. Let me go talk to her for a few minutes. You gentlemen can go to the sanctuary and start the wedding. I won't be long. We will be there on time." He walked to the door and walked out with Sara.

"Hello, Gregory. Are you ready for this?" Angela asked when he walked into the room.

"I am ready. And you will be in a moment."

"I am ready." Angela looked at herself in the mirror. She looked ready. What did he notice that she didn't?

"You, young lady, are at the threshold of your life when major changes are about to transform you. You won't notice them today. Today is all about the ceremony and the celebration. Today you may start your life together in the eyes of God and everyone here. Tomorrow you will start your life as a married couple. A couple with a bright future together can last a lifetime if you give one hundred percent of yourselves and work fifty / fifty on the workings of living together. You hold in your mind and heart a pure love for each other. It shows to all who see you. Keep that purity. Keep the lines of communication open. Share everything about your life with each other. Never be afraid to speak your mind. Be honest and truthful, always."

Angela listened to every word he spoke. His wisdom was from experience. From lessons learned along the way to ways he knew had worked for him and his soulmate. She reached out and hugged him.

"Thank you, Gregory. When I first spotted you on that park bench, something told me to stop and get to know you. Whatever that force was, I am grateful."

"That was God. He works in mysterious ways sometimes. We never know when or how our lives will change if we just listen and obey where He sends us and what he directs us to do. One day you will see all of that. His blessings will last you a lifetime."

Sara motioned for them to get ready. She heard the music playing and saw Heather walking towards them.

With a deep breath, bouquet in hand, Terri walked out with Heather to begin the procession of her sister's wedding.

The door opened in the back of the chapel as the music changed for Terri's walk down the aisle. She smiled, knowing that her husband was the one changing the music. The song playing for her walk was one he suggested and was a love song directed at her. She looked to the front of the chapel and saw Jay's smile. Her smile changed, but not so anyone would notice. There, in front of her, was her past love. Her emotions momentarily mixed. Then she noticed Jeff and returned her mind to their special day. She truly wished them the best.

The music changed again after Terri stood in her spot for the ceremony. Everyone turned to watch the bride enter.

Gregory held his bent arm out for Angela to place her hand on his forearm. They looked at each other in silent understanding. They both turned their faces to the front as they slowly walked down the aisle.

Gregory's heart overflowed with love for this special lady he had only recently met. He knew that she would soon understand that love. He looked at the guests as they walked. Angela only saw Jeff. Her smile grew with each step.

The music played for a few moments after Gregory placed Angela's hand into Jeff's. As Gregory turned to take his seat, he looked back at one particular guest. One he knew from years past.

~~~~~~

Angela and Jeff turned to face their guests. The minister had just announced them as husband and wife. Nothing could be better than the feeling they each had. This was the beginning of their life together.

The guests stood and applauded as the newlyweds rushed down the aisle, hand in hand. They were followed immediately by Jay and Terri, who looked at each other and silently agreed not to hold hands as they walked.

The two couples stood in the back of the chapel for a few minutes. The photographer took photos of the ceremony, including as they walked out. He wanted to take posed photos at the gazebo and on the grounds while the guests went to the reception. He promised not to take too long; since they did not have a lot of family members there, it would be easy. Angela asked him to find Gregory for a few of the photos. Gregory gladly joined them.

The wedding group headed for the reception when the photo session was over. Their guests were waiting for them and already enjoying drinks and appetizers. Angela and Jeff made their grand entrance and headed to the bridal table, where their plates of food were waiting for them. Terri and Jay sat on either side of the bride and groom.

Adam played quiet love songs while everyone began to eat. He took a cue from Jeff and started to play their wedding song. Angela took Jeff's hand as he stood up. Their smiles never dimmed as they began to dance to their wedding song. It was another song written by Adam. "I

Give My All to You." Halfway through the song, Adam walked to his wife and reached out his hand. Terri took it and joined him on the dance floor. Jay was already walking towards Carrie when she stood and met him to dance. By the time the song ended, several couples had joined the bridal party on the dance floor.

Angela and Jeff continued to dance the evening away. When it was time to cut and serve the cake, Karen had to get their attention. They gladly took a break from dancing, and once they sat down, they realized how worn out they were.

Guests began to leave after they had eaten some cake and had spoken to the newlyweds one more time. Some had words of wisdom for them, others congratulating them.

Adam stopped playing the music when people stopped dancing. Angela led Jeff out of the room to get changed for their honeymoon escape before everyone left. As they walked away, she noticed Gregory leaving with Larry. She wanted to make sure she said goodbye to him before they left for the night.

Gregory had watched Angela and Jeff as they danced and mingled with the guests. After they had cut the cake, he decided it was time to see if the man he had noticed at the wedding ceremony was still there. He looked around the room and noticed the man he saw at the ceremony. He excused himself from his son and walked over to Larry.

Chapter Forty-One
Reconnected

"Hello, Larry. How are you?"

Larry turned and faced Gregory. Larry was unsure how he would handle talking to him when he saw him with Angela. Now that the man stood before him, there was no choice but to be friendly.

"Hello, Gregory. I am fine. I am surprised to see you here. I didn't realize you knew Angela and Jeff."

"I just met Angela a couple of months ago. She came to the lake to write a story, and we instantly connected."

"I see." Larry wondered what story Angela was searching for.

"Nothing to worry about, Larry. She was there to discuss the area and the people. Not to dig into anything."

"I didn't say she was."

"No, but your facial expression said enough. I will keep your secret."

"Secret is out. Many years ago, that came out. It is the only way I am now living here. A long story."

"I have time. I know what happened at the lake, but how did that bring you here?"

"Ah, so, you don't know the whole story?"

"I know you saw someone for a few summers when you were young and fresh out of college. And that the last summer, she was pregnant. I know that she never stayed over the winter months. And that after she had the baby, she never returned alone again. What I don't know is how that brought you here? Or did it have anything to do with this move?"

"It had everything to do with this move. Shall we go outside to talk?"

"Sure. I would love to hear the details of your involvement with a married woman. And the fact that your parents seemed okay with that."

The two men walked outside to continue their conversation. All those years ago, all the time spent living in the same area and never a word between them. Now, some eight hours away, they meet at a wedding. Now, Gregory wanted details.

Larry never did understand why his father and uncle quit talking to each other when he was young.

"Why did you stop talking to my parents?" Larry got right to the point.

"Stupid decision when I look back. I was an upright, strict Christian, heavily involved with the church. When my brother talked to me about your behavior, I told him you had to make things right and ask the church for forgiveness. I was almost forced to step away from your family when you didn't."

"That is a stupid reason. Family should always come first."

"I see that now. I kept an eye on you over the years. How could I not? We lived in the same town."

"So I don't understand; why do you want to talk to me now?"

"I didn't plan on it. My brother died, and then you moved away. I thought there was no chance of finding you to tell my side of the story. I had let it fester and then just let it all go—until today. I never thought I would see you again. I had no idea where you and Grace moved to. What brought you here?"

Larry smiled. He knew what he was about to tell his uncle would either shock or make him smile. "You may not believe me when I tell you this, but it is because of my son."

"Wait, you and Grace don't have a son." Gregory stopped speaking and looked into Larry's eyes. "Explain."

"That married woman you thought I was having an affair with all those years ago? Well, she was divorced at the time. That baby? Is my son. His name is Andy."

Gregory didn't say a word. His mind tried to make sense of what his nephew was telling him. "But how did that bring you here?"

"That woman? And now my son and his siblings own Bella Rose Estate."

Gregory was speechless. Larry did not know how to continue.

"Let me get this straight. The woman you were seeing was the owner of this place?" Gregory raised his hand in a sweeping motion to indicate the whole area.

"At the time, her parents owned it. When they passed away, she became the owner. After she had the baby, Andy, she returned home to her parents to raise him. She then reconnected with her ex-husband, and they remarried. Her children inherited it when she and her husband died several years ago."

"But how did you?" Gregory didn't even know what to ask.

"How did I learn about Andy? I always knew. Susan wanted the truth to stay a secret, so we never told anyone. Andy never knew. Until after his mother died. His story is long. I'll just say that he found out. It took a while for him and his family to accept the truth, but we are in a good place now. His family accepted me with open arms."

"You are blessed."

"Yes, I am. We all are. The key to it is telling the truth."

"The truth is always best," Gregory remembered all the years he had wasted not talking with his brother and nephew. "Can you ever forgive me?" he asked Larry.

'Of course. That is what family does. I understand now why you did what you did at the time. I am not sure I would if it happened today."

"Today, there is a different attitude about a lot of things. Plus, I am not as strict in my beliefs. Everyone deserves to be loved and have a family."

Larry reached into his pocket and pulled out some keys.

"What are those for?" Gregory asked.

"These are for different things in the manor."

"Why do you have them? Do you work here?"

"No, and there is no need to explain why I have them. It is, however, time that I return them where they belong."

"What are you saying? You stole them?"

"In a way, yes." Larry hung his head. He was now so ashamed of his actions.

As he held them in his hand, Sara approached them on her way to the manor. She spotted the keys in Larry's hand. She stopped in her tracks. She had heard part of the conversation, but it was not until she saw them that she realized what keys Larry was discussing.

Larry stared at Sara when she stood in front of him. He swallowed hard. He felt Gregory looking at him. There was no way out of facing the horrible truth.

He reached out his hand above Sara's outstretched, open hand, took a deep breath, and loosened his grip. The key ring of antique keys dropped into Sara's hand.

"You have some explaining to do." Sara felt empowered about Larry, even though he was much taller than her, and most people initially felt intimidated.

He hung his head and agreed. His days of dishonesty and holding a mystery over people would soon be over.

Gregory watched the two of them without saying a word. He noticed Angela and Jeff leave the reception hall. He quietly walked away from Larry and Sara.

Sara almost yelled at Larry before continuing her walk to the manor. This was not the time to confront him. Something told her that Larry would be in her office the next morning to explain his actions over the years. She could only assume and wonder about the anger inside him.

The next morning Sara opened the door to her office, then walked to her desk and opened the top center drawer where the key to the safe was. She smiled when she saw it was still there. With the keys that the former guest had returned and the ones Larry had just relinquished, she hoped she had the full assortment. Now was when she would have loved seeing Raymond enter her room or her mind. Maybe tonight would be the night Raymond returned. Her belief in ghosts was growing, but not to the fullest extent that some people believed. She had never seen an actual ghost. Her experience was the feeling of the air around them. The brush of air in the attic. And the visions she had just a few days ago.

Sara heard a door close. She wondered if it was Larry. When she looked up, she saw Angela and Jeff walking in. They didn't live far away but had chosen to spend their honeymoon night at the manor. Sara smiled to herself and momentarily forgot about the keys.

Chapter Forty-Two
Confession

Larry could not sleep. His mind would not stop thinking. How was he going to face Sara? Even more so, how was he going to face Andy? All those years of hiding and playing tricks on a family he had come to love. He should have never moved to Tennessee to be near his son. None of this would have happened if he and Grace had stayed in Pennsylvania, minding their own business. He looked at his loving wife sleeping soundly by his side. He felt he had betrayed her all these years, as well as his son.

He climbed out of bed and poured himself a drink. It was the wrong thing to do at three in the morning, but he didn't care. He wanted to avoid reality. Determined to confess to Sara as soon as possible to get it over with and let the truth be known, he wondered what the outcome would be. Would they hate him? Would they understand or even attempt to understand? Had any of them loved someone so much they would do anything to hold on to that person? Even if it meant destroying what he had?

He heard Grace walking down the hall towards him. He hung his head. She needed an explanation too. He had put her through a lot over the years that she had accepted. He wanted to cry but refused to allow emotions to take over.

Grace sat next to him and put her hand on his leg. She reached for his half-empty glass and took it from him. She did not say a word. She knew he hurt. She knew he was in turmoil with himself. Larry looked at his wife and slowly shook his head. A tear escaped and started a flood of them. He had no words. Not yet. Grace held him. She would stand by him no matter what he had to explain or what she assumed he felt.

241

Several emotional moments passed before Larry said anything.

"I am so sorry," was all he could finally say.

"No matter what you have to tell the family or me, I will be by your side."

"How? How can you? I have put you through so much over the years. And now this. This thing that I have kept from you."

"Love. That is all I have. Love."

Larry shook his head and stood up. He would never understand. He started to walk away when Grace joined him and took his hand, leading him back to bed. They lay beside each other in silence. Larry finally fell asleep. His dream woke him as the sun was coming in through their window. He knew what he had to do. And he knew he had to do it that morning.

Grace was making coffee when Larry walked into the kitchen. "I need to go talk to Sara." He said as he walked out the door and got in his car. Grace smiled as she watched him drive away.

~~~~~~

Sara was in her office when her door opened, and Larry walked in. He sat in the armchair across from her as she sat at her desk. She looked at him and raised her eyebrows. Without her asking anything, Larry began to talk.

"I am so sorry. I know you and your family deserved peace after Susan died. I tried to give you that. I tried to protect you all from finding the truth. I was more afraid of how you would react to the truth than how you would react to my horrible behavior against all of you."

"How did you know about the keys? How did you know about the journals? How did you know anything we eventually discovered? That's the first thing I want to know."

"I did not know everything you would discover. I only knew the secrets between Susan and myself. I knew the agreement she and I had made when Andy was born. I knew she did not want the truth found out. We did our best for all those years, and I was not about to let her death bring shame to your family, especially our son."

"Once we did find out, why continue to hide the keys?"

"Because you started discovering more and more secrets, and the more you found, the more I wanted to protect you from more pain."

"But how did you know any of it?"

"I didn't. That is the funny part if there is a funny part. Which, there really isn't."

"Did you know about Raymond and Rose?"

"Yes, I did. Susan knew about her mother and the affair. She told me about it years ago. She told me about Raymond and the work he had done and about the keys. She said that Rose told her all about it when she was a teenager. Something about her not wanting her daughter to make the same mistake."

"How ironic."

"I know. A few differences between the two circumstances, but agreed, ironic."

"So, I still don't understand it all. Mostly how you knew so much about the secrets you were trying to protect us from, as you say."

"I don't expect anyone to understand it. None of it. How could two people keep an agreement for life about a child they had together? How could a mother not want her child to know his biological father? I might understand if the father was terrible, but I am a good man. Okay, not perfect, but good. I honored her request. Maybe too far and for too long."

Sara took in all he had to say. Somehow, she took him at his word. It made sense that he loved Susan so much that he did everything he could to keep their secret. He had sacrificed a life with his son to honor her, even after her death. Only a man of integrity could do that.

Sara lifted the keys from the desk. She had laid them out that morning to make a point to Larry when he showed up. She was angry with him. When she first saw the keys in his hand and heard what he told Gregory, she wanted Larry out of their lives. Now, after hearing his story and remembering reading about their secret in both the journals, she almost understood.

"How does Grace feel about your continued love for Susan?"

"She told me this morning that she would stand by my side, no matter what. Although she doesn't know everything yet. I have put her through a lot during our marriage. Her acceptance of Andy, when she found out, was more than any man could hope for. I am blessed with an amazing woman."

"You are blessed, lucky, fortunate. Take your pick. You never stopped loving Susan, did you?"

"No, not one day of my life did I stop loving her. And for Grace to know that and still love me, knowing a part of my heart would always belong to another woman? I do not deserve her."

"Larry, you are an amazing man. I was angry with you after last night. I wanted to make you and Grace leave town; heck, I wanted you to move back to Pennsylvania."

"And now?"

"Now, I want you to tell my family the truth. The truth about the keys and your love for our mama. The truth about everything."

"Set up a family meeting. I will tell them everything and answer all their questions. First, I need to confess to Grace."

"You have not told her?"

"No, not completely. She knows most of it but not about the keys. She knows about my love for Susan."

"Okay. You go tell Grace, and I will set up a family meeting; for tonight. You don't have long to confess to your wife." Sara's anger was starting to show again. She took a deep breath.

"I hope the rest of the family understands as easily as you do."

"They will. You may know a lot about us, but you don't know how resilient we are and how we regard deep love."

"Thank you, Sara. I will call you later to find out when you want me here tonight. Hopefully, Grace will join me."

"I think she will. She loves you."

Larry stood to leave but was stopped by Sara's action. She walked around her desk to him and reached up to give him a hug.

"Thank you."

"For what? I caused your family so much pain."

"All for love. You did what you thought was best and what our mama wanted. I think she always loved you, too."

Larry returned her hug and smiled as he left the office. He took a deep breath. His confession time was not over yet. His heart was heavy.

When Larry returned home, Grace sat in their living room enjoying a cup of afternoon tea. He hung his head as he shuffled over to her. He was not proud of what he had done. He was shocked that Sara had taken it all so well. He prayed his wife would.

"How did things go with Sara?"

"Better than I expected." He sat next to Grace.

"I am glad."

"Now, I need to tell you."

"I know. And I would understand if you are not ready."

"I have to be ready. There is a family meeting tonight with Sara, Heather, and Andy, and I must tell you first. And before you tell me that you will stand by my side no matter what. I will understand if you do not."

"Okay. I won't promise. Although I am not sure what you could say would make me not love you."

"Grace, I have shared almost every aspect of my life with you. I have loved you for all these years. You learned about my past and Andy and continued to love me. What you don't know is." Larry fell silent as he feared her reaction to what he had to tell her.

Grace set her cup down and turned to face her husband. She put her hands on his that were folded at his knees as he sat looking down. "I know. I know. I have always known. You never stopped loving the mother of your child. The love you had for Susan held in your heart. And I even know now it still does."

"How? How did you know? And why did it not bother you?" Larry lifted his head and looked into her eyes.

"I didn't know who had won your heart before we met. I just knew someone had. I just knew a part of your heart would always be with that person. When you and Andy figured out who you both were and connected, I was honored to be a part of that reunion. I was blessed to finally know or know about a lady whose love was so powerful to hold your thoughts for so long."

"I have more to tell you."

"Okay." Grace sat back a little. She had no idea what was about to come.

"Do you remember being at Bella Rose Manor several years ago and Sara and the kids talking about missing keys to the attic and then the secret room they found?"

"Sure. It was always a mystery. Did they ever solve that?"

"Sara did today. Heather and Andy will tonight."

"What do you mean? How do you know they will find out tonight? I thought they had a family meeting, and we needed to be there."

"Yes, we need to be there. Because." Larry swallowed hard and looked at Grace. "Because I am the one who moved or hid the keys."

Grace sat back and looked at him. "How? Why?"

Because I was trying to protect them from finding out the truth about Susan and me. And even about Rose and Raymond."

"Who?" Grace sat all the way back. She let loose of one of Larry's hands and just sat in silence.

"Rose and Raymond. Susan told me about her mother having an affair with a man named Raymond. It didn't last long. Rose wrote about it in her journal. There were no children involved in it."

"What does that have to do with the keys, the journal, and your relationship with Susan?"

"Come to find out, Raymond and Rose had things to hide too. One is his threat of revenge on the family. I somehow found out about that. I moved the keys but never said a word about any of them. I was trying to protect the family from the truth. I thought they were better off not knowing how their ancestors were. They had a perfect life after Susan died. Who was I to ruin it with ugly truths?"

Grace looked at him, not saying a word. She needed to process what he told her.

~~~~~~

The family gathered in the dining room, but Sara suggested they retire to the great room. The guests were all gone, and it would be more comfortable for everyone.

Larry and Sara sat near the fireplace. Their spouses sat by their sides. Andy and Karen sat on the loveseat. Heather and Ben sat on the sofa. Everyone looked toward Larry and Sara.

Larry looked at everyone and began without hesitation. He told them about what he knew, how he felt all the love in the family, and how he wanted to be a part of it. He told them about the keys and how he tried to keep things secret. He told them about Rose and Raymond. He shared his emotions with everyone.

In the end, the siblings looked at him and smiled. His love shined through. His love for Susan, Andy, and all of them, including his love for Grace. They looked at Grace and saw her love for Larry and them.

"Larry, I think I can speak for the family, and this may sound odd, but. Thank you. And Grace, thank you too." Sara said.

Everyone nodded in agreement.

The mystery of Bella Rose was solved. Larry had moved all the keys occasionally to protect them from what to some would seem cruel. To them, it was love.

Pure, deep, unconditional love.

The evening ended soon after Larry's confession. Everyone returned to their homes.

The mystery may have been solved about the keys. But Sara knew there would always be another one involving their family. She drifted off to sleep, wondering what would happen now.

She didn't have long to wait.

Chapter Forty-Three
Beauty of Love

Jeff and Angela arrived at the airport with plenty of time to catch their plane for their cross-country honeymoon trip. They were headed to a hideaway. Jeff had not even told Angela where they were going. She had suggested places she wanted to go that she had never been to, but he told her he would take care of it. She trusted him wholeheartedly and had long since overcome her dislike for surprises.

As they walked to check in, Angela looked at the destination board to guess where they were going. The only places on the list were outside the United States. She smiled. Jeff looked at her and winked.

"Did you figure out where I am taking you?"

"Almost," she shook her head.

Jeff reached for her hand and told her they were going to Jamaica. He told her he knew someone who lived there and would take them around the island better than any tourist trap company.

"You know someone in Jamaica? Wow! How did you meet him?"

Jeff laughed. Holding her hand a little tighter, he shook his head.

"No? I don't understand."

"I know a lady who lives in Jamaica."

"Oh, an old girlfriend?" She attempted to pull her hand out from his.

"No, well, sort of. I grew up with her, and we have been friends all my life. We tried to date in high school, but that was a failure. We remained best friends over the years. We have each other's back when things get rough."

"I love that. I know a few people who are opposite sex friends. Not enough people are. And few people understand that it can happen. Most people think that whenever a man and woman are together, they are a couple in love."

"Glad you understand. You are right. I did not know how to tell you about her without just making it a surprise and hoping you would be okay with it."

"Of course I am. I love you. I will always love you."

Jeff reached over and kissed her as they heard the call to board their plane.

A layover in Charlotte gave them time to stretch their legs and grab a quick bite to eat. Angela was excited about their destination but unsure about meeting the lady Jeff knew. But she didn't say anything. She would wait to see what happened once they arrived and settled into their hotel room.

Jeff watched Angela as they flew. She had leaned on his shoulder and fallen asleep. She was so beautiful to him. He rested his head on hers as they drew close to the airport. She stirred as the plane turned to reach the airstrip. He kissed her as she raised her head. Her smile reassured him of her love.

~~~~~~

Georgia was waiting for her childhood friend at baggage claim. She had not seen Jeff in several years but looked forward to their getting together. She knew he was on his honeymoon and was interested in meeting his wife. He had told her about Angela when he called to make arrangements for their honeymoon.

Angela asked Jeff if they were going to rent a car while they were there. He told her that Georgia was picking them up.

"That is nice of her. I am anxious to meet this woman. She must be special if you stayed in touch with her all these years."

"She is. I think you will like her. I hope you will."

"I am sure I will."

"Well, there is something else I need to tell you."

"Yes?"

"We are staying with her while we are here."

Angela turned to look at him. They were not off the plane yet, and he was throwing her another curveball. How could he do that to her without asking her?

"Why? I thought you had made reservations."

"I did. But it is at her place. She owns a bed and breakfast here in town."

"How convenient."

"What's that supposed to mean? Are you upset?"

"A little. It is our honeymoon. Time to be alone and have fun."

"We will be. Most of the time."

Angela took a deep breath. "Okay. I guess that is all I can ask."

They walked off the plane and to baggage claim. After they picked up their luggage, Jeff heard his name being called. He turned around and saw Georgia standing about ten feet away. Jeff took Angela by the hand and met up with his childhood friend.

"Angela, this is Georgia. Georgia, this is my wife, Angela. It is so good to see you again."

"Hi, Angela. It is good to finally meet you." Georgia reached out her hand to her. Angela reached out and shook her hand.

"It is good to meet you also. So nice of you to meet us here and let us stay at your bed and breakfast."

"I would not have it any other way. Jeff has been there for me so often. I could never repay him enough."

"Okay, ladies, can we get out of this airport and to someplace more comfortable?"

"Of course. Let's go." Georgia said. She led them to her car and drove them to her Bed and Breakfast.

~~~~~~

The morning after Jeff and Angela arrived in Jamaica, they and two other couples enjoyed an island breakfast Georgia had made for her guests.

Knowing they were not the only ones there eased Angela's mind. She had reservations about their past relationship getting in the way of her honeymoon.

After breakfast, Jeff and Angela walked down to the beach to enjoy the day relaxing. The weather was perfect. Sunshine, warm, with a beautiful ocean in front of them.

~~~~~~

The week went by too fast for the newlyweds. They had enjoyed so much of the island on their own and with Georgia's help. When she drove the couples to the airport, everyone thanked her for all her help. Jeff stayed behind for a few extra minutes to talk to his old friend.

"Thank you so much for all your help. I had no idea how I would impress my bride until I spoke with you. You saved my marriage that did not have a rough spot yet."

"You are welcome, my friend. I love seeing you so happy. The love between the two of you is genuine. I can see it every time you look at each other and talk about each other. That love is rare, my Friend. Rare. Never let it go. Never let her go."

"I do not intend to break that bond we have. One divorce was enough in my life. This one is forever. I hope she never leaves me."

"The way you look at each other…. She is never letting you go. I am glad I was not hoping for anything to happen between us while you were here. I could tell you loved her when I heard you talk about her and make your reservation. I do not think you or I could have had that love."

"Thank you, Georgia. One day you will need to come to Tennessee to visit us. Or to wherever we are at the moment."

"Are you saying you may move away?"

"I am used to moving around. Angela is used to moving, but not like I have. Time will tell."

"Yes, time will tell," Jeff said. "Goodbye, dear"

They hugged for a moment before Jeff turned to leave. "Goodbye. You know I will always love you." She winked at him and turned away. She would never forget her first love. She also knew he had found his forever soulmate. She smiled as the door to the airport closed behind her.

Chapter Forty-Four
Family Bonds

Sara returned to her writing the family history. With the added information and confession from Larry, it did change several things about their background. It had an added mystery that made it all that more interesting.

Gayle had been helping her mother with some of the writing. Her desire to become a detective when she finished school continued. She loved being from a family with so much intrigue.

One day while Sara was finishing a chapter and about to close the office, Gayle walked in and sat down. Sara looked up, surprised.

"Why are you here instead of at the house? I'm about to head that way."

"I knew you would still be here, and I did not want to wait until we all got home to discuss this."

"Oh, it is more than just telling us something; it is discussing something." Sara sat down in her office chair. Whatever her daughter had to say sounded serious.

"It is not anything bad. I think it will be fun, but I will need your help."

"Is this a school project? And what do you need help doing?"

"Our assignment is to write about our family history." Before she had time to finish, Sara was laughing.

"Family history?" Sara tried not to laugh more.

"Yes. I know for us that sounds funny, considering our family. However, I want to write it as honestly as possible. My family is not a normal family. It is quite interesting when you think about it."

"Interesting is one way to describe it."

"Well, it's not dysfunctional. It's not crazy. It's not weird."

"Some may say it is all of those things. And once they read my book, I am sure more people will think that way. So, how do you want to portray your family?"

"I want to be honest about it, to a point. I know I will not dig into the generational background you all have discovered and are writing about. I want to concentrate on the time I was a foster child leading to the time you adopted me. I want to talk about that issue and how your friend, Barbara, is working with the foster system."

"You could do it without Barbara's involvement. Write about how we adopted you and how Terri and Andy foster an infant. Rachelle and Bob are fostering an older child."

"I want to emphasize the love it takes to be foster parents. And then the total commitment when you decided to adopt me."

"That sounds amazing. Are you sure you are ready to write about all of that?"

"It is the only family I know. It is the one I belong to. So, yes, I am ready."

~~~~~~

Gayle spent the next few days watching her parents. She made a point of spending time with her aunts and uncles. She visited Barbara and quickly gathered as much information about the foster system as possible. She talked to her mother to find out how it felt to make the decision to adopt her. And asked why they never fostered any other children.

When she had all the personal information, she researched articles by so-called experts on families. And the dynamics that create what families are.

What she deducted was how loved she was. That was what she was going to emphasize in her report—love.

It took Gayle a week to do the actual writing of her report. When she finished with it, she took it to Sara.

"Mama, could you read this for me and tell me what you think? I need to know the technical issues, grammar, spelling, writing structure, and your overall opinion."

"I am honored to read it. I will give it my best review." Sara accepted the report her teenage daughter had written. Sara expected a positive article. What she read was far beyond all her expectations.

Sara took the article to her office to read in her private time. She wanted to digest it and critique it for her only child.

Gayle's writing took Sara's breath away. It captured her heartstrings. It made her feel important for what she and Randall had done for her over the years. When she reached the section about the overall system, she was impressed. Gayle had captured the essence of a child's longing for family, the process of becoming a foster parent, and the joy and heartache of adults opening their lives so they qualified as a parent. It was not a simple process. Sara almost wished couples with their own children would need to undergo the process to qualify for the life-long mission.

There were times that Sara shed a tear as she read it. To think that her daughter had written such a beautiful piece about the topic was amazing. To be included in the real-life story made her feel loved.

Gayle returned to pick up the article the next day. She had two more days before it was due and needed time to make all the corrections needed for a good grade.

"You are a beautiful writer," Sara said as she handed the report to Gayle.

"Thanks, Mama. I take after you in that field."

Sara smiled and shook her head.

"What?" Gayle asked, seeing her mama's reaction.

"We are not related by blood. I didn't think you could pick up those traits unless you're related."

"Part of it is when people are blood-related, but it is possible to pick things up just by being around people long enough."

"Promise me you will only pick up the good points of your family."

"I promise. The good parts of my family are the best."

"You are sweet. Our family has a lot of quirks and bad habits."

"I know. Learning about all the secrets and mysteries of this family, I could not imagine belonging to any other one."

Sara gave her daughter a hug. "I hope your teacher gives you a good grade."

"I hope she chooses mine to be presented to everyone."

"Presented? What are you talking about? These are being presented to all the students in school?"

"More than that. A few of us will read them or at least present them at our school appreciation night."

"When is that program?" Sara asked. This was the first she was hearing about it.

"Yes. Next Friday night at school, I think. I will get you all the details. I would love for the whole family to attend."

"Yes, get me the details, and I will talk to everyone."

~~~~~~

The school's assembly hall was full. They rarely had that many people at any event or meeting. Gayle looked out from behind the heavy curtains and looked for her family. She smiled when she saw them sitting two rows back in the center.

The school's principal addressed the audience and shared the details of the program. It would be a mixture of little skits, musical numbers, and readings put on by the students in each grade. The theme, as it was each year, was family. She warned everyone that some of what they would see and hear may be disturbing, others would be funny, and a few would be serious and full of love. Their purpose this year was for the students to be honest in their depiction of family. He added that not all were from personal accounts but research and creativity.

Sara looked at Randall. "Gayle's reading is true."

"I am sure it is. I noticed she did a lot of family research with us."

Sara smiled and reached for her husband's hand. "Yes, she did. She's going to make a good detective or reporter one day."

After a few skits and musical numbers, it was time for the students to read the reports they had written. Gayle was first.

"Good evening, ladies and gentlemen, family, friends, and fellow students. I am here tonight to share with you my family story."

Gayle went on to talk about how she was placed in foster care at a young age. She briefly described the living conditions in a few foster care homes. Then she mentioned Sara and Randall and how they became her foster parents.

"I was still little at that time. I did not know the difference between being a foster child and being adopted. I didn't know that once you were adopted, you were stuck in the family forever!" The audience laughed.

"I was also still young when they adopted me. However, by then, I knew they loved me and wanted me to stay with them forever. It was the first time in my life I felt secure. I felt like I belonged somewhere. For a while, I still feared being taken away. Now, I know I belong right where I am. I know they love me, as do my aunts and uncles and even the friends who are as close as any family could be."

Gayle continued. "I learned a lot about my family these last two weeks. My extended family combines biological children, adopted kids, and foster families." Gayle smiled. "In my research, I found both good and bad of being a child or being foster parents. I learned all the statistics of unwanted children and children tossed around in the foster care system. Those fortunate children who are adopted. And those blessed to be born into a family that does and is capable of being what most people call a normal family."

"Let me tell you about 'normal.' At that time, Gayle looked to the right of the stage. The lights went dim, and music began to play.

Sara looked at Randall and shrugged her shoulders. She had not been made privy to more than Gayle's written story.

Some of Gayles' classmates entered the stage a few minutes later, with music softly playing. The scenes in the background showed families sitting around the kitchen table eating. Then it changed to kids playing outside. The last scene was a mother reading a story to a young child.

When it ended, Gayle took center stage again. "That is the idea of a normal family. I can see many of you shaking your heads. We all know that is not a normal occurrence. Families fight, and kids disobey the rules. Parents discipline their children. Today's families seldom sit at the kitchen table to eat dinner together. That is today's normal. And all of that is all a child in need of foster care wants. A family who cares for and treats them as their own child.

Gayle was silent for a moment. She looked around at all the people in the audience. "If any of you would like to share your love with a child, come see me, and I can connect you with someone who, through pure love, is changing and improving the foster care system and placing qualified families with amazing children in need."

The audience rose as Gayle turned and walked off the stage. Cheering the loudest were Sara and Randall.

After the school program finished, Gayle walked to the edge of the stage and waited. It was not long before three couples walked to the front to talk to Gayle about becoming foster parents. Barbara walked over to Gayle and sat with her. Together they worked with the couples to get them started in the process. Sara and Randall waited in the back of the auditorium and watched. They were so proud of their daughter.

~~~~~~

After the school program was over and the three couples had left, Sara and Randall met with Gayle and her teacher. Her teacher told her parents how proud she was of all Gayle's hard work in class. Sharing that she was the best student she had. Gayle humbly hung her head. She did not handle all the attention well. She did not think she was that special.

On the way home, Randall asked Gayle if she still wanted to become a detective or if she wanted to be an actress.

"Don't be silly, Dad. I still want to be a detective. Maybe even study family law."

"Why family law?"

"In my research, I learned so much about families and the issues they face. I want to work with Barbara in the foster family field."

"I am so proud of you," Sara said. Gayle was sitting in the back seat of the SUV and never noticed how big her mother's smile was.

Chapter Forty-Five
Kindness

A month after Gayle was in the school program about family, she was called into the principal's office. Before opening the office door, Gayle saw her parents sitting inside. Her mind raced over reasons why she would be in trouble. That was the only time parents were called to the principal's office. When nothing came to mind, she opened the door and smiled at Sara and Randall. When they smiled back, she knew something else was going on.

"Gayle, Sara, Randall, could you please come into my office?" The Principal asked when she opened the door to her inner office. She held her office door open as they all walked past her.

After they had all taken a seat, she sat facing them. She smiled before speaking.

"I know you are all curious about this meeting. Coming here is not usually a positive encounter. I assure you, this one is."

"Good," Sara said. "I will say you had us worried when you called. I was relieved when your secretary said it was nothing bad. Although we are confused."

"I will get to the point. Last month Gayle did a piece for the Family program that grabbed our attention. Not only our attention here at the school but the attention of people in the community."

Gayle sat in silence. This conversation could go in several directions. She caught herself holding her breath.

"Gayle, I understand you want to work as a detective when you finish school. I also heard you want to work in family law and the foster system."

"Yes, Ma'am. That is all I have wanted for a few years."
She looked at her parents, still wondering where this
meeting was headed.

"As you may or may not know, this school has several
students who are in the foster care system. Some of their
stories are heartbreaking. Some are nothing more than
miracles that they can be here."

"Yes, we have a few foster children in our extended
family, too," Randall added.

"Your family has been such an asset to this community.
It is time the community helps you."

"How?"

"I was approached by the mayor, of all people. He was
here the night of the program. Apparently, he went to the
next town meeting and presented a proposal that drew even
more interest from the community leaders."

"Okay. Am I in some kind of trouble?" Gayle asked.
She was still worried that all her work and information had
somehow sat wrong with someone.

"Oh, quite the opposite." The principal reached into her
desk drawer and pulled out an envelope. She handed it to
Gayle. "This is a token of appreciation for all the work you
put into investigating this topic we often avoid discussing."

Gayle looked at the envelope and then at her parents.
She hesitated to open it.

"Go ahead and open it." She smiled as Gayle carefully
opened the envelope. Then she pulled out a paper, which
she unfolded. Staring at her was a check. She looked at the
principal with raised eyebrows.

"What is this for?" She handed the check to her parents.
When they saw the amount, they also asked about it.

"The town has raised money for you to continue your
education in the field of your choice. We know you want to
be a detective and study family law. Those fields of study
are not cheap. We know you are not ready for college for a
couple more years, so this check is just the beginning."

"The beginning?" Randall questioned her statement.

"The town has voted to grant you a scholarship. This check is for the first year of school. Or if you want to study something over the summers before you reach college age."

"Why?" Gayle asked.

"Because you are the next generation, and we believe in you to improve this town and maybe the world."

"I'm just one person. A woman at that. And only in high school." Gayle was overwhelmed.

"Yes, but one person, doing the right things with the right attitude and initiative, can do wonders."

"Thank you. I don't know what else to say." She looked again at the check in her hand. It was more money than she had ever dreamed of having at her age. She took a deep breath.

"I will put it to wise use and do my best for this town and all the foster children and families. They need so much more than Barbara has been able to give. She is doing her best and has made a difference, but there is more to do, and she could use the help. I am honored by the support of the town."

"And that is another thing. We want you to work with Barbara as you have time to learn from her."

"That will be easy to do. In my spare time, of course."

"Oh, yes, your spare time. No skipping school." The principal rose from her seat to dismiss the family.

"I have one question."

"Yes, Mr. Williams."

"Why did they choose Gayle?"

"She's one of our best students. She is kind to everyone she meets. She knows no stranger, and helping others comes naturally to her. Or seems to. You have done an amazing job raising your daughter."

Sara reached for Randall's hand. "We try. When we first became foster parents, we had no idea what we were getting ourselves into. Once she arrived, we knew she was special, and it did not take long to know we wanted to adopt her."

"Whatever you are doing as parents is working. I wish more foster, adoptive, and biological parents would do more for their families."

"We appreciate your kind words. And we thank you so much for believing in our daughter."

"It has been my honor to have her in our school system."

Gayle was listening to the adults talk about her. It was humbling. She was herself. She didn't know any other way to be.

A few minutes later, they all left the office. Gayle returned to her classes, and Sara and Randall drove home.

"Kindness." Sara shook her head. "Just be kind, and people will notice."

"Some people will notice. Others still may not." Randall said as he parked their car at the house. They both were smiling as they walked inside. Both of them were proud of their daughter.

~~~~~~

Angela and Jeff easily adapted to married life following their extended honeymoon. A month after they returned home, Angela received a phone call from a local attorney. He asked her to come to his office. When she inquired about the reason, he told her that she had been named in a gentleman's will but that he could not disclose who until she came to the office. She was confused but made an appointment for the next day.

She told Jeff about it, and he had no idea who it could be.

The next day the couple arrived at the attorney's office fully expecting to be told it was a mistake. Neither one knew of anyone who would name Angela in a will.

"Thank you for coming in. Please have a seat." The attorney directed them to chairs opposite his desk. He picked up a file that was on his desk and opened it.

"I received this a couple of days ago from a fellow attorney in Pennsylvania."

"What is this all about? You said a gentleman left me something? Who from Pennsylvania would even know me?" Angela asked and knew the answer as soon as she said it. "Gregory?"

"Yes. Do you know him?"

"I met him when I did a photojournalism story on that area. We became close. We invited him to our wedding. His son brought him, and I had him walk me down the aisle."

"So you were close to him?"

"As close as two people can become in a short amount of time."

"Angela, I hate to be the one to let you know, but Gregory passed away three weeks ago."

"What?" Angela's heart skipped a beat. She reached for Jeff's hand. She was at a loss for words. Tears formed and rolled down her face. She had trouble breathing. Her body began to tremble.

Jeff put his arm around her to console her. Angela wrapped her arms around him and sobbed uncontrollably for several minutes.

"Angela, I know his death is hard to accept. According to the documents, you meant a lot to him in the short time you knew each other."

"How do you know he felt that way?"

"Let me just say that you meant more to him than most family members. He left you an inheritance."

Angela wiped her last tear and stared at the attorney. "What inheritance? Why me?"

The attorney moved the papers toward Angela. She looked at the top sheet and then leafed through the others

267

until she reached the last one. When she looked at it, she immediately looked from the paper to Jeff, then to the attorney.

"What does this mean?"

"It means, Ms. Angela, that you inherited two million dollars and his estate in Pennsylvania."

"His what? Why? Why did he not leave it to his son?"

"Oh, he left his son enough as well. There is nothing for you to be concerned about there."

Jeff and Angela were speechless.

"And to answer your question of why. The word I received when I asked was because you were kind to Gregory from the moment you met him. Your kindness at that time meant the world to him."

Angela was awestruck. It was just her nature to be kind to people. She smiled and shook her head.

"What are you thinking?" Jeff asked. He knew something was going on in his wife's head.

"Being kind. It is so natural for me to be kind, and now it has brought me two things that have changed my life."

"Two things? How's that?" the attorney asked.

"I was kind to a man in an airport once. He was alone and looked like he needed someone to talk with." She reached over and touched Jeff's leg. "I married him not too long ago. And now an older gentleman, who happened to be sitting alone on a bench, who I thought needed some company, has given me more than anything I could have imagined."

"You have been blessed with a gift, young lady. And you have used it wisely."

"I don't think of it that way. It is simply the way I am."

The attorney smiled. He wished more people were that way. If they were, his work would be so much easier. Dealing with this case gave him hope in mankind again. Kindness. Simple kindness.

Chapter Forty-Six
Decisions

Life never stood still for anyone involved with Bella Rose Estate. The family was growing. Goals were changing. New people were joining the family. Friends were more like family. And the children were growing.

Sara and Randall were proud of Gayle and her life goals. When they first took her into their home as a foster child, they had no idea what to expect. They found a love for her they never expected, and it was easy to decide to adopt her. Little did they know what she would grow up to be. Her desire to be a detective was because of the research the family did. The secrets and the mysteries surrounding them made Sara glad they included her in their work and with her writing. Her influence on her daughter had been positive, even though she sometimes wondered about what they found and if it was a positive or negative thing for the family. Now, she knew it was positive if only to encourage Gayle to be whatever she wanted to become. She and Randall would support her.

Gayle arrived home from school near the end of the school year with information about summer classes, research to do, and an invitation to participate in a two-week training session on detective work. When she talked to her parents about it, they warned her that it would not be a fun summer if she took all of it on. She said she was done having fun. She was grown up and wanted to get involved. After much discussion and working out the details, Gayle was signed up for everything she could manage to do during her summer break. Gayle went to bed that night and dreamed of solving cases. She woke up the next morning eager to finish school to follow her passion.

Angela and Jeff sat at their dining room table with the papers from the attorney in front of them. Jeff had poured them a glass of wine to calm their anxiety.

"What are we going to do with all of this?"

"I have no idea. First, the money, and then to find out Gregory gave us his estate. Do you even know where it is in Pennsylvania?"

"I have an idea. I know where I met him, and he showed me a little bit of the area. We also discussed it after I returned home, but I've never seen it."

"I wonder why he didn't take you there?"

"Maybe because I would not be in town that much longer when I met him. We didn't have time."

"That makes sense. The trouble is we have no idea if the place is a mansion or a cabin in the woods."

"I'd say a cabin in the woods, but how did he have two million dollars to give us?"

"Give to you." Jeff corrected.

"Okay, give it to me. However, we are married, so technically, it is yours too."

"Cool. I'll take mine in small bills."

"Very funny," Angela laughed and took a sip of her wine. "We still need to make plans."

"You're correct. We need to know what we will do with it all."

"First, we must go to Pennsylvania to find the place and see what we have to deal with. We may want to keep it, or we may want to sell it. Donate it, maybe."

"Donate it? What are you talking about? Why would we donate it? And to whom?"

"I don't know, just a thought. We've got the two million dollars to take care of us. Do we really need the property Gregory gave us?"

"It may be worth something. Let's make arrangements to go look at it and investigate a little more about the area."

"Sounds like a good plan to me. We go to the bank first to deal with the money. Then take a week off work, and enjoy a road trip."

A week later, Angela and Jeff drove to Pennsylvania. She had the address and contacted Gregory's son, Anthony, for more details. His son told her he would meet them at the hotel when they arrived.

The ten-hour trip went quickly. They took turns driving and enjoyed the conversation without interruptions. Angela had always loved the road trips for her magazine work, but this trip was different and meant more.

Angela called Anthony after they had arrived at the hotel and freshened up. They agreed to meet at the local diner in the center of town. Angela looked around at the area as Jeff drove. She smiled at the things she remembered and took in a few things she had not noticed. She wondered which property was now hers. Or if it was even visible from the road. If she remembered correctly, the place was surrounded by woods. Her mind drifted to what it would look like, and she wondered what in the world they would do with it.

As the three ate, they discussed plans for the next day. They would meet after breakfast and go to the property. Anthony shared photos of the property. He told them that his father had used the land and house as a vacation home that he let family and friends use whenever it was available.

That night, Angela and Jeff discussed what they would like to do with the place. They could do the same as Gregory had done if they wanted. Or they could even move to Pennsylvania. Angela could work from anywhere. Jeff could easily find work. They fell asleep in each other's arms with decisions on their minds.

Sara looked at the manuscript laying on her desk. She had finished editing the night before. It had taken a few years to write, but she smiled as she looked at the finished product. So many secrets, mysteries, and discoveries lay within the words of the book. Her family history was about to be exposed to the world as soon as she downloaded it for publication. She looked at the book cover she and her siblings had created. She called Heather.

"Hi, sis. How are you?"

"I'm good. What's up?"

"Would you like to join me as I download our family history into a book?"

"I will be right over," Heather said. When she hung up from Sara, she called Andy to join them. He told her Sara had just texted him. He would see her there.

Heather and Andy stood behind Sara as she downloaded their story, which was now in book form, into the publishing program. Their story would be available to the world in a matter of days.

Sara was emotional when she pushed the button to publish the book. Her hand shook as she lifted her finger from the button. Heather and Andy put their hands on Sara's shoulders. It was a memory they would never forget. What had begun as a condition to an inheritance from their mama had become so much more. Sara took a deep breath. A sense of release came over her. Her life had changed over the last several years. Now she wondered if it would change again. Her decision to go public now made her smile. It felt right.

~~~~~~

Gayle sat at her desk in her bedroom, finishing her last writing assignment for school. Sara walked into her room and asked if she could read the report. She smiled as she read it. Her daughter's writing was high quality, and the content was powerful.

"You are an amazing writer, Gayle. I know you will be good in your desired field. Your attention to detail is impressive. I am proud of you."

"Thank you, Mama. I am proud of you too. Not everyone would be willing or able to write about their family. Especially one so full of secrets and mystery."

"The truth needed to be told, and I was the one to tell it."

Gayle smiled at her mama, knowing how right that was.

Sara left her daughter's room and thought about what Gayle had said. Her daughter was proud of her. That made all her hard work worth it. She must be doing something right.

Randall saw her smile as she approached him in the living room. "Why the smile?"

"Oh, nothing. Just happy." Sara wanted to keep that conversation a secret between mother and daughter.

274

Chapter Forty-Seven
Separated

A month into summer vacation from school, Gayle headed away from home for a couple of weeks. Heather and Ben had plans to go on a two-week vacation. Andy and Karen also wanted to take time away. Sara and Randall needed a break. Rachelle and Bob agreed to step in and run the manor for the two weeks everyone would be gone. It was the busy season but easily handled with the two of them. Barbara and Steven always stepped in to help when they could.

It had been quite the beginning to the year. When Sara looked back over all that had happened since the holidays, she had to shake her head. Her book sales ranked high on her list of accomplishments. She had not anticipated such an interest in the Bella Rose Estate. She knew their guests loved it there, but once the story about the history and the family began circulating within the community, she had been in demand.

Sara received phone calls nearly every day at the manor from someone who wanted to know more. She hated to be the bearer of bad news to them, but there was no more. The book was a tell-all book. She wondered if she should have left something out.

She needed a break from all the demands. Randall took time off work so the two could spend time in their vacation home. It was the first time they would be alone there in several years. Ever since they had fostered Gayle, they had included her. This trip would seem empty.

Ben and Heather had decided they needed time away from the manor. The kids were a little older, making travel easier for them. Ben wanted to surprise Heather with their destination but had to tell her what clothes to pack, which gave it away. She smiled when she knew they were going to the beach. She could do with a little sand in her toes. And the boys were old enough to enjoy the sand and the water.

Andy and Karen were taking their family to Pennsylvania. Summer would be busy but beautiful there. The kids were still young, but Karen hoped their experience of the lake would be something the older children would remember.

When Randall pulled out of their driveway and drove down Rose Lane, Sara looked behind her through the side mirror. Randall noticed her strange smile. "Why that look? You seem quiet."

"I just realized it is the first time our family has taken separate vacations since Mama died. We have done everything together since reading her will. She wanted us to be together for the first five years. We went beyond that, but I think she would be pleased. I wonder what she would think now?"

"She'd be proud of each of you. You gave Bella Rose and each other so much these last several years. You have always been there for each other. Most families don't manage that closeness."

"I feel bad for those who can't. This time has been amazing. We have learned so much about one another. And to have the family close so the kids can grow up together. That is special."

"Your family is a rare breed. I will give you that." He laughed.

"Hey! I resemble that remark." Sara laughed with him.

Sara's cell phone rang when they had almost arrived at the vacation home. She saw it was from Gayle and immediately answered.

"Hi, Sweety. What's up?"

"Nothing, I just wanted to call and let you know we have arrived at our destination, and all is going well. I already made friends with a couple of the other kids."

"That is great, Honey. I hope you learn a lot while there, but I also hope they let you have some fun."

"We will. We had fun on the bus trip here. I am sure they won't work us too hard."

"Good. Daddy and I are almost at the vacation house. Stay in touch as much as you can. I won't interrupt your work."

"Okay, Mama. I love you."

"We love you too, Sweety."

Sara hung up and looked at Randall. "Our daughter is so grown up. I'm not sure I'm ready for that."

"You will be fine. It's not like she is moving out. She has more school to complete, and I feel we could not get her to move out if we tried."

"You better never try to make her move." Sara reached over and gently hit his leg.

"Not even on her worst day. She is our daughter."

Thirty minutes later, they arrived at their vacation home. When they walked inside, they felt relaxation overtake them. It would be a well-deserved time away from the hectic way life had been for them for the last six months.

~~~~~~

Ben and Heather packed their car and loaded their children into their car seats. It was the first family trip they had taken since their boys had been born. They always felt the kids were too small to take them anywhere. Once they were on the road, it seemed like a normal thing to do.

"Why have we put this off for so long?" Heather asked about an hour into their trip.

"I don't know. So far, it has been an easy trip. I expected the boys to act up more."

"Don't jinx us," Heather said. She looked into the seat behind them and saw the boys asleep. She shook her head as she turned to face the front. "I hope they stay asleep for most of the trip. Although then they may stay awake all night."

"We will get them walking on the beach for a while and playing some once we get there. They will sleep."

"All that fresh air should do it for them. And for me."

Ben smiled as he anticipated a good vacation away. No matter what happens, being away from the manor felt good. And if he was being honest, it felt good to be away from the family. He loved being a part of them, but it wasn't always easy.

"What are you thinking about? You look far away." Heather asked.

"Thinking how good it feels to get away."

"I agree. Both from the manor and from the family."

"You too? I was afraid you would take it wrong if I said it felt good to be away from your family."

"Are you kidding? When was the last time we were away from all of them?"

"Before your Mama died."

"I know. Far too long. We had a good life on our own before that. I'm not saying it has been bad with the changes Mama required from us, but a lot has happened and kept us far too busy."

"I never knew a family could have so many secrets and mysteries."

"Neither did I. Never dreamed our family was anything but normal."

"I would not go that far. I knew your family was different when I met you, but it did become a lot to grasp."

"I am so glad Sara took it upon herself to put it together and write her book. We questioned letting the public know about our history, but I think it will benefit us."

"It already has increased the guest registrations."

"I know. Which makes me happy to get away now. Another month and we will be so busy we won't be able to leave."

"Don't remind me. Let us enjoy this time away and not discuss your family."

"Deal. We will concentrate on our little family."

Several hours later, Ben pulled into the parking lot of the hotel they had reserved. Stepping out of the car and feeling the salty air made them both smile. They both opened the back doors and lifted their kids from their seats.

~~~~~~

Andy and Karen sighed as they pulled away from Bella Rose. Karen had not been away in a while. Andy had been away on his own. This was different. It felt good to be headed to Pennsylvania again. Karen deserved to see her hometown. Andy missed the lake. Their children were old enough to enjoy the lake and to remember it when they were older. Andy had reserved a lakefront Airbnb.

As they neared the lake, Karen began to smile more. She had not realized how much she missed the area. She had fallen in love with the mountains of Tennessee, but there was something about Lake Wallenpaupack that held her heart.

Andy noticed her smile. "Almost there, Babe. I know you have missed this area. It is why I decided this is where we needed to spend our vacation."

"Thank you. I didn't realize how much I missed it until now. Having Larry and Grace live near us helped, and I thought that was enough. I guess it isn't."

"We will try to rejuvenate you while we are here. I hope you know the people and places you want to visit while we are here. I know most of your friends will love to meet the kids."

"I know. They have only seen the photos I've shared on social media."

"Our first stop will be the marina and resort. Larry asked me to stop and see how things were going."

"Of course. I hope the new owners are taking care of it and maybe even making improvements."

Andy turned left and drove along the lake for a while. When Karen saw the marina, she opened her window to get a better look. She was impressed. People were everywhere. The parking lot was full. Then she noticed a new building. She looked closer and saw that it was a new restaurant.

"Wow, they have a new restaurant! We may need to eat there one night."

"We can eat there tonight if you want."

"Let's see what the resort looks like first. Then, we can return after getting settled into our Airbnb."

Andy drove the few extra miles until reaching the resort. He pulled into the paved parking lot and stopped the car. Karen looked around before opening her car door to get out and go to the gift shop.

"Can't resist the gift shop, can you?"

"No, you know me well. It holds amazing memories. Even the ring I stole and what that led to is a good memory."

They walked inside and were met by the owner. Karen smiled as she hugged Renee. "You are still here?"

"I am the new owner. I bought it about six months ago."

"Good for you. It all looks amazing." Karen said. She was impressed with the changes in the resort and the marina. Larry would be happy.

Andy watched his wife wander around the store, talking with Renee. Her smile was all he needed to see to know he had done the right thing for her.

Getting her separated from his family was the answer to his concern. He wondered if the rest of his family felt the same about the separate vacation destinations. He hoped so.

Chapter Forty-Eight
A Small World

Angela and Jeff met with Anthony on the second day. After a good night's sleep from the long trip, they felt refreshed and ready to address reality. Whatever reality was. To be given such a gift from a man they barely knew still had not sunk in. They had seen the photos of what was now theirs. Now it was time to physically face it.

Anthony met them at their hotel to lead them to his late father's property. He had wanted to own it all his life and now faced his father giving it to a complete stranger. He would do his best not to show his resentment.

Anthony stopped at the gate to the property. He had given Angela the code to the gate the night before, but instead of opening it and driving through, he motioned for them to get out of their car so he could show them other things of importance hidden at the entrance. His father had been a mysterious man and enjoyed things other people never noticed.

"I need to show you a few things here that only those close to Dad know about. Considering he kept to himself much of the time, that is very few people."

"You gave us the code to open the gate; what more is there?"

"There is a switch to turn the lights to the entrance on or off. There is also a plug to hook up holiday lights if you wish to decorate the area. There is a cord in this hidden metal box to connect lights or other electrical items." Anthony moved the limbs of the bush aside to reveal a camouflaged metal box that matched the shrubs.

"Does he have a lot of things like this on his property?" Jeff asked as he looked at Angela, wondering what they were getting themselves into.

"First, it is your property now, not his. But yes. There are numerous secrets to this place."

Angela shook her head and laughed. "Oh boy. I guess we are in for a treat."

"A treat or a lot of tricks. Dad liked to play games and create magical ways of living."

"Interesting, I think," Jeff said as they returned to their cars.

While they drove up the driveway to the house, Angela noticed a smaller structure on the right side of the driveway. She wondered what its purpose was, yet was almost afraid to ask. She knew she would find out sooner or later.

The photos did not do the home justice. Anthony parked his car on the right side of the house, allowing Jeff to park in front of the two-car garage. Angela's eyes opened wider as she opened her car door and stood up. She could not move. The house was huge.

Anthony walked over to them and smiled. "A little more than you expected?" He looked from them to the house as he spoke.

"A lot more than I expected. This is beautiful!" Angela joined her husband, who had walked to the front of their car while looking up at the mansion.

"What are we going to do with this?" Jeff asked as they walked up the walkway to the front door.

"I have no idea. It's too big for just the two of us. Plus, I don't want to move again."

"Are you sure? Look at this place!" Jeff tried to take it all in. He turned to face away from the house to see the vast property. There was more than he could have imagined. He was beginning to think they could live there. Until he looked at his wife. She looked worried. "What's wrong?"

"I can't. I can't grasp that Gregory just gave us this." Her emotions held her immovable.

"Believe it. After Dad met you, he contacted his attorney as soon as you left. The attorney contacted me to verify my father had not lost his mind." Anthony laughed. "I assured him that my father knew what he was doing. Now, come on in and explore your home."

The three of them entered the home. After the initial surprise at what the outside looked like, they were more shocked at the inside. Twelve-foot ceilings, a chandelier that hung from the ceiling at the top of the staircase, a fireplace with a solid mahogany mantel, and brown leather furniture placed facing the fireplace. Real wooden floors welcomed them from the moment they walked inside. Angela and Jeff were speechless while taking in the front room. There was so much more to explore.

They followed Anthony into the kitchen. Again they were impressed. The stainless steel appliances looked new, like the kitchen had been remodeled. Angela looked around and noticed the dining room to the right of the kitchen.

"When was this house remodeled? It almost looks brand new."

"Dad had it completely remodeled two years ago. He knew he probably would not be around much longer and wanted it to be the best for whomever he gave it to."

"Did you know he may give it to someone other than you?"

"Oh, yes. This is his second home. I inherited his first home and that property."

"Is that far from here?"

"No. It is about ten miles from here. Also, on the lake."

"If his main house was on the lake, why did he have a second one here?"

"He rented this one out most of the time. It was his second income for most of his life. In his later years, he let people stay for free."

"How could he do that?"

"After renting it for so long, it was paid for many years ago. He saved the rent money after it was paid for and one day decided to offer it to people who needed to get away but could not afford it."

"Talk about kindness. Gregory was a leader in that blessing."

"Yes, he was. Everyone who knew him loved and admired him."

After the trio finished walking through the house and around the property, they walked to their cars. Angela told Anthony they would need to discuss their options before making a final decision. He told them he totally understood.

As Jeff drove away, he looked over at his wife. "What are you contemplating? I can see your wheels turning."

"You know me well. I think I want to do the same thing he did. Let people who need to get away stay there for free or a low fee for a week or two."

"I agree. Unless you want to move here."

"No. And after seeing that place, our place, I don't think I could live there. It is too much for me to handle."

"How do you want to handle the rentals? Make it an Airbnb or a full-blown bed and breakfast?"

"I am thinking of an Airbnb. Rent out the whole place. We don't need to be here. We can hire someone local to manage it for us. Once in a while, we can make the trip and stay here when it is empty and to check on everything."

"I think that is a good plan. We can discuss it more over dinner. Where is a good place to eat around here?"

"We can go to the Dam Diner."

"What?" Jeff laughed.

"The Dam Diner. It makes people laugh, but it's a great place to eat. And before you ask me where it is, it is near the dam on the lake."

"Very funny. That makes sense. Let's go." Jeff turned left towards town, knowing the dam was on the way.

~~~~~~

Karen and Andy loaded the kids into the car and headed out to eat. They had not been to the local diner in so long. Karen wondered if the same people owned it. They would soon find out. Andy parked the car and helped his wife get the children from the back seat. As they entered the diner, Karen heard her name being called. She looked towards the reservation desk expecting to see her old friend she grew up with. Instead, she saw Angela.

"What are you doing here?" She walked over to where Jeff and Angela were sitting.

"Us? Why are you here?"

"I grew up in this area. It is where Andy and I met."

"I never realized that. I remember hearing something about you coming from Pennsylvania, but I never knew exactly what area. This area is beautiful. You had some childhood." Jeff said.

"Some would say that. I like it here and miss it sometimes. What are you doing here?" Karen repeated her question.

"We just inherited a piece of property."

"You what? Wow. What property? From who? Oh, never mind. It's none of my business. Sorry. I tend to be a little noisy from time to time. And this being my old stomping grounds, I am just curious."

"It's ok. We are not keeping it secret. Not now, anyway. We kept it quiet until we arrived and saw the place. Do you remember Gregory? The gentleman who walked me down the aisle at our wedding? That is who gave it to us."

"Yes, I do. I didn't realize he lived here. So many people live around the lake it is hard to know everyone, even when I grew up here."

"We came to see the house and land and talk with Anthony about it."

"It's a beautiful area. You will love it here."

"Oh, we are not planning to move. We are thinking of making it into an Airbnb."

"That would be great here on the lake." Karen turned as Andy motioned her to their table. "We need to get together while you are here. I will call you later. Enjoy your dinner."

"Thanks. Yes, call me later." Angela said as Karen walked away.

"Do you believe she doesn't know who Gregory is?"

"Sure, why?"

"I got the impression she knows something. Maybe something about the family or the property."

"Well, she is going to call me later. We can get together and talk with her before we talk to Anthony again."

"I think that would be a good idea."

They finished eating and stopped to say goodbye to Andy and Karen before they left. Karen promised to call them later that evening.

Chapter Forty-Nine
Truth Revealed

Karen and Andy put Ryan, River, and Ravyn to bed in the Airbnb. They listened for several minutes until the kids fell asleep. It didn't take them long due to how active they were all day. The kids loved spending time in the water. Karen loved seeing some of her old friends again.

Andy knew Karen had things on her mind. She had changed her attitude after talking with Angela and Jeff at the diner.

"What's on your mind, Babe? You've been quieter since dinner."

"I need to tell them about Gregory. He has always painted a positive picture of himself and what he has when talking to strangers."

"He seemed nice when I talked to him at their wedding. Angela liked him so much she had him walk her down the aisle."

"That's just it. He seemed nice to everyone."

"Then what is it about him that has you concerned?"

"His property. The way he acquired that huge place. And then there is the type of people he always invited to stay there. They were not the best people in the world."

"So tell me about him. What do you know?"

"I need to tell Angela before she makes a major mistake."

"You said you would call her this evening. Call her and see if they want to come over for a drink. We can talk and enjoy the evening together."

"You're the best." Karen already had her phone in her hand, calling Angela.

"Hello, Karen."

"Hi. Andy had a great idea. Would you and Jeff like to come to our Airbnb for drinks? I need to talk with you about Gregory, too."

"You had mentioned that. Yes, Jeff and I will be over in a few minutes."

"We'll be waiting."

Andy opened the door when Angela and Jeff arrived. After pouring glasses of wine for everyone, they sat in the living room.

"It is nice of you to invite us over. We love the area and can only imagine how wonderful it was to grow up here." Jeff said.

"It was a great place to grow up. I miss it once in a while." Karen looked at Andy and smiled. "But, not enough to move back."

"What do you have to tell us about Gregory? We need to give Anthony an answer sometime tomorrow about what we want to do with the house and property."

"That is why I wanted to talk to you tonight. There are things about him and his business dealings that you need to know about before you decide what to do. Personally, I'd sell it. The decision is up to you after I tell you what I know."

Angela sat up straight. Something about the way Karen was talking made her more curious. Jeff looked at Andy, who just shrugged his shoulders. Karen had not told her husband anything yet.

"Let me begin by saying I have known Gregory and Anthony long enough to know the truth about the family. As you recall, they did not speak with me at your wedding. I do not think it was because they did not know who I was. I think it was because they did not want to raise any suspicions."

"What would be suspicious about you and them? You are both from the lake region."

"Yes, we are. Gregory, or even Anthony, might have thought I would cause trouble for him by telling you about him. I would never do that to you. Not at that time. You had chosen him to walk you down the aisle. You knew the good side of him. It is the only side he shows. His truth is secret."

Angela sat at full attention. What could be so bad about him? What was it about the property? She waited for more details.

"No one knew Gregory when he first arrived at the lake. He lived in an apartment for a long time. No one seemed to pay attention to him. That was until he bought that property. The house had been for sale for years. It stood vacant for as long as I could remember. The community was surprised when this stranger bought it."

"Why was it so odd? People buy property all the time. And property on the lake should be quick to sell."

"Not this one. The price was higher than other similar places. Some people spread the rumor that it was haunted."

"Is it haunted?"

"No. Not that we know of. The secret is that Gregory bought it with drug money."

"Drug money? How so?" Angela asked. This news could mean trouble.

"Gregory was from New York. You saw his appearance and how he dressed when you met him. That is how he was the whole time we knew him. He looked poor and homeless."

"Yes, he did. That was what drew me to him. I wanted to see if I could help him. He looked so downtrodden. When I spoke with him, he was full of love and compassion, and his stories touched me." Angela felt sick for being so gullible to a stranger.

"That is how he was with everyone. When he bought the property, and it was discovered that he paid cash for it, it raised many red flags in the area."

"Why wasn't he arrested for something?"

"The investigation led the police nowhere. The police could not connect the dots to make a case against him."

"Maybe because his drug dealings were false?"

"No, it was true."

"How do you know?"

"After he bought it, he remodeled it and turned it into a type of Airbnb before it was popular. The people who stayed there came from Gregory's home area in New York. When the suspicions came to light, more surveillance was placed to watch the house and Gregory's involvement with his tenants. It was through one of them that the police were led to suspect the drug traffic."

"But they didn't arrest Gregory for anything?"

"No. Once he found out they were on his tail, he shut down everything. He closed the house for remodeling. His acquaintances stopped coming to town. And he apparently disposed of all evidence. He covered his tracks so well that the investigation was halted. The townspeople eventually forgot about it as they watched the remodeling, and Gregory changed his ways."

"So, is that the whole story of the house and property? That is nothing to be concerned about, in my opinion," Jeff said and shrugged his shoulders. He expected a mysterious death or stories of ghosts. Something more disheartening.

"I don't see anything wrong with it either. Unless there are more drugs hidden someplace in the house. Then we might have a problem."

"Nothing was ever found. I guess I just wanted you to know a little of his background story that he never shared with people. To the stranger, he was a poor man living alone. He rarely spoke of Anthony or any family. We assumed he was a widower since Anthony never spoke of his mother. The two of them kept to themselves most of the time."

"I got that from him. To me, he was a loner. He didn't seem to have a lot of friends. You are right. He never spoke of any family except Anthony to us."

"I had forgotten about him until seeing him at your wedding. I never said anything at the time because I didn't want to ruin your wedding."

"I appreciate that. I will always admire Gregory. Even hearing what you say about him. He was a kind soul. In my eyes, anyway," Angela smiled. Nothing would change her opinion of Gregory.

"Okay. I wanted you to know the truth about the property and Gregory before you decide what to do with it."

"I think I know what I want to do with it. Jeff and I will need to discuss it, but I know what I want."

Jeff looked at his wife. They may be newlyweds, but he shook his head, knowing what she would discuss later.

~~~~~~

"I want to keep it," Angela told Jeff later that night.

"I knew you would. It was that story that clinched the decision, wasn't it?"

"You know me well." Angela nodded. "Before that story, I was thinking of selling it. With that history behind the estate, we have an amazing story to tell."

"Ever the journalist." Jeff took his wife in his arms. "I love you, Babe. We will keep it. Rent it out or something."

"No."

"No? No, what? You don't want to rent it out? A BnB?"

"Nope." Angela looked into Jeff's eyes.

"You're joking. You want to move here, don't you? We just bought a place in Tennessee. Now you want to move to Pennsylvania?"

"Not permanently. We need to retain the place in Tennessee. We will move back there after a while. We can rent it out for now. I want to investigate the history of this estate and see what we discover."

"We?"

"Yes, we. I can't do this without your help. I can do the writing, but I need your help doing the digging. Both figuratively and physically."

"Physically? We're going to dig into the ground?"

"No, we will dig in the basement AND the ground. Gregory hid the drugs somewhere here. The fact that no one found them does not mean they are not here."

"You have got to be kidding," Jeff looked at the pleading eyes of his other half. He knew she was not kidding. She believed there were drugs on the estate they now owned. "What happens if or when we find them?"

"By that time, I will have a story written about Gregory and this place. And some about where he grew up in New York. His life has become very interesting. My subscribers will be fascinated."

"Always working, aren't you?"

"I can't help it. This was dumped in our laps. I cannot stand by and let it fall away with the wind."

"We will call Anthony in the morning and tell him our plans. He will be thrilled."

"I hear your sarcasm."

"You sense the same thing. I am sure Anthony was hoping we would sell it. He knows the truth about his father. He knows this place has secrets and may know where those secrets are. The fact that his father didn't give it to him when he died speaks volumes."

"Anthony was hoping to inherit this instead of the other place. His enthusiasm about the way his father dealt with his wealth is fake. He is just glad to have something. If we put it up for sale, he may put an offer on it with the money his father gave him. If we keep it, all he has is that other place and the money his father gave him. Which, according to him, is less than he gave us. I felt sorry for him at first.

Now, I am not so sure. Maybe Gregory knew how his son would be if he owned this. Gregory hoped the truth would stay hidden."

"If Gregory wished for it to remain hidden, shouldn't we honor his wishes and not attempt to find something that may or may not be there?"

"Probably." Angela hung her head in silence. A moment later, she lifted her head and smiled. She looked at Jeff, who shook his head. "Right! Like that is going to happen with me owning it. You know me. I want to find the treasure."

"Maybe that is it. A treasure instead of drugs."

"That would be something. All the more reason to investigate. Prove one way or the other what Gregory was all about."

"Okay. You have convinced me. We will move here. Temporarily. Only temporarily."

"Agreed." Angela hugged her husband. Life was getting interesting again.

Chapter Fifty
Adjustments

Sara walked along the trail below Bella Rose Manor. When she and her family were away at the vacation home, they had gone for short hikes in the surrounding woods. She realized while away that she needed to find a new purpose in her life.

School was back in session, and Gayle was busy with her schoolwork. Sara's book about the family and Bella Rose was selling well in the stores in town. Andy had worked with her to publish it online, and those sales were also starting to come in. She had help running the manor and was not needed there as often. She found herself at a loss for what she was to be doing.

Sara stopped at the bridge on the trail and leaned out, looking at the mountain view. She smiled. Life had been good to her over the last several years. Her decision after her divorce from her first husband to return home and help her folks had been a good one. She felt stuck with the work when they died, but it became a blessing for her and her siblings. Life was good. Her life was, what was it? She felt lost.

Later that day, she sat at the desk of the manor. Heather knocked on the door and walked in. It had long since been established that people just walked into her office without her saying anything. When Heather sat down on the easy chair and didn't say anything, Sara knew something was wrong.

"What is it, Sis? Why the long face? The boys alright?"

"Yes, the boys are alright. Before you ask, Ben is fine too."

"So what is it?"

"I'm not sure. I just feel empty." She slumped in the chair as she spoke. "While we were on vacation at the beach, I realized something. I realized I am getting old."

Sara laughed. "Old? You? Heather, you are not getting old. Well, technically, you are getting older, but you are far from what is considered old. What makes you say that?" Sara asked and leaned onto her elbows on her desk. She was not about to admit she had the same feelings.

"The boys are already in school, work is going great here, but I feel something is missing. I have free time that I didn't have before, and I am unsure what to do with it."

Sara smiled. "Enjoy it. Take a breath and enjoy the peace and the time."

"That's just it. I don't know how. I have had so much going on in my life since Mama died that now I feel a change coming on that I am not ready for. I don't know what it is, but something is about to happen."

"Maybe you are going through the change."

"Don't say that. I am not That old!" Heather stood up laughing. "I think something else is going on."

"Okay. What do you think it is?"

"Well," Heather faced away from her sister as she spoke almost in a whisper. "I took a test this morning,"

"A test? What kind of a test? One of those aptitude things on the internet? Why would you take one of those?"

"No, not one of those. I took a test. Three of them, to be exact. And they all said the same thing."

"Okay. It must not have been what you expected. What was the test, and why do the results make you feel old?"

"Because I thought I was done. I thought I was moving on. Now I am going to be starting over. And I am not sure I am ready to handle it again."

"Heather, what are you talking about? Again?" Sara stood up when she realized what her younger sister was saying. She walked to Heather and turned her around. She smiled when she saw the look on her sister's face. It was far from sad.

Heather hugged her sister, and the two started laughing and dancing around. "Yes, I am pregnant again!"

"That is wonderful news! I am so excited! That is just what this family needs, a new member to love! Oh, sis. I am thrilled!"

"So am I. I have not told Ben yet. He was already out the door this morning when I took the tests. He knows something is up because of how I have been acting since our vacation, but I just shrugged off my mood as just the way I get sometimes."

"He will be as thrilled as you are." Sara's spirits were lifted from her earlier reflection on her life. That was what she was thinking about. Something new needed to happen. She thought it would be about her, but maybe her thoughts were about the family. They had gotten closer than ever this past year. She smiled. A new baby in the family, how amazing.

"I hope so. We talked while on vacation that now, with the boys in school during the day, it would give me more time to expand the business. Funny when you think about it. I guess I am expanding." She rubbed her belly. She was not showing yet, but she loved the idea that a new life was growing inside, and sometime in the spring, a new person would join their family. Secretly she hoped it would be a girl.

~~~~~~

Andy and Karen were busy getting the kids ready for the day at home. The twins had started preschool. Ravyn was into her terrible threes. Karen laughed when she thought about it. Her daughter had been such a sweet happy infant. She even sailed beautifully through the terrible twos. Then she turned three. Now she was making up for her sweetness. Karen did not need to wonder why. She knew. Ravyn missed her siblings while they were in preschool and did not know how to act when they were not around.

"Do you think you could help me at the manor later today? I am trying out new recipes and could use your help."

"Sure. What made you want to try new recipes?"

"I realized I was stuck in a rut of always making the same thing for our guests. They deserve something fresh and new."

"Considering most of our guests have been first-time guests." Karen began.

"That's just it. They are now more repeat guests than new ones. The ones returning year after year need something new to come here and experience."

"I like how you said that. Food to you has never been something you just make and eat. Food to you is something to experience. From the time you look at a recipe or see something made, to the process of you making it, to watching the guests and even family eat it. To you, it is an experience. Something to take in with all of our senses. You are an amazing chef. Of course, I will come to help you." Karen wrapped her arms around her husband. He had spoiled her since the day they met at the lake. It was her turn to spoil him.

~~~~~~

Sara called Rachelle and told her that she would be away from the office for a few hours. Rachelle said she would listen for the phone and anyone coming in while she cleaned the guest rooms.

Sara told Randall that she would be back as soon as possible. She'd stop and pick up something for dinner if she ran late. He didn't question where she was going or why, although he knew something was on her mind.

298

Sara drove to town, and after parking in her favorite spot by the park, she walked across the street into the café. There she was met by Terri, who happened to be the person she was looking for.

"Good afternoon, Sara. How are you? I'm not used to seeing you here at this time of day. Is Randall joining you for lunch?"

"No, it is just me today, and I'm not here to eat. I need to talk to you about something. Do you have a few minutes?"

"Of course. What's up?" Terri led them to a back table away from her other patrons. She motioned to her waitress that she was taking a break.

"I spoke with Heather this morning. And I noticed something about Andy the other day that has me thinking."

"Okay, what is on your mind?" Terri loved when Sara had ideas.

"I would like to host a party here for my family. I know it sounds odd with the facilities we have at Bella Rose, but this needs to be when my family does not have to lift a finger to put together a celebration."

"A celebration? What are we celebrating?"

"For now, we are celebrating a new beginning. I think we all felt something changing while we were away on our vacations this summer. Something is new about each of us. And I want to make this time special. I want my siblings to know that starting something new is good and that I support them in whatever it is."

"What is new about everyone? Do you have a theme in mind?"

"Not sure yet. I will get back to you on that. I was wondering when you had an opening or a good suggestion for when to have this party."

"Let me check the calendar." Terri rose from her chair to go to the office.

Sara waited for Terri to return and heard the back door to the lounge open. She turned and saw Steven walking in.

"Hi, Sara. How are you?" Steven said when he saw her.

"Hi, Steven. I'm well. How are you?"

"I'm good. Came in a little early to get ready for a special night here."

"Oh? What's going on? I may need to come back," she smiled. She didn't come to the lounge very often, but it was a nice break once in a while.

"A private party coming in. You are welcome to join us if you want. It's not exclusive. Just need to set up a section for the group."

"I will talk to Randall and see if he wants to come to enjoy the music tonight."

Terri returned as Steven tested the sound system for the music and karaoke later.

"Love the music Steven and Adam play here. That addition to the café has been a blessing."

"We're not here very often, but we enjoy it. My guests talk about it all the time. They love the local entertainment."

Terri opened her calendar to the current month. "I have an open Saturday night in three weeks. Would that work for you?"

Sara looked at the date and thought about other things that were coming up. She nodded her head. "That will be perfect. It will give me just enough time to invite the group of people I want and for them not to forget about it." They both laughed.

"It's amazing how fast people forget things, isn't it? I write things down so I don't forget. I learned not to rely on my brain for such things long ago."

Sara stood to leave, but Terri asked her to stay for a few more minutes. She had something she wanted to ask.

Sara sat back down. It was rare that Terri asked her anything.

"Adam and I are thinking of taking on another foster child. What do you think? Should we?"

Sara smiled. "Any time you want a foster child, just ask Barbara. I know she tries to limit how many children go to one family, but if you want more, that is amazing. Have you thought about adopting Makenna?"

"We have, but her parents will hopefully turn their lives around and be able to take her back. She needs to be with her biological family if at all possible. We have talked to Barbara about that. She keeps track of what her parents are doing and how they are improving their lives so they can have her back. I will miss her when she is gone, but know it is for the best."

"Being a foster parent is amazing. Randall and I were blessed to be able to adopt Gayle. I can not imagine my life without her."

"I know what you mean. We have fallen in love with Makenna, even though she will leave our home someday."

"Easy to do with some of the children. I hope Barbara can help you. She is always searching for the best matches."

"Thanks. I will let you know what happens.

Sara left shortly after talking more with Terri. She headed home with a new idea of what she wanted to do with her life now that she had more time.

Randall noticed a difference in his wife when he arrived home from work. He hugged her and gave her a kiss. He had learned a long time ago to let her tell him what was on her mind without him asking. She needed time to process things first. He felt this time, it would take a little longer to process. He smiled as he turned to walk away.

"What is that smile about?" Sara asked. She knew the difference in his smiles, and this one was secretive.

"Not a thing. I know you will tell me about whatever is on your mind when ready."

"I get the sense that you have something on your mind too."

"In due time, my dear. In due time."

Sara shook her head. Secrets. They never end.

Chapter Fifty-One
Escape

It seemed life was changing for everyone. Sara noticed the different facial expressions on her siblings, the spouses, and the children. She did not know if the seasons were changing for them or if every person she knew had something new they were doing or thinking about doing. Would anyone be willing to share? Or should she let sleeping dogs lie? She watched them for over a week. And she paid attention to her own behavior. She felt the need for another family meeting. A sense of growth. Maybe that was it.

Gayle bounced into the room and stopped when she noticed her parents' expressions and quietness. Something was going on, and she feared the worse.

"Hey, you two. Why such faces?"

Sara blinked and looked at Gayle. "Nothing to worry about if that is what you think. We are just discussing our future."

"Your future? Don't rush that away. Take your time. I want the two of you around for a very long time."

"Oh, we plan to be. We are just deciding on our next adventure."

"Okay. If you say so. Remember that if it is these next two years, you can cut it back to one year."

"What are you talking about? Talk about us looking suspicious. What are you trying to tell us? You are NOT quitting school. I worked hard to get you where you are now."

"Oh, I would never quit school. I have too many goals. No, today I talked with the guidance counselor. I am going to take both junior and senior classes this year."

"How can you manage that?" Sara asked with her full attention focused on her daughter.

"I only need a few classes that are senior level in addition to my junior year classes. I talked to my guidance counselor, and she said I could take those during my free periods and graduate this year instead of next." Gayle was beaming with excitement. All she needed now was her parent's permission.

"That is amazing!" Sara and Randall said at the same time.

"I am so proud of you," Sara added.

"Thank you. All I need is your signature giving approval."

"We will gladly sign it as long as you believe you can. Will it still give you time to work with Barbara in the foster care system?"

"I can work with her in my spare time."

Sara laughed. Gayle may not be her biological daughter, but she certainly was her daughter. They both were hard workers.

"I need both of your signatures. Seems some kids were only getting one, which was causing issues." Gayle hesitated. "Which makes me wonder, what do they do if a student only has one parent at home? I guess I understand their policy, but it needs some flexibility."

Randall shook his head. "Where did we ever get such a smart and caring daughter?"

Sara looked at her husband and smiled. "She picked us. We took her on a trial basis; she made it so that we had no choice, and I'm glad she did." Sara hugged Gayle. It had been a wise decision in all aspects.

After Gayle left the room, Sara talked with Randall about wanting a family meeting. He agreed it was time for one. And admitted that he sensed something major was about to happen, although he could not explain it.

Sara called Heather that evening and told her sister she wanted to schedule a family meeting. Heather agreed it was time to meet and discuss what was new with them again. Once they set a date, Sara called Andy to let him know. Andy also agreed and asked if it was just for the three of them, or also for their spouses. Sara said spouses were included this time.

Three days later, the three couples gathered in the manor's kitchen around the island. The tradition would never end for them. It had been a symbol of their togetherness while being separated from the rest of the world. An island unto themselves.

Sara began telling her family she felt lost since her book was published and selling well. She no longer felt a purpose in her life. She was going to find something to do with her life, but only with their consent.

Heather nodded her head in support of her sister. "You deserve whatever happiness you find." She addressed her sister. Then she added, "I think part of what you are saying is that we have been under the bind of our mama even after the time limit she set. I know we discussed this a while ago and agreed to stay as we were as a family and as the owners of Bella Rose. Since then, we have each grown more. Our families have grown. The kids are mostly all in school, which has freed up some of my time. This has given me time to dwell on what is next for me and us." She glanced at Ben."

The room was quiet for only a moment before Andy spoke. "I hear both of you. Karen and I talked the other day about changes we want to make. We discussed working together on new recipes and food for the manor's guests. And about adding a brunch menu either on Saturday or Sunday."

"I suggest Saturday since many of our guests return home on Sunday, and the new ones arrive in the early evening."

"That sounds like a good plan for the two of you. I am proud of you, Andy. You stuck it out, as they say, for longer than you were requested. I honestly thought you would move on when the five years were up."

"I thought I would too. But finding Karen and then the family made it easier to stay and start a new life. I no longer have the need to escape in solitude as often. I still get that wandering urge, but I have learned to postpone it until it makes sense to make a journey on my own for a little while. Having Karen by my side the other fifty weeks a year helps me keep a balance in my life that I never had." He air-kissed his wife, who smiled.

Karen stood when Andy took a moment to catch his breath. "If any of you have other things you want to do in your life, I can speak from experience that you need to follow your dream. I was stuck in my rut at my resort. I thought it was the only life for me. It had been for my parents. Then, Andy arrived and changed my life. I will tell you that if you do not follow your dream, you will regret it later."

"But what if we don't have a dream?"

"We all have dreams." You may not realize them since you are and have been so busy with life that you lost how to live."

The room grew silent again. They each were soaking in Karen's last sentence.

"Too busy with life to enjoy living," Sara said just above a whisper. "You are so right. When Mama died, we went from living to a life we had to live."

Randall looked at his wife. Soaking in the repeated phrase, he realized he was doing the same thing with his work. Work had become life.

"Maybe it is time for a major change for all of us?" Ben asked.

"Maybe. But are we willing? Are we able?"

306

"Sis, have you forgotten our inheritances? Of course, we are able. None of us need to work. We all do it because we love it and want to keep the manor running and in the family. Its history almost demanded that it be that way."

"No, its history showed that it had been closed a few times yet survived years later."

"But, it stayed in the family all those years."

"True. Except for when Rose almost sold it before returning to her senses."

Randall noticed Sara's concerned expression. "What is bothering you, Dear?"

"I am wondering if we are all thinking the same thing, but one, are afraid to say it, and two, realizing what it could mean to our family bond."

"Our family bond is stronger than ever. Nothing could break what we have welded together over these past years."

Sara stood up to speak. What she was about to say could alter life as they knew it.

"Okay. I will say it." She hesitated as she looked at everyone's facial expressions. She reached for Randall's hand for emotional support. After she felt his hand squeeze hers, she took a deep breath. One final look around, then a look at the ceiling. An attempt for God's guidance in what she was about to announce.

"It's time to sell Bella Rose."

Silence.

Tears fell from her face. A glance at Heather. A look at Andy. Her two siblings stood and walked to either side of her. They joined in a family hug as tears fell from everyone. Jointly they all knew that Sara spoke the truth. It was time to escape the rule of Mama.

Chapter Fifty-Two
Transition

The siblings had cried and held each other for a while after Sara's proclamation to sell Bella Rose. It was something they had all felt. They had discussed it a few years earlier. This time, it was a more serious decision. This time they were all in agreement that it was time to change their lives. Time to control their lives instead of life and the business controlling them. Karen had said it best. Don't be so busy in life that you forget to live.

At the end of their family meeting, they had agreed to give their decision a week's thought before meeting again to discuss it. Sara told them to go home, discuss it with each other and come up with as many pros and cons as possible. When they reconvened, they would make a decision one way or the other.

Randall thought he knew which way his wife thought about the estate. She had been hinting at the need for change for a while. He had even looked at new homes in case they needed to move. He knew that if the family sold the estate, that would most likely include all of their homes. He had not kept his place after they married. They did have their vacation home, but that was too far away for him to commute back and forth to work.

Sara had been quiet for a couple of days. She was not ready to have a discussion about the future. Not even with Randall. She understood his need to be included in her decision but needed to internalize the process to develop the best argument. She kept wavering over what would be best for the family.

It was three nights after the family meeting before she told Randall they needed to talk. He smiled when she worded it that way. He often associated that phrase with a couple having a difficult time in their marriage. He was confident his marriage was secure.

After dinner, Gayle went to her room to work on her homework. She knew her parents needed to have a serious discussion about something. She had noticed how quiet her mama had been. When she closed her bedroom door, she had the horrible thought that her parents may be separating. She had heard about how that happened with many of her friends. She occupied her mind with her schoolwork, so she did not have to think about what might be happening in her family. They would tell her about it when it was time for her to know. They never kept secrets from her. At least not that she knew.

Randall poured glasses of wine for Sara and himself before they sat down to talk. He would support the love of his life in her decision.

"Thank you for giving me time to think things through these last couple of days. You know me so well. This situation is an important one for all of us."

"Giving you time has always been what I do best. I waited several years for you, remember?"

Sara laughed. That he had. "Yes, I know." She took a sip of her wine.

"After tossing all the pros and cons around in my head, writing them down on paper, and wondering what Mama and Daddy would honestly want us to do, I have decided it is time for changes. I am not ready to move or sell our family legacy to anyone else. I think we need to find a management company to take care of everything. Once I talk with Heather and Andy, I will see how much they want to stay involved. I know Andy and Karen were talking about making new foods and adding brunch on Saturdays. That was before the idea of selling it. Heather has her event business, but she can still do that if she wants. She can work that business from anywhere and use the reception hall and chapel."

"You have given it a lot of thought. I'm proud of you. If you want my opinion, I can share."

"Yes, please."

"I have been looking for a new home for us if you wanted to sell and move away."

"Really?"

"I wanted to be prepared. I am happy you want to stay here."

"This has been my home most of my life. I lived away from it for several years, but this is where I belong. Mama knew what she was doing."

Randall reached over and kissed his wife. "I agree. He knew that family belonged together if at all possible."

~~~~~~

Thanks to Andy arriving at the manor before his sisters, coffee was hot and fresh when they arrived. He handed everyone a cup as they arrived. Life was about to change for all of them. He could feel it. He was anxious to hear what the rest of his family had decided.

After the last family meeting, Andy and Karen discussed their original goal of improving the meals they served. They wondered if that was what they needed to do or if something else was in the wings for them. Andy said maybe it was time for them to travel. Karen wondered if his bringing that up meant that he had the urge to run away again. He assured her that those days were over, but he would love to travel with her and their children. At the end of their conversations, nothing was set in stone for them. Andy was willing to go with the flow of the rest of his family. Karen was happy living in Tennessee but was open to change if that was coming. It would not be easy to move with three kids in tow.

Heather and Ben walked in, holding hands and smiling. Andy wondered what they were thinking. He knew Heather had been through a lot over the last several years. Maybe she was ready to move on to a simpler life somewhere.

Sara arrived after her siblings. She usually was the first person to arrive anywhere. When she and Randall walked in, they noticed the looks of Andy and Heather.

"What? Why those looks?" Sara asked as she accepted her mug of coffee.

"You are late. You are never last to arrive anywhere. Is everything okay?"

"Everything is fine. We had to help Gayle with her homework before we came over."

"That's right, she's taking extra classes this year. How is she doing with that?"

"She's doing great. Still an honor student. And she has been helping Barbara on the weekends while learning more about the foster care programs. I think she will be a great asset in that field."

"She has the heart for it. I think she gets that from you, Sis."

"I agree. Gayle certainly didn't get that heart from me." Randall added, which made everyone laugh.

The laughter broke the tension in the room. Sara took a sip of her hot coffee and began to talk about the topic of change.

"I assume you all have had time to discuss the future of Bella Rose since the last meeting?"

"The future of Bella Rose and our personal lives, too," Ben said flatly. To him, this potential change affected the rest of his family, not just Heather's side. He had Barbara and Steven to think about. He had recently found his sister, his twin. He did not want to move away and leave her.

Heather touched Ben's forearm. She felt his concern. They had talked about it during the previous week. A change would affect everyone and everything they had become.

"True. The potential change affects us to the core. We have put so much of our heart and soul into this estate. Our parents and grandparents did as well. We have remodeled, built additions, and expanded our services. We have grown closer as a family." She took another sip of her coffee, allowing someone else to speak.

"I know, to us, selling Bella Rose would feel like cutting out part of our family. I may not have been here for several years, but since we have returned, this is home. This is who we are. Yes, it is hard work. We have times we want to walk away from it. We want a break at the busiest time of year. We forget to care for ourselves while doing our best to care for our guests. Then we see how happy they are, and it changes everything."

"You are so right, Sis." Sara smiled, realizing how big her little sister's heart was. "We do tend to overwork ourselves for most of the year. We see the rewards through the eyes and words of our guests. Our folks and grandparents had a dream. We need to keep the dream going."

Randall looked at his wife. That was not how he imagined she was going with her ideas of change. "Are you sure?"

Sara looked at Randall and then at everyone else in the room. She scanned the room. A tiny cup on the small corner shelf by the window made her smile. "I am very sure." She smiled and raised her coffee mug into the air. "This day will go down in history as a day of change."

Everyone had lifted their mugs to meet hers, then stopped mid-air as she said the word change. "I thought you said we were staying?" Andy asked.

"We are. At least, I want us to. Is everyone in agreement?"

"Yes," everyone said in unison. Their mostly empty coffee mugs clanged together in agreement.

"Then it is settled. Today we begin fresh." Sara said.

Heather stood from her stool. "I have a few words to say while we are here." She looked at Ben, who smiled and nodded his head. Sara looked at her and winked. Ben stood up to join his wife.

"We have something to announce," Ben said. He took Heather's hand as they said the next words together. "We are pregnant."

"Congratulations!" Sara was the first to respond. She had known of Heather's suspicions but had not heard the confirmation.

"Yes, congrats Sis!" Andy said.

Karen reached over and hugged Heather. "Oh, the joys of having three." She laughed. Welcome to chaos."

"Thank you, Karen. I know it will be a challenge. We are looking forward to having a little one again. Miss them being tiny."

"I know the feeling. Tiny humans are amazing."

"Oh, and just to answer your silent question, I had green tea, not coffee, this morning." She raised her empty cup.

"I was wondering about that. You need to take all the precautions you can with this baby."

"We know. Dr. George is keeping a close eye on me."

"We are all here for you. Whatever you need, just say the word." Sara said. She hugged Heather and whispered, "you know, at your age."

Heather shook her head at Sara. She knew it was all in fun. Heather and Ben had talked to Dr. George about that very thing. Which was why they were taking precautions during this pregnancy. She was what they called a Geriatric pregnancy, which put her at high risk.

~~~~~~

Life transformed once the mutual decision was agreed upon by the family. There was no need to tell anyone about the momentary idea of selling. It made no difference to anyone since they were all staying.

Andy and Karen began working on the meal planning and changes in the menu. New recipes were discovered, created, and family-tested before they were served to the guests.

Heather took it easy as much as she could during her first trimester. Her boys were old enough to be told of the new baby coming. Marc and Maddex both wanted a sister. Ben wanted twins. Heather told him to put that idea out of his head. That just because he was a twin, he may not be ready to be the father of twins. They got some good laughs over the concept.

Sara and Randall spent a lot of time helping Gayle with her schoolwork so she could maintain her grade-point average and graduate a year early. They were proud of her determination and her goals in life. They also began working on a new plan Sara had. They kept it secret while they developed it, just in case it did not work as they hoped it would.

～～～～～～～～～～～～～～～～～～～～～～～～～～～～～

Four months later, Christmas arrived once again. Another ball was planned, with Santa returning to Bella Rose for the foster children and families. This time Santa had more help. Bob played Santa as he had for the previous three years. One of the elves was new. Gayle had designed her outfit for the event and stood with Santa handing out gifts and hugging each child that approached Santa wanting to sit on his lap. Her joy in helping showed on her face and radiated from her eyes.

"You do have a way with the children, Gayle," Barbara told her near the end of the evening. I am impressed. I am also proud of you for your hard work."

"Thank you Ms Barbara. I do not know why I feel so close to them or this mission, but I don't think I could walk away from it if I tried."

"I am so glad your family decided to stay here," Barbara commented, assuming Gayle knew about the family decision.

"Decided to stay here? What are you talking about? Were they going to relocate this event?"

"Oh," Barbara realized she had misspoken. "No, sorry. There is always the possibility the agency would want to hold it elsewhere. I fight to keep it at Bella Rose." She covered up reality.

"I know. This building will be big enough for many years. At least, I hope it will. I know the agency is needed, as there are always children that need foster care, but it would make me so happy knowing our services were never needed. The goal is to know that children are safe and loved in their homes."

"That would be the ideal." Barbara loved Gayle's positive approach to all the situations they had faced since she began helping. She would support Gayle in all her efforts to become the person she wanted to be. Her enthusiasm spread to the other volunteers.

Gayle loved her work with the foster families and spent all her free time with them over the Christmas holiday.

Bella Rose Manor was normally closed for January, but they were booked into Spring due to the book's popularity and word on the internet they had agreed to stay open.

Andy and Karen made a special meal for the guests for New Year's. The reception hall was hosting a New Year's Eve party. The large group arrived early to decorate so Heather could take it easy while she supervised.

The weather was unexpectedly warm, inspiring them to decorate the gazebo. Fireworks were supposed to be shot off in town at midnight and would be visible from outside at Bella Rose.

Sara had invited family and close friends to join them for the New Year's Eve party. Most people accepted the invitation. Terri and Adam declined because they were hosting a party at the lounge. When Sara contacted Jay and Carrie to invite them, she learned they were going to the lounge for their party. She had been amazed at the connection and friendship between Terri and Jay. It was rare for ex-couples to remain friends. The added interesting factor was Terri's sister married Jay's brother. Sara always laughed at that connection. Somehow they made it work.

Thinking of Angela and Jeff, Sara knew she would miss them when they moved to Pennsylvania. She understood the desire to move but was surprised they made that decision so easily. She hoped they would not be away long. Angela was a joy to be around. She had spunk and was not afraid to try anything. Her magazine articles were proof of that. Adventurous destinations were the main focus. Her team was amazing at their work. Jeff was especially good at his job. Sara assumed he loved to travel. Even though his job was with the hospitals, she assumed Jeff liked to travel. He had easily moved to Tennessee. With the move to Pennsylvania, Sara assumed Angela was working on her best story ever. Why else would anyone move there when they did not have to? She hoped Jeff could find a job there.

She laughed at herself when she realized what she had thought. They could have asked the same thing about her family moving to the tiny town in Tennessee.

Sara broke from her thoughts as guests started to arrive. She was headed out the manor's door when she heard the main phone ring. She hesitated but returned to answer it. If someone had wanted her to bring anything, they would have called her cell phone or sent her a text.

317

"Hello, Happy New Year," she answered.

"Happy New Year, my dear." Sara smiled as she recognized the voice. It may have been a long time since she had heard it, but the lady was one she would never forget.

"Rhea! How are you, young lady?"

"I am nothing near a young lady, but I am doing well. I called to wish you and your family a happy new year."

"Thank you. We wish the same for you. Is your granddaughter spending the holidays with you?"

"Yes, Laura has been here. She moved closer to me to spend more time with me. She says I am getting old and need her company."

"She may be right, you know." Sara laughed. Something told her Rhea would be fine on her own no matter what age she reached.

"Oh, I know. The staff takes good care of me at the assistant living. I do love it when she is here or takes me places."

"And are you still seeing that gentleman?"

"Yes, we are still together. At our age, it would feel wrong to break off a friendship like we have." Sara could tell Rhea had a smile of love on her face.

"That is good. I don't want to come there to give him a hard time for dropping you."

"Well, I do hope you will come here this spring." Rhea hesitated before sharing her news.

"We would love to come. It will need to be after school gets out for the summer."

"That's perfect. The wedding is on the first Saturday in June."

"The what? Wedding? Rhea, are you getting married?"

"I am!" Rhea's joy was evident.

"Send us the information, and we will be there! That is so exciting! I will let the others know!"

"Thank you. I would love to have the wedding there, but we are not traveling very far at our age, even if Laura brings us."

"I understand. Don't worry about that. I am thrilled for you."

"I could not let the new year start without telling you. He just proposed at Christmas. It took us a few days to decide on a wedding day. Not like we have a lot going on, but we wanted to make it so our family and friends could be here to celebrate with us."

"June is a perfect month."

"I will let you go. I assume you have a large party to get to. Tell everyone I said hello, and I miss them."

"I will. Talk to you soon."

"Love you, Sara."

"Love you, too, Rhea. Happy New Year." Sara smiled as she hung up the phone. Life was full of surprises.

Chapter Fifty-Three
Opportunities

A blanket of heavy snow could be seen falling on the world through the windows of homes and the guest rooms at Bella Rose Estate. As everyone rose to welcome the new day and the new year, they gazed outside into the beauty of winter.

Sara rose from her bed with a smile before she had coffee or looked out the windows of her home. Sleep had lured her into dreams of happiness. The happiness remained as she opened her eyes and stood. A special quiet filled her room. She knew that sound. She smiled. The peaceful quiet of silence as snow absorbed all outside sound. Their guests would be staying until the roads were cleared.

She poured herself a cup of black coffee before she finished getting dressed. Randall was already up and out of the house. She peered out the front door and saw her husband shoveling the path between their home and the manor. Nothing stopped them from connecting with the people who had chosen to spend the end of one year and the beginning of a new year full of possibilities with them.

Standing at the front window, sipping her hot coffee, she caught Randall's eyes and waved. He waved back the continued shoveling the snow. Sara looked toward the sky and saw tiny flakes floating to the earth. She pointed up, and Randall tilted his head to look. He stuck his tongue out to catch a snowflake. Sometimes Randall wished he was still a child and only had the fun of snow on his mind. Sara smiled at him as he caught several more before shaking his head at Sara. She always managed to bring out the child in him.

Randall finished plowing and shoveling the paths to the manor and their cars. They were not going anywhere, but it was better to clear the walkway early in case it froze later that evening.

Sara nodded her head. Randall was indeed her hero.

She hated winter when she had to be out in it. Gazing at it from the warmth of her home had always been her preferred style of enjoyment.

Her phone rang as she dressed and finished her cup of coffee. She answered it without knowing who the caller was. At that hour, she imagined it was Heather or Andy.

"Happy New Year," Sara said.

"Happy New Year to you too, Sis. How are you?"

"Except for the snow and needing to get out, I am good. How about you? Did you survive the party last night?"

"Yes, I survived. I pushed myself, but I think we are all okay. So, the baby survived too?"

"Yes, I am happy to report that the baby did very well for its first big party." Heather laughed.

"Good. What can I help you with? Are there guests who want to leave, or are they all wanting to stay an extra day?"

"All of them want to stay an extra day. Do we have the room?"

"Yes, we do. I have not booked anyone until the middle of the week. This forecast was in the works early enough to plan accordingly. Plus, it was New Year's Eve, and I was not sure who might be unable to drive home even in good weather."

"Good. Because I do not feel like cleaning either."

Sara laughed. "I don't blame you. But Andy is making a good brunch, I hope. I need to call him to make sure. They should be awake by now." She looked at her watch.

"I do not have plans for today. Too risky on the roads. The snow makes it worse. I think I will bundle up and head over to the manor to see if Andy needs help. And to see if any guest needs anything we can get for them. The view should be pretty today."

After brunch, the guests joined some of the family outside to play in the snow. A few built a snowman in the front yard. A snowball fight brought lots of laughter as the adults reverted to the joys of childhood.

By mid-afternoon, most of the snow had melted from Rose Lane, and everyone could drive on it, but no one did. When Andy and Karen realized the guests were staying another night, they planned an evening meal for everyone. Andy used most of the leftovers from the party, added a few other specialties, and created a feast.

Later that evening, everyone gathered in the great room to enjoy one last night together near the fireplace. The first day of the new year was coming to an end. Along with it, new friendships had already been made amongst the guests.

~~~~~~

Two weeks later, Heather called Sara in a panic. Ben had been gone all day, and Heather was in so much pain she could hardly move. Sara rushed over and drove her to the hospital. Dr. George met them in the emergency room and quickly assessed her condition. Ben arrived just as the doctor began telling Heather the news. It was not what they wanted to hear, but it was not the worst.

"You knew from the beginning that you had a high-risk pregnancy. I cautioned you of all the possibilities."

Heather held Ben's hand as they all listened.

"I am putting you on bed rest for the remainder of your pregnancy. By taking this precaution, you should be able to carry the babies to full term."

Heather looked at Ben. Ben looked at Dr. George. Sara raised her eyebrows. That word was new.

"Babies?" Heather repeated slowly.

Dr. George smiled. "Yes, babies, as in twins. When we did the ultrasound, we heard two heartbeats and saw two babies."

"How? How did you not see or hear two before now?"

"Even with our modern technology, we occasionally miss. Babies like to hide. Years ago, parents did not know they were having twins until delivery."

"Oh, that would be scary. This is scary enough." Heather said. She turned to Ben. "Well, babe, you got your wish. It's twins."

"I certainly did. No wonder you were getting so.."

"Watch it, buddy! Don't say another word."

"I was going to say no wonder you were getting so beautiful." He smiled big and hoped that would work.

"Good try." Heather made a fist and gently hit his upper arm.

Sara walked over and hugged her sister. "Let us know what you need from the rest of the family. We are here for you. We will take care of the boys, cleaning, and cooking. Well, maybe not me for the cooking, but I can do the rest." Everyone knew she was not a good cook. That was Andy's domain.

"I will. I need to check my calendar for any events scheduled. I limited them closer to the due date, but not this far out."

"Rachelle, Karen, Terri, and I can handle the events. Andy can cook. We all can clean."

"Hey, Hello. I can do most of those things." Ben said.

Sara smiled. "I know you can. We are here, though. It won't be easy to do it all. And once the babies arrive, we will continue to help."

"Thank you, Sara."

Dr. George handed Heather a list of instructions. "These are for you to follow. Plenty of liquids, eat healthy, bed rest with short sessions of time out of bed. You need to hang on to these babies as long as possible. Oh, and are you sure you do not want to know what sex they are?"

Heather looked at Ben. Maybe with two, they should find out that detail. So they could be prepared. They nodded to the doctor.

"Okay. You are having fraternal twins."

Ben smiled. "Perfect." He reached down and kissed his wife on her forehead. "I love you," he whispered.

"Well, we need to double up on baby gifts for you now." Sara laughed. "I can't believe you are having twins. Let the fun begin."

"We still have a few months," Heather said.

"When can I take her home, Doc? She can come home, right?"

"Yes, she may go home. We will keep a close watch on her progress. I may stop at your house occasionally since it is on my way to work. That will save you a trip she does not need to make unless necessary."

"We appreciate that."

Dr. George left to see another patient. Sara helped Heather get ready to go home while Ben drove the car to the hospital entrance.

Once again, life changed for the core of the family. Plans originally set were reevaluated for importance. Life was the only important thing. The life of two new family members. These babies took control before they were born. A sign of what was to become the future of Bella Rose? Only time and years could answer that question.

Word soon spread to those close to Heather and Ben about the twins. Gifts started arriving well before a baby shower was planned. Strangers were sending money in cards. At least they thought they were strangers. Until Gayle put it together with a list of the recent guests at the manor and at the last two events at the reception hall. The only question was, how did word spread so far and wide? Gayle denied any initiation.

Angela and Jeff inquired about their move to Pennsylvania. They were not family but said they would stay if needed to help. Heather and Ben appreciated their offer but assured them they would be well taken care of by the rest of the family.

Angela made a phone call to Anthony and let him know the date they planned to arrive. He assured them that their home would be ready by that time. He had worked with them regarding repairs it needed before they moved. He hoped they would find their forever home there. His father had thought the world of Angela. Anthony was glad for the connection. He did wonder why his father had not given anything to Larry and Grace since Larry was Gregory's nephew and his cousin. He understood the disconnect for most of their lives, but once they made amends, it would have made sense to do something for Larry. Anthony put the idea out of his mind. He had work to do for Angela and Jeff.

~~~~~~

Gayle was finishing her high school classes as spring arrived. She had worked hard to achieve her goal. Sara and Randall were proud of their daughter. Her goals for her future were impressive.

Gayle was preparing for her graduation. Two more weeks before she would prepare for her summer vacation and volunteer work with Barbara, she faced a decision. One Gayle could not make alone. A conversation with one of her teachers gave her an option she had not considered in her life choices.

Randall noticed the change in Gayle and asked her what was on her mind. He wondered if it was the realization of graduation.

"No, I'm good with graduation. I love school, but college sounds inviting."

"So, what's wrong?" Sara joined the conversation. They were eating supper together as they did as often as they could.

"I have an opportunity to do something this summer that I never thought of doing."

"Okay. Would it take you away from working with Barbara? You made a commitment to help her this summer."

"I know I did. That is what makes this so hard to consider. One of my teachers is putting together a group of students to go hiking this summer."

"Okay. That doesn't sound like such a problem. You like to hike. When is the hike? I'm sure Barbara can work around that day. You won't be working seven days a week all summer."

"That's just it. The group will be hiking part of the Appalachian Trail. For a month."

"A Month!" Sara almost choked on her food.

Randall was quiet as he calculated the time and distance in his head. "That is only part of the trail. No one can hike the entire trail in a month."

"No, it wasn't for the whole trail. But it still is a month away."

"When are they starting?"

"Two weeks after graduation."

Sara looked at Randall. Was he calculating the time she would be gone but still be able to help Barbara for most of the summer as she had promised?

"Randall?" Sara looked at her husband. She could not believe he was considering letting her go.

"What? I think that if she wants to go and if Barbara works with her, it will be an amazing experience. We will talk to the hiking group leader about all the details. Then we will discuss it further and then maybe. This will be the opportunity of a lifetime. When else is she going to have this chance?"

Sara took a deep breath. Once again, her husband was correct. When would Gayle be able to do this again?

"You mean it? I can go?" Gayle was surprised they would consider allowing her this chance.

"We will investigate it," Randall said with a hint of her detective ambition.

"Understood. I will talk to my teacher tomorrow for more details."

"And we need to schedule a meeting with her."

"It is a him, not a her," Gayle corrected.

"Oh. Well, are there females joining you? Adult females?"

"Yes, mama. His wife is going as is another teaching couple."

"Okay, that makes it better. Once we talk to them, you will talk to Barbara. You may want to discuss the possibility with her before we talk to them. No sense in talking to them if Barbara needs you more."

"I will call her after dinner."

Gayle gulped her water and finished supper in record time. "May I call Barbara now?"

"Yes, you may." Sara shook her head as she said it.

After Gayle left the room, Sara looked at her husband. "Our little girl is almost all grown up."

"Yes, she is." The two smiled as they heard their daughter's muffled voice on the phone in the other room.

Chapter Fifty-Four
Adventures

Barbara was more than willing to change her plans for Gayle if she decided to hike with the school hiking group. Her words to Gayle were the same as Sara and Randall's. When would she have another opportunity to experience such an adventure?

Armed with that approval, Gayle arranged to discuss the details with her teacher. During their conversation, she requested a meeting with her folks. The meeting was set for later that evening.

Randall was prepared with several questions about the trip, the equipment needed, safety measures used, food, and more. Each was answered to their satisfaction.

Sara asked a few more questions. And then, the teacher and his wife added more information that had not been discussed. When the meeting ended, Sara and Randal said they would need to discuss it at home and asked how long they had before making a final decision.

Gayle was concerned her parents would not let her go. The only thing that seemed too much for her was the distance they expected to hike in the month's trip. She was also concerned about being gone for so long. She had never even spent a night away from home since being their foster child and then being adopted by her folks.

Two days later, Sara and Randall told Gayle that she had their permission to go. Gayle smiled as she heard the news. It certainly was the opportunity of a lifetime. It would transform her life. She looked at each of the parents and shook her head.

"I have made a decision I hope I will not regret for the rest of my life. I am not going on the hike."

"Why not?" Sara was thrilled but confused.

"I made a commitment to Barbara before this came up."

"Nope, that excuse will not work. She gave her approval to go. She's run the foster program independently for several years and can do it for another month."

"Yes, I know she can. It is just that I feel I owe her to stick with my summer plans for the sake of the children."

"Gayle, this chance will most likely not present itself again. Are you one hundred percent sure this is what you want to do?" Randall asked. He was concerned that she would regret not going later in life.

"I am sure. I know I brought it up and needed your permission to go on the hike, but I feel, in my heart, that hiking is not where I belong this summer. I belong here with all of you, helping Barbara and the children with no home to go to each night. I was a foster child once. I will give up a month of a selfish desire to help the foster children."

"Gayle, going on the trip is not selfish. You can learn a lot through others and what you observe along the way."

"I know that. Yet something is pulling me away from the hike so I can spend time helping others."

Sara and Randall wrapped their arms around their daughter. Such a mature child to understand life and living for others more than herself. They were more proud of her. Sara was relieved that Gayle was not going but never let that show.

～～～～～～～～～～～～～～～～～～～～～～～～～～～～～

Angela and Jeff finished loading the moving van. One last look around their home, and they closed the door. Behind them stood a house that would wait for their return. Ahead of them was a ten-hour trip to a place they would call their temporary home. A location that beckoned them from the moment they heard it was theirs.

The moving van pulled out of their driveway, followed by Jeff driving their SUV. Angela looked behind her to their home as it slowly grew smaller as the distance progressed.

The trip took nearly twelve hours due to stops along the way for food, fuel, stretching their legs, and a traffic delay due to an accident that was cleared by the time they reached it.

As they entered Pennsylvania, the road changed. Angela had fallen asleep but woke up when she felt something different about the drive. She opened her eyes and laughed. "We were warned about this."

"Yes, we were. I didn't notice it last time, but there is a difference in the roads here. I am sure we will get used to it."

They pulled in behind the moving van parked in their driveway an hour later. They stepped out of their SUV and stretched before walking to the front door. A sign was hanging on the door. "Home Sweet Home. Welcome."

Jeff and Angela smiled as Jeff unlocked the door and waited for Angela to walk ahead of him. "Welcome home, Babe."

"Thank you." Angela turned as Jeff walked in to join her.

This was the beginning of a new adventure. They wondered what it had in store for them.

The next morning they were met with their first challenge. It had snowed during the night. Ill-equipped to deal with the white stuff, they were glad it was not more than two inches. They could deal with that and hoped it would melt quickly.

They enjoyed fresh coffee before beginning their day unloading the moving van and setting up their house. As they finished drinking their third cup of coffee, there was a knock at the front door. Jeff answered it and invited Anthony inside, where it was warm.

"Good morning, Anthony. How are you on this early spring day of winter?" Angela shook her head.

"I am good. This late-season snow is normal around here, so I am used to it. I forgot to mention it to you earlier. I hope you can manage with it."

"We will be fine. We know about snow, but it usually doesn't snow this late in the season at home."

"This is home, Babe," Angela reminded him. "At least for a while."

"Yes, Dear. I know." Jeff winked at his wife. He already missed Tennessee and warmth.

"What may I help you with today? I am at your service to help unload, answer questions, whatever you need."

"Thank you. We can use your help. Let our adventure begin." Jeff put the empty coffee mugs into the sink. He grabbed his jacket, and he and Anthony headed out the door. Angela watched and smiled. She hoped this had been a good move.

~~~~~~

Terri called her sister after she arrived at the Café. She had not heard from her since they left the day before.

"Hey, Sis. How are you? How was the trip? Are you moved in and settled yet?" Terri smiled as she left the message on Angela's cell phone. Terri shook her head. The idea that there was no cellular service where her sister lived now came to mind. She laughed. If that was the case, she knew her sister would not last living there very long. She needed the internet and her cell phone for her work.

Terri went about her day preparing for her customers. When she heard the front door open, she realized she had forgotten to lock it after she had arrived that morning.

Steven walked inside and gave his boss a look of unbelief. "You left the place unlocked?"

"Yes. I came in through the front door this morning, had my sister on my mind, and just forgot. I'm just glad it was you. I don't cook breakfast here."

"You could start," Steven suggested.

"That is not going to happen. What we have already is enough of an adventure for me. By the way, why are you here so early?"

"I came to town for a walk along the pond but noticed the lights on and wanted to make sure everything was alright."

"Thank you. Good to know people are looking out for us."

"Are you okay? You seem a little down." Steven walked closer instead of heading out for his walk.

"I am fine. Angela and Jeff moved to Pennsylvania yesterday, and I've not heard from her since they left."

"I am sure she will call you as soon as possible. You two are close."

"I know. I just worry about her sometimes. It took her so long to move closer to me, and now she has moved away again."

"They kept their house here, though. They will be back." Steven assured her.

"I know. Although she likes to move around with her work. I was hoping Jeff would make her settle down here. I realize that he is a wanderer too, so for them to stay in one location for very long is highly unlikely."

"Such is living a full life. Sounds like they have it figured out."

"They do. Now, go on your walk. Enjoy your day. The lounge will be here when it's time to work tonight."

"Thanks. You need to have a good day too. Angela will call you when she can."

"Thanks." Terri turned and walked into the kitchen. Breakfast sounded good. Maybe she would make herself something to eat while she was there.

Her phone dinged as she began cooking bacon and eggs. She smiled when she saw it was a text from Angela. A short message and a photo of snow. Terry replied with a laughing emoji. That was enough to make her happy for her sister.

Steven walked along the path of the pond slower than he normally had. He had a lot on his mind lately. None of which he had shared with anyone. When he reached the pond, he sat on the bench overlooking the water. Eight Canadian Geese floated across the water in a group causing ripples to move toward the shore. The trees were beginning to show signs of budding. He looked up to the blue sky and smiled. Life was good, no matter what was on his mind. He needed to find a way to talk to Barbara about it. And he knew it should be soon.

A man on a bicycle approached the pond. Steven didn't pay much attention to him until he stopped and joined him on the bench.

"Good morning. How are you this morning?"

Steven looked at the man and smiled. "Good morning, Joe. I am good. How are you?"

"I am great. However, by the look on your face, something is troubling you."

"Man, you psychiatrists are something."

"It's been my living for so long, I can't help it. A curse sometimes. I'm here if you want to share." Joe said, shrugging his shoulders. "Free of charge for this session," he added.

"How can I say no to free?" Steven took a deep breath. He wasn't sure if he was ready to talk but decided it was worth an attempt. If nothing else, it would prepare him for when he talked with Barbara.

"Well, I do have something on my mind. I have not told anyone about it yet, and don't know how to tell Barbara."

"Use me for practice."

Steven looked at Joe. He started to shake his head but knew it was best to talk about it. "Okay. Thanks."

Steven proceeded to tell Joe that an opportunity had presented itself that he was conflicted about. He had wanted this job before he met Barbara, but when he met her, his focus was all on her. Now he hated to take away from her life and career growth.

"Is it something you can do from here? It sounds like it might require a move?"

"It does require a move. That is the issue. I don't want to uproot our lives. Especially hers. My wife finally found her family, her place in a field she is amazing in and is making a difference in many lives."

Joe listened. Without saying a word, he knew Steven wasn't going anywhere. His wife was his life.

Steven kept talking about the pros and cons. The more he spoke the words out loud, the more he understood his role in life. He stopped talking for a moment and looked at Joe. "I guess I have my answer, don't I?"

"I think you do. All you had to do was talk it out. Find what is most important in your life and decide."

"Thanks. You people have a way of giving great advice."

"I only listened. You made up your mind on your own." Joe stood up and picked his bicycle up to continue his ride. "Anytime you need to talk, you know where I am. Good luck with your new adventure. Barbara will love you even more for it."

Steven watched Joe ride away. He smiled as he stood to finish his walk. His new adventure. He shook his head. He would do anything for the love of his life. Even keep the old adventure alive.

Chapter Fifty-Five
It's Settled

Bella Rose. To anyone looking on the internet for the perfect place to stay in a small town with the most beautiful mountain views – this was the place to be.

The history documented in *Bella Rose - Secrets, Family and Love by Sara Williams* was selling well and brought more guests to experience the depths of its mystery.

Guests continued to write in the journals left in their rooms. Couples continued requesting weddings in the chapel and the gazebo, with the receptions and parties in the reception hall.

Susan's dream had come true. Her children had come together to live in harmony. To raise their children. To welcome strangers who became friends. And to give family, friends, and guests their love and care.

The discovered secrets were accepted if still misunderstood by some. Most found fascination with the land, the buildings, and the family.

Years of hard work, tough decisions, tears, and happiness showed through the photos, stories, and memories shared by the family.

Spring had transformed into summer. The skies radiated with sunshine and warmth after the bitterly cold winter and damp spring. The heat of July erased memories of cold.

Sara sat alone in the attic on a rare day of solitude. She glanced at the furniture that was left in the room. Her eyes darted to the secret room that had remained as they found it. Too difficult to touch anything that had truly made Bella Rose what it was, the siblings had decided to leave everything the way it was. Maybe one day, the entire manor would be a destination tourist museum, and the tours would include a glimpse into the secret room. Until then, only the family occasionally peeked inside. Today was one of those days for Sara.

Rarely had anyone entered the secret room alone. No one feared what would be found. No one gave ghosts a thought while anywhere near the place. Not anymore.

Sara reached for the door and opened it, allowing her eyes to focus on the darkness inside. She reached for the light switch, then changed her mind. She wanted to experience it as the girls had as they hid. Sara sat cross-legged on the floor in silence. She listened for the past to reveal itself. She closed her eyes so she could hear better.

Breathing. Whispers. A movement. Then a sound at the door.

The door opened, letting light inside. Sara jumped and opened her eyes. She turned her white face toward the door. Her eyes grew wide open. Her hand clenched into a fist. Prepared for what the stories of old told. Suspicious and leary of what could be encroaching on the stillness.

Gayle held her hand out in self-protection against her mother.

"Mama, it's just me."

"What are you doing here? How did you know I was here?"

"Where else would you be on the anniversary of Granny's death?"

Sara relaxed her fists and reached up for her daughter. Gayle crossed her legs and sat next to her Mama. She leaned her head to rest on Sara's shoulder.

"I didn't think anyone would remember that. Sara whispered.

"You forget I'm a numbers person like you." Gayle smiled. She loved her odd fascination with numbers.

"True. There are not many of us."

"What feeling did you get this time?"

Sara shook her head. Only her daughter would realize she had been up here more often than the rest of the family. "A feeling of closure somehow. The vibes are different this time. The voices are quieter. The cold air feels warm, besides the fact that it is July. There is a stillness in here this time."

Sara closed her eyes again to feel the room. Gayle looked at Sara and closed her eyes too. She listened, as her mother was. Maybe this time she could feel the past like Sara always had.

~~~~~~

Heather looked at the calendar in her kitchen. She had meant to look at the clock. Linda Ann and Lance Andrew, her newborn twins, had been napping longer than usual. She stared at the date instead. When it hit, she shivered. She sat down on a kitchen chair, momentarily forgetting the world around her.

She wondered if Sara had given the date a thought. Normally they talked about it. This year it almost slipped her mind. She silently told her Mama she was sorry. Sorry for forgetting the anniversary of her death.

How could she manage to forget finding her on the floor that day? How could she forget the rest of that day and the following weeks? How could she wipe out those sights and sounds?

At that thought, she heard the cries of one of the twins. It made her jump. They had been born perfect despite being a product of a geriatric, high-risk pregnancy. Now at two months old, they were still perfect.

Heather walked into the nursery and picked up Linda Ann. Her little girl's smile could melt any bad day.

She fed Linda Ann and then heard Lance Andrew cry as he woke. Heather was thankful they did not always wake up at the same time. She was left alone for most of the day, and they seemed to sense that and were already considerate. Almost. They still woke up in the middle of the night most nights.

Her phone rang as she put Randy into the playpen with his sister. They could not do much damage while there. Heather gave each a small toy to play with for a few minutes.

She saw it was Sara calling and felt bad for making her wait.

"Hello, Sis, How are you?"

"I am okay. How are you? I noticed you have not brought the babies to the Manor recently. Is there a reason?"

"No, no reason except that they are so small. You would think that I have had no experience with babies."

"I understand. They are still tiny. I'm calling to see if you remember what today is," Sara said.

"Yes, I meant to look at the clock but noticed the calendar and realized what day it was. Hard to believe Mama has been gone so many years already. I don't think I will ever forget that day."

"Neither will I, Sis. It changed our lives. And we have a great life now, thanks to her and her ways."

"We didn't see it that way for a while."

"That's for sure." Heather laughed. "The many good memories overshadowed her final wishes for us."

"Yes, they did. I miss Mama every day, but I am glad she brought us all closer together through her death."

"I agree."

"I think we need a family dinner if Andy is up to it. Not a meeting, but just a dinner in memory of Mama, and Daddy."

"I'm good with that. Give him a call and let me know what time. Do we want to go out or stay here around the island?"

Sara smiled. "Stay in. That island is our family space."

Heather smiled. "Yes, and I like that we have that."

340

"Let me call Andy. I will call you back when we decide when and if we can do it tonight."

"I'll be here. The twins are calling." Heather said before hanging up.

~~~~~~

It was two nights before the family could arrange for everyone to get together for family dinner. Their lives were busier than normal.

Andy made a special meal of their Mama's favorite foods. Topped with Susan's favorite triple chocolate cake. Wine was served with the meal, and coffee accompanied dessert.

Everyone met in the dining room while Andy and Karen set everything out on the island. The younger children were seated at their children's table. Karen took special care and put a fancy tablecloth on the small table for the kids. They deserved the best sometimes too.

As they gathered at the island to sit down, Sara noticed the centerpiece. She touched the bouquet of flowers. The red roses, mixed with white baby's breath and greenery. She looked at Ben and smiled. He always knew the right thing to do with flowers.

As she took her hand away from the vase, she noticed an object sticking out from under it. She touched it, then lifted the vase slightly as she pulled the object out. She almost dropped it. As she pulled it out, she noticed a paper underneath it. She carefully pulled them both out and looked around at her family.

They looked at her with wide eyes. What lay on the table in front of them was nothing they ever expected to see again.

Sara lifted the object as if it was about to explode. Everyone looked at it in her hand. No one said a word.

Randall reached over and picked up the paper. It was a sealed pink envelope. There was nothing written on the outside. Sara looked at her husband and motioned with her head to open it. Randall looked at the other family members. They shrugged their shoulders and then nodded their heads. A mystery was inside, and it was best to find out what it was as soon as possible.

Randall carefully broke the seal without damaging the paper. He pulled the paper from inside, laid the envelope back onto the table, and then unfolded the one fold of the note. He handed it to Sara.

Sara looked at it. Her face turned white. The paper felt hot. Seeing the handwriting gave her chills. Heather looked at her sister and then at the paper. Her eyes opened wide, and a chill ran through her. Andy glanced at it from across the table. He had not seen the details until rising from his stool.

"OH!" was all Andy was able to voice.

Sara scanned the first few lines before saying anything. When she gathered her bearings again, she began to speak.

"I have no idea what is happening here, but this note is in Mama's handwriting." She shook as she felt more chills that she thought must be filling the room because her brother and sister were rubbing their arms, trying to stay warm.

"As with the others we read, I will read this to us."

Sara took a deep breath and began to read:

> *You, my family, have succeeded beyond my hopes and dreams.*
>
> *I know these last years have not been easy. My demands or requests put pressure on each of you. The challenges of normal life can be enough to break people, both individuals and couples. If you are reading*

this together, you faced each challenge and won.

Unable to do it alone, I hope you leaned on each other.

I do not know if or how your families, my family, has grown. I hope you have each found true and lasting love. I hope you have children to love and who love you. I hope you are a pillar of the community and positively influence everyone you meet.

I hope you forgave me a long time ago and accepted the life I led. I assume you know all my and the family's secrets by now.

My words to you, my children – live life to the fullest. Take every opportunity God and others present to you and experience it. Life is too short to worry, fret, debate, fight or miss out on something because you are stubborn and set in your ways of being the only ways.

Continue to support each other. Be there through hard times and the good. Celebrate life often.

Know that I loved you every day. Also, know that I loved and held Glen and Larry dear to my heart. Having all of you in my life was a blessing.

Now – Go! Be the best people you can be. It is settled.

Life is full of mystery, secrets, love, compassion, twists, and turns. Face them all with all your hearts.

Love,
Mama

Oh, and this key? It goes to nothing. That last piece that Raymond was going to build for my Mama – never got made.

Tears flowed from everyone at the table. A combination of shock, love and overpowering emotions filled the room. The girls looked around the room, expecting to see a ghost. They rubbed their arms, expecting to feel the touch they once had. Andy watched his sisters' reactions. Maybe he was the stronger one now. He didn't feel the emotions as deeply. He felt her message was telling them to move forward. Move on if that was the case. She finally gave her written permission to be who they were meant to be. She was relinquishing her power over all of them.

Sara skimmed over the note again without reading it out loud. She looked around the room again. Who had placed it there? Larry, who had moved all the keys years ago, was out of town. He could not have been the one.

"So, who knew about this and placed it here? Andy?"

Andy shook his head as he backed away and raised his hands. "Not me. I knew nothing about any of that."

"You saw my reaction. I certainly did not place it there."

Sara looked at each person in the room. Each one shook their head. All denied involvement.

Sara took a deep breath. "Okay. At least we know the key has no purpose. There is nothing more we need to search for. No more secrets to uncover. No more mystery to unravel."

"Except the one about who put it there," Ben said.

Karen stood up. "In the meantime, does anyone want to eat? Dinner is getting chilled."

Laughter filled the room. The ice of suspense was broken. Sara folded the note and placed it inside the envelope. She placed the antique key inside, too, and placed it on the counter behind her. They would chase that mystery later. Now was the time to celebrate their Mama. Her and the mysteries she provided.

~~~~~~

Two days later, Sara's phone rang. She saw that it was Grace. Usually, Larry called her, so she wondered why it was not him.

"Hello, Grace. How are you?" She answered.

"I am well," Larry said.

Sara laughed. "Good one, Larry. Why are you calling from Grace's phone?"

"Because I was not sure if you would answer if you saw it was me."

"Why would that be?" Sara asked. Then her mind clicked. "Unless."

"I assumed you would hate me for what I did—again."

"Larry? You and Grace are out of town. How did you manage to put that last note on our table? And furthermore, how did you know we would have a family dinner that night?"

There was silence for a brief moment. "Don't be mad at her."

"Mama?"

"Gayle."

"Gayle? What did she have to do with any of it? Wait. Gayle!" Suddenly, Sara was putting things together. Her own daughter was working with Larry. Her little detective, sneaky daughter.

Sara sat down on her sofa. She was glad she was home and alone.

Larry broke the silence. "I had to get your Mama's last letter to you. The key was part of her letter, so I reluctantly included it. I figured you would suspect me even though I was not in town. I also did not want you to think it was a ghost doing it all along."

345

"I don't approve of you involving my daughter or giving it to us as you did. We knew the other keys had been moved by you. Why didn't you just give us the letter?"

"I can not answer that. I knew the other occurrences had been on the sly. I guess I wanted to keep the mystery going that Susan had begun."

"Well, now that I know, I will tell the rest of the family."

"Sara?"

"Yes, Larry."

"I am so sorry. For all the trouble I caused your family for so many years."

"Larry, it is all behind us. Mama made her decisions a long time ago. You are a part of our family. I am glad things worked out for all of us."

"Thank you. That means a lot to me. And Sara, Please don't be too harsh on Gayle. She is an amazing young woman."

Sara smiled. She knew he was right. She also knew she would talk to her daughter about her actions.

Chapter Fifty-Six
Final Decision

Summer came to an end all too fast. The busy season at Bella Rose was slowing down. Sara, Heather, and Andy met once again around the island of the manor's kitchen. With the final answer to the mystery of the estate and their mother, Sara looked around at her siblings. Her smile was telling without her saying a word. Her siblings knew it was time.

Sara placed the folder on the island in front of her. Andy poured them each a glass of wine. Quietness filled the room as they each understood. Sara lifted her glass in a toast. Andy and Heather met her glass, and the silence broke when the glasses clanged together.

"To us," Sara said.

"To Bella Rose," Heather added.

"To love, family, our past, and our future," Andy concluded.

They each sipped the sweetness of the wine.

"We all know why we are here one more time," Sara began. "Once again, we are faced with a decision."

Andy and Heather nodded.

"I, for one, am tired. I know you all are, also. We have been down this path before and agree on the same thing each time. This time it is a little different." She opened the file and removed the papers. "This time, we have this." She handed each one a copy of the top page.

Andy glanced at his and looked at Sara. Heather looked at her copy and opened her eyes wider to look again.

"What is this?" Andy asked.

"This is an offer to buy Bella Rose Estate," Sara said bluntly. There was no other way to share the obvious. They had someone who wanted to buy their homestead.

"But why? Why would someone want to buy it and take it out of the family after all these years? Who is this person?" Andy had not read who the potential buyer was.

Heather looked at the bottom of the page and turned hers over for more information.

"I have not revealed who the buyer is. I want you to consider your thoughts if you did not know and if they would be different if you knew who wanted to own it."

"Mine would be. If we decided to sell it, I would want it to go to someone we knew. Someone we knew and trusted to take care of it and leave it as it is."

"I agree with Heather. I do not want it going to anyone who wanted to destroy what we and our parents and grandparents made it into."

"What if I told you it would change? What if I told you an organization wanted to buy it?"

"What organization would want to own a bed and breakfast?" Andy tried to imagine who it could possibly be and who would take on such an undertaking.

"What if I also told you that we could remain in our homes."

"How is that possible?" Heather asked. She did not want to pack up and move with four children to take care of, two of whom were still infants.

Sara smiled. She personally loved the idea of what she was about to share with her family. Sara picked up the next page in the file and gave each of her siblings a copy. Then she waited for their reactions.

"Barbara?"

"Really? Why"

A knock came at the back door before Sara had time to answer their questions. Andy went to answer it as Barbara walked in before he reached the doorknob.

"Hello, everyone. I hope I timed this right." She looked at Sara and smiled.

"Your timing is perfect," Sara said. She handed Barbara a glass of wine she had poured while Andy had walked to answer the door.

Barbara took the glass of wine and joined them at the island. "I know you may be confused and concerned about my proposal. It has taken a lot of work, planning, legal avenues, and prayers to offer this. I know you may never have given this option a thought, but I think it will work for all of us."

"You are correct that it never crossed our minds for consideration," Andy said as he skimmed over the papers.

"So, if I am reading this right, you want to purchase the manor and land, but we get to keep our homes?"

"Yes. On the simple side of it. My organization and I are proposing and offering to purchase everything except your homes. We will do what needs to be done to survey and divide the property as best we can so that you will own your own property and homes. We will own the rest. We will make minor changes to the manor to fit our needs, but the rest will remain. Put simply, we want to transform this into a foster landing home for unwanted children and those that find themselves homeless for whatever reason. You all know that there are times when children are removed from their homes due to the conditions of the home or their family. Some children run away from home for one reason or another. Other times parents drop their babies off, and they need loving homes."

"That would seem to need more room than the manor has."

"Which is why we would do some remodeling and expansions. However, overall this land is perfect for our needs."

Everyone listened without comment. Their minds were attempting to take it all in.

"How are we able to stay in our homes? They are built close to the manor."

Sara spoke up. "There is an opportunity for all of us by living here. I understand it will change our lives, but it could be amazing if we all work together."

Heather started to say something, then changed her mind. "Go on. We're listening, Sis."

"Okay. The organization could use our help. We would be paid for it, but we have the skills they need to help run the foster pre-home."

"Foster pre-home. That is an interesting name," Barbara interrupted.

"Not sure what else to call it." She continued. "I can help run it. Andy, you and Karen can work in the kitchen and be creative with more meals. Heather, you could help organize events and work with the children on projects. Ben could stay on to work the grounds."

"Okay. Wait." Andy stopped the conversation. "I understand this is a matter between the three of us whether to sell or not. However, you are talking about bringing our spouses into the picture to help, and they are not here. I think we need to bring them in and see if they are willing to do the work."

"You are right. Can you call them?" Sara agreed. It was unfair to assume the spouses would want to change their work.

Andy called Karen, and Heather called Ben. They were there with kids in tow in less than thirty minutes, albeit confused. Neither had been given the reason to come to the family meeting.

"We're here. What's going on?" Ben asked. He looked around at the wine glasses and added, "Where's ours." And laughed.

Andy retrieved two more wine glasses, poured them for Ben and Karen, and then refilled the others who wanted more.

Sara took a sip of her wine before filling Ben and Karen in on their discussion.

When she finished, Ben had one comment, "I'm all for it, depending on all the specifics, of course."

Karen looked at her husband. "What do you think? It would mean more work for you, for us. And to a different group of people. Children of all ages as well as adults. Not fancy meals like you enjoy making."

"This is true. However, you and I have been discussing expanding the menu. And I have wanted to cook more than breakfasts for a while now."

"This is true. And it would certainly allow for that."

"Could I continue to do my events and the weddings in the chapel and reception hall?" Heather asked. It had become her passion over the prior few years.

Barbara looked at her and thought about it. "I have brought that up with the board. We would consider leaving those buildings to your family and then simply renting them from you when we need to use them if that would work better for all of you."

"That divides the property up even more. And more complicated." Sara said. Her mind was working on other options.

The room grew silent as they thought about this complication.

"What if we maintain ownership of most of the estate? We keep our homes, the reception hall, and the chapel. Keep it under Bella Rose Estate. Then lease, or sell the manor and property immediately surrounding that alone to you and your organization?" Sara stated as she continued to think.

Barbara thought about what Sara offered. She pulled out the map of the property to configure the layout and property lines. She drew an imaginary line of how that would look. "If we buy it, we need a separate driveway put in."

"We can have it drawn up as a shared driveway. The lane would stay the same as a dead-end county lane. We already have driveways from the lane to each of our homes."

Barbara nodded her head. "That seems like it would work."

Sara looked at her siblings and their spouses, waiting for more feedback. She could see their minds working. Their eyes drifted back and forth as they visualized the changes. Both in the property and in their lives.

"So, who would I work for?" Ben laughed. He saw himself working for Bella Rose Estate and the foster care organization.

"That is a good question. I would say you could work for both. Be an independent landscaper/contractor, and take us both on as your customers. This will also allow you to hire on at other places if you want. We could form a contract with you for certain work regularly, but have the understanding that we are not your exclusive customer."

"Sounds like you would be back to what you were doing before Mama died and change everything for us." Heather laughed but was serious.

"That is what it sounds like. I can do that." Ben agreed.

Sara felt a sense of relief. She never thought she would be relieved to sell Bella Rose. It had been in her family for generations. It had been her home. She was raised on this property. She helped build it into what it was. She was surprised at how calm and content she was with their final decision.

Epilogue

Bella Rose took on a new look, a new meaning. The memories and history stood and will stand the test of time. Sara's book preserved the treasure of the mysteries. The facts were better than any fiction anyone could create as they preserved the truth of the family who stood tall and strong through all they endured through the generations.

The community joined to transform the manor into a temporary home for foster children waiting for foster families and permanent homes. Heather created fundraisers to help pay for the changes. Ben donated some of his time to the remodel. He reached out to Donovan and his construction crew to help in their spare time. Barbara was impressed by the support she had received. Opening day of the home was celebrated by a special event to raise more money for the children.

Gayle remained involved with the foster care program while attending college. Her studies led her to expand her education to include legal studies.

Sara and Randall settled into their roles as parents to a young lady. Sara found herself able to step back and oversee all the operations of the Estate as well as become the assistant running the foster home.

Heather and Ben continued in their roles. The transition had been fairly easy for them. They had a family of four, which took up a lot of time, but they learned to manage it well, and the children were thriving.

Andy and Karen tackled their roles of cooking and nutrition for the children and workers of the home. Andy enjoyed making new dishes to serve. Karen enjoyed helping her husband, making desserts, and raising their family with her husband.

The family stayed close, with everyone taking on new roles and staying busy but working together. Every once in a while, Sara climbed the stairs to the attic room and into the secret room. When Barbara designed the remodel, the family requested that those two rooms remain as they always had been.

Almost a year after the remodel, Sara was again in the attic. It was the anniversary of Susan's death. Sara sat on the one chair that remained and looked around. She envisioned her Mama writing at her desk like she had for many years. Sara walked over to the desk and wiped her fingers gently across the top. This was one of the last places she knew her mama had been. Sara knew one of the last things Susan wrote was the final letter to her and her siblings.

In the room's silence, Sara wondered what her mama thought when she wrote it. Did she know her time was near? Did she just happen to write it on a whim, or did she have a sixth sense about life and death? Does anyone have that awakening in them when their time is near?

Sara walked to the door of the secret room. She reached above the door for the key to open the door. They had left the antique key and lock as they had been even when they remodeled some of the room and doorway. She looked at the key in her hand, and all the memories flashed through her. The ones of discovery for her and her family. The imagined memories of her grandparents and their activities. The young girls who gave all they had to survive and have their babies live. Sara felt a moment of sadness, remembering that not all the babies had survived.

She lowered her hand, now holding the key. She looked at the key with a fondness for the story and mysteries behind all the keys. She took a closer look.

"Truth" was engraved on the length of it. She had never noticed that before.

The End

The writing of the story of Bella Rose Estate has come to an end. The twists and turns, mystery, secrets, family dynamics, and emotions of the characters filled these six books.

I hope you have enjoyed getting to the characters, fictionalized locations, and the lives led by Sara, Heather, Andy, their family, and friends.

My desire is that you were touched somehow during this storyline and that it has given you things to think about in your life.

You may follow my writing by joining or following my group, "The Flowing Pen," on Facebook.

https://www.facebook.com/groups/theflowingpen